Convincing the Cowboy Billionaire

A Chappell Brothers Novel: Bluegrass Ranch Romance Book 8

Emmy Eugene

ISBN-13: 979-8459002768

CHAPTER 1

Ian Chappell's hands slipped, and the hay bales he'd been carrying tipped. "Whoa!" he yelled as he felt himself slanting to the right. He stumbled that way, abandoning the bale he'd started to bobble.

The window loomed right there, and he had a flash of himself falling out of it, tumbling three stories to his death below. He managed to hurl the hay bale onto the conveyor and catch himself as his hand came down against the wall.

"Comin' your way!" he called just as he bashed his shin against a metal beam in the loft. All kinds of swear words streamed through his mind, but none came out of his mouth. Mom would be so proud.

He instantly took all the weight off his right leg, realizing that idiotic beam had probably saved him from going out the window, but holy-mother-of-pearl, it had just injured him something fierce.

"You okay?" someone asked, but Ian had forgotten who

he was working with in the loft. He definitely took his turn doing chores around the family owned and operated ranch, and he'd never minded loading hay onto the conveyor belt to get it out of the loft and where it needed to go.

He blinked, the pain still shooting up into his hip and radiating down into his foot. His toes tingled, as if he'd hit a nerve, and he steadied himself against the wall of the barn and pulled in a breath. He didn't dare put any weight on his foot, though.

"Yeah," he managed to say, glancing over to Lawrence, one of his brothers.

Someone yelled from below, and Lawrence turned to see what they wanted. They were probably mad about the double-bale coming on the belt, but Ian *had* warned them. His fingers ached from the way he'd been clenching them around twine and lifting fifty-pound bales for the past hour.

He tried putting weight on his right leg, but his shin gave a violent protest in the form of another blinding wave of pain. He groaned and collapsed onto the nearest thing— which of course, was the bale of hay he'd had in his left hand. He'd been injured dozens of times on the ranch. Spur, his oldest brother, barely had any feeling left in his fingertips for how often he touched hot things. Blaine, the second oldest brother in the Chappell family, had once broken his leg and then worked on crutches for eight weeks. Daddy sure didn't see a reason not to be out in the fields or stables, broken legs or not.

He *had* taken a break a couple of years ago when he'd

had hip surgery, but Ian suspected his mother had enforced that more than his father would've.

"Ian got hurt," he called down from the big window where they'd positioned the belt.

"I'm fine."

The belt started to slow and then stop, and Ian's mood worsened. He didn't want the spotlight on him. Now that he was the last remaining brother to get engaged or married, it seemed to be shining directly in his eyes at all times. He'd been one of the first to get married originally, but that relationship had been such a disaster—and he hadn't even seen it until it was too late.

Almost too late, he amended silently. He'd gotten out of the marriage without any children and without having to pay a whole bunch of money. It helped that it had only been six months old, and that Minnie had been a pathological liar.

"You're not fine," Lawrence said. "Your pantleg is soaked with blood." He crouched in front of Ian, who looked down at his leg. He moved his foot further from his body, but even that slight motion sent stars into his head. Sharp, steel stars that sliced at his senses harshly.

His vision went white along the edges, but he still managed to see the bloodstain on his jeans. "Great," he said. "I just washed these." His attempt at humor fell on deaf ears in Lawrence, who hadn't looked away from Ian's shin.

"I'm going to pull it up," Lawrence said as Blaine yelled from below. Neither Ian nor Lawrence answered him. Lawrence met his eyes, and Ian reached up to grab a bar that had been nailed into the wall. Probably a steadying bar, which he could've used as he was falling toward the open window.

He nodded, quick little pulses of his head. "Okay," he said. "I'm ready."

Even moving the jeans around his wound made his teeth grind together and a groan come out of his mouth. "Holy heavens," he said, the words bursting from him in mostly air. "What did I do?"

Lawrence didn't answer, and that wasn't a good sign. He whistled a warning like *I can't believe what I'm seeing, you're in so much trouble*, and stood. "I'm getting everyone up here. You've got to get to the hospital, and you're not putting any weight on that to get down the ladder." He moved over to the window despite Ian's protests.

As Lawrence yelled for Blaine and Trey to come up and help, Ian took a deep breath and closed his eyes. He wasn't exactly squeamish about blood. He could deal with horse injuries, Conrad—the brother he currently lived with in the corner house on the ranch—cutting his hand while washing a glass, and any other number of slices and scrapes...as long as it wasn't his *own* blood.

There was something eerie and equally disturbing to see his own blood leaving his body, and he hissed through his teeth as Lawrence returned and started to pull his pantleg down. "We'll want to cover that," he said. "You don't want it getting any dirtier than it already is. I'm gonna call Spur and let him know we can't finish up here. Maybe he can send over a few guys."

"It's that bad?" Ian asked, his heartbeat suddenly free-falling through his body. He was supposed to be taking Anita Powell to dinner that night. Their first real date, one he'd thought would never happen.

He'd texted her a lot over the course of a couple of days, and then suggested they could get dinner together. She hadn't answered for two more days, during which time he'd imagined every terrible thing that could've happened to her or her phone, and then he'd started in on himself for being so bold and so assuming.

He'd asked women to dinner before. Lots of men did it. It wasn't like he'd proposed.

No, that honor had gone to Conrad, who'd gotten engaged only a week ago.

He looked down at his leg, a shocked gasp flying from his mouth.

"No," Lawrence said, pawing at his pantleg now. "Don't look, Ian."

It was too late. Ian had seen the bloody mess that was his shin, with long, weeping fingers of red liquid moving down his leg to the top of his boot. The hay loft started to spin. He groaned, and Lawrence knelt in front of him and said, "I'm going to kill you for looking. Don't pass out on me."

He closed his eyes, but the image of his bone—so snowy white and so jagged—right in the middle of all that blood didn't go away.

"I'm sorry," he slurred, because he was definitely going to pass out.

"Help!" Lawrence called. "Blaine, get up here now!" He braced himself against Ian's chest, and the last thing Ian heard was Blaine's voice mingling with Trey's as they arrived in the loft. He passed out before he heard or felt anything else, not a single thought in his head at all.

"There he is," Blaine said, and Ian's eyelids fluttered again. "I told you he wouldn't be out long."

"How long?" Ian asked, his tongue so thick in his mouth. He wasn't on the hay bale anymore, but lying on the floor of the loft, looking straight up at the pointy part of the roof. Bales had been moved to block the window, and he wished for a breeze to come cool him down. In the next breath, he trembled with cold or pain, he wasn't sure which.

"Maybe three minutes," Lawrence said. "Come on, we still have to get him down."

"Maybe he could ride the conveyor," Trey said.

Even Ian gaped at him. Daddy had said he'd tan their hides if he ever found them treating the bale conveyor as a toy.

Trey shrugged. "I know it's not ideal. It's not something we'd normally do, but TJ does it at our place. He hasn't died yet."

"TJ is seven years old," Lawrence said. "Ian weighs at least ten times as much as him."

He groaned and closed his eyes again as the roof above him began to spin.

"And can't stay conscious," Blaine added. "No, he has to go down the ladder."

Lawrence: "He'll pass out from the pain."

Trey: "Call Spur."

Blaine: "What's Spur gonna do? He's not a doctor."

Ian just wanted them all to stop talking. Didn't they know their voices were driving a wedge between the halves of his brain with every word they spoke? He opened his eyes and sat up, though even that seemed to pull on his shin bone and send a wave of pain through his body. "I'm fine. I can go down the ladder."

"How?" Lawrence demanded. "You cannot, in any way, put weight on that leg. I'm pretty sure you cracked your shin. It could splinter."

He really didn't have time for a broken anything. Helplessness cut through him, because even moving his leg left to right with no weight on it hurt.

"I'm calling Spur," Trey said, and he paced away from the three of them to do it.

"Moving me is going to hurt," Ian said.

"I'm calling an ambulance," Blaine said. "There's no way we can drive him to the ER. He'll be bouncing all over." He stood and started tapping.

"I don't want an ambulance."

Lawrence crouched in front of him again. "Ian, you're in a bad way. Let us figure this out."

"I'm sorry," Ian said again, and Lawrence wore understanding in his gaze. They were only fourteen months apart, and he'd been close to Lawrence growing up. Once Conrad had shown his skill with the training, though, Daddy had always partnered he and Ian together, and Lawrence had gone his own way.

"It was an accident," Lawrence said. "They happen."

Ian nodded, pressing his teeth together in frustration and pain.

Blaine: "The ambulance is on the way."

Trey: "Spur and Duke are on their way. They're gonna grab Conrad from the family stable."

Lawrence: "I'm texting the work thread."

"That's everyone on the ranch," Ian complained. "Everyone doesn't need to know."

"Yes, they do," Lawrence said, his fingers flying only inches in front of Ian's face. "They need to move vehicles and we might get some volunteers to come help finish the loft."

All Ian could think was that Nita would get that text. Lawrence would push it out to everyone who worked at Bluegrass, as they had a lot of people come and go on the ranch. They ran one of the biggest boarding stables and training facilities in the Lexington area, and Nita worked as a trainer with one of their long-time rowhouse renters.

Within sixty seconds, more voices filled the air, and Ian consigned himself to his fate. No one suggested moving him, and when the paramedics got there, they took one look at his leg and then each other, the deathly still expression in their eyes speaking volumes to Ian.

"All right," one of them drawled. "We're going to strap you to a board." He stayed down on his knees, close to Ian, his voice calm and oh-so-even. He knew exactly what he was doing, and Ian trusted him. "It's like a stretcher, but it'll hold your head still—and that leg. Then we'll send you down the belt. It's going to be fine."

Ian nodded, those short bursts happening again. "All right."

Spur: "Daddy's here."

Blaine: "Don't let him climb the ladder. They're bringing him down."

Trey: "I'll get everyone away from the conveyor and go get it moving again."

Movement happened around Ian, but he didn't twitch a muscle. He said nothing. The paramedics used the belt to get their "board" up to the loft, and they sent everyone except Conrad and Duke down.

"It's okay, brother," Conrad said, reaching for Ian's hand. They gripped each other's fingers, and the paramedic said, "Good. Hold on tight, cowboy. This is going to hurt."

Both of them moved him then, and Ian yelled out as white-hot waves of pain cascaded through his whole body.

"It's okay," Conrad said on his left, Duke on his right.

Ian panted, the echo of his scream still caught in his head. He felt wild, frantic, and he needed some meds now.

"When we get him down, we'll start a drip," the first paramedic said. "Morphine and fluids. We can only take one in the ambulance."

"Don't come," Ian said through gritted teeth. "I'm fine. Daddy can come."

"I'll go talk to Daddy." Conrad left, because he was

closer to the ladder. Ian looked at Duke, who wore such a sober look on his face.

"All right," the paramedic said. "Easy now. You've got that side?" They inched him over to the belt, and it was smooth as butter as they laid him on it. He couldn't watch the sky flow by, as it made him dizzy and nauseous, and thankfully, keeping his eyes closed also meant he didn't have to see how many people were staring at him coming down that blasted conveyor belt out of the hay loft.

The belt beneath him started to slow, and Trey said, "It'll stop in time."

Ian opened his eyes as it did indeed stop, but he could only stare straight up. The paramedics hadn't made it down the ladder yet, but he felt like he'd just landed on the moon —he'd just taken one giant step for mankind—by getting from the loft to the ground.

Spur appeared above him. "Okay?"

Ian couldn't nod, so he employed his voice to say, "Okay."

He leaned closer. "Nita wanted to know if you'd like her to bring dinner to your room tonight." His dark eyes sparkled with something Ian couldn't name. He wasn't teasing Ian, because Spur didn't do that. He sure seemed happy though. "She asked me real privately, and no one overheard."

Ian normally would've nodded, but once again, found he could not. "Okay," he said again, and the paramedics arrived.

The crowd started to applaud in reverence—there was

no whooping or hollering as could often be heard among cowboys—and Ian could definitely see out of his peripheral vision.

Nita stood right at the bumper of the ambulance, and their eyes met. She wore worry in hers as Ian's humiliation and embarrassment doubled and then tripled.

"Sorry," he muttered, to which she said, "See you at six."

The last text she'd sent him, right after she'd given him her home address so he could pick her up all Southern-gentleman-proper had been *see you at six*.

As he got loaded in the back of the ambulance and Spur helped Daddy climb in with him, Ian couldn't help smiling to himself.

See you at six.

He hoped they wouldn't give him so many drugs that he couldn't enjoy his second hospital experience with the lovely Anita Powell.

CHAPTER 2

Anita Powell suspected she'd throw up on her next breath. When she didn't, she thought, *The next one.*

Nope.

Next one.

She managed to keep her breakfast where it belonged, though that had been hours and hours ago. She'd skipped lunch when she'd gotten the text about an injury on the ranch, and she'd spent the afternoon cleaning stalls and organizing paperwork—anything that didn't require too much mental energy.

All of that was currently going to Ian Chappell.

She'd texted him right after Lawrence's text had hit her phone, and he hadn't responded. Word spread fast on a ranch, even a big one like Bluegrass that housed boarding stables and training facilities. Besides, everyone knew Ian. He was a god among trainers, the last three horses he'd devoted his time to going on to win huge money prizes in some of the biggest races around the world.

Most people knew about three races: the Belmont Stakes, the Kentucky Derby, and the Preakness. They were, by far, the most popular races in the US. But Australia had massive money prizes, as did the UK and the United Arab Emirates.

Even if Ian didn't stay with them throughout his career, she knew he consulted with the new owners of the horses he'd raised and broken. The ones he'd taught initially. She'd been around Bluegrass enough to know how they worked, and they were a breeding, working, training ranch that specialized in Thoroughbreds.

Now that the Chappells had started their own race, they'd only been adding to their pool of money, and everywhere she looked at Bluegrass, she saw dollar signs.

"Fifty-four," a man called, and Nita looked down at her receipt. She was fifty-four. She held up her receipt and stepped through the to-go crowd to pick up her barbecue dinner. "Family rib meal," the man said, pushing everything toward her in Styrofoam and plastic bags.

"Thanks," she said, and she tucked her receipt in her pocket and picked up her food. She couldn't *believe* she was headed to the hospital. The last time she and Ian had been there together, they'd gone to see one of her fellow Glenn Marks trainers, a man named Rome.

She was fairly certain he hadn't planned on taking her back to the hospital cafeteria for their first official date. He'd told her that he didn't count the meal they'd shared a few minutes before the cafeteria had closed as a date. Tonight, though, would've been. That much had been clear to Nita. She was still shocked Ian had asked at all. She'd felt sparks for hours after he'd delivered her back to her truck the evening they'd gone to see Rome. Every time her phone dinged, her stomach swooped, because it could be Ian.

She hadn't thought she'd caused the same—or even a close-to-similar—feeling inside him. They did spend a lot of time talking about horses, but she also knew he loved authentic Kentucky barbecue sauce and mashed potatoes with plenty of country gravy—not brown. She could definitely take him a good meal tonight, and that thought alone got her back to her pick-up and on her way toward one of the tallest buildings in Dreamsville—the hospital.

Her father called as she pulled into a parking space, and she tapped on her screen to answer it. "Hey, Dad." She'd met with him last week to go over the proposal, contracts, and final logo. His new wife, Janet, hadn't seemed overly enthusiastic about the splitting of Glenn Marks, but Nita didn't much care what her dad's new wife thought. This was something she'd been talking about with Glenn since her uncle's death. They both wanted her to take over the stables, and Janet really had no say in the matter.

"Where you at, sugarbaby?"

She looked toward the half-circle entrance to the hospital that stuck way out from the main building. "Taking dinner to a friend."

"I heard there was an accident at Bluegrass today."

"Yeah," she said. "Ian Chappell got hurt in the hay loft. I

haven't heard if he broke his leg or what, but they strapped him up tight to a stretcher and sent him down on the conveyor belt."

"That's terrible," he said. "I'll call Jefferson as soon as we hang up."

Nita should probably tell him that she was about go inside the hospital and see what Ian needed. If he was really as injured as a broken bone, she wouldn't be able to take care of him the way he had her. He'd come over to Glenn Marks a couple of times to help keep the horses fed and clean and healthy. Now, when she saw Conrad or Ian talking to one of her champions, she smiled and thanked them, and she'd started to feel like part of the community at Bluegrass where she'd always felt on the outskirts.

"Okay," she said, not mentioning the family barbecue rib meal on the seat next to her. She didn't need to get anyone's hopes up—least of all, hers. She knew tonight's dinner was intended as a fishing expedition for Ian. He wanted to see what a real date would be like, and if she didn't meet his standards, she felt certain she wouldn't hear from him again—at least not about personal matters.

With Ian, a person usually only got one strike. She'd shown up at his house and yelled at him to stay out of her stables, and she'd still gotten a second chance to bat. She knew she wouldn't get a third.

"Casey said he'd have the paperwork ready to sign in the next week or two."

"Okay," Nita said again. She didn't want to think about taking half the stables from her dad right now. The weight of that might crush her lungs, and she just wanted to try to enjoy her evening with Ian. If she was lucky, it would last an hour, as neither of them seemed all that loquacious. She'd actually made a list on her phone of things she could ask him, because it had been a long time since she'd been out with a man, and certainly forever since that man had been as talented and as handsome as Ian.

"I can tell you're busy," her dad said. "I'll let you know if we're going to do something for the Chappells."

"Sounds good," she said, only because she didn't want to say *okay* for a third time. The call ended, and Nita decided she didn't want to waste any more time. If she didn't go in now, she'd drive the family meal back to her perfect little house on the edge of some woods and eat the whole thing— even the country gravy she didn't particularly like.

She collected the bag and got out of the SUV, her mind running through the mundane tasks she needed to do when she got home to that perfect little house on five acres, with a gorgeous view of the river from the front porch and the windmills from the back.

She needed to switch her laundry from the washer to the dryer, and if she didn't give her little dog a bath soon, both of them were going to be paying for it.

"Nita?"

She looked up, her pulse skyrocketing at the disgust her name had been said with. She looked right into Judd Rake's eyes, and a groan pulled through every muscle in her body. "Judd." She said his name with as much respect as she could muster, which admittedly, wasn't much.

"What are you doin' here?" His gaze slid down to the plastic bag in her hand. Thankfully, Blue Barbecue cared more about their flavors than having fancy sacks to carry it in, and she could've been taking in groceries for all Judd would know.

"Nothing," she said, though Judd would hardly let that stand. No one just came to the hospital for fun.

"Did you hear about Ian Chappell?" he asked.

"Yes."

"We just saw 'im," Judd said.

She really wanted to ask him who "we" comprised. As far as she could see, only he stood in front of her. She clamped the remark behind closed lips and nodded.

"You're not here to see him, are you?" Judd asked, moving out of the way as a mother and her two small children exited the hospital and couldn't quite get by him.

"It's really none of your business," Nita said. "I have to go. Excuse me."

Judd narrowed his eyes at her, but Nita walked away, choosing to enter the hospital by one of the side doors instead of having to shuffle along in that rotating automatic door. She couldn't shake Judd's eyes until she stepped onto the elevator that would take her to the second floor, where she'd learned Ian's room sat.

Her nerves assaulted her again, but she kept her feet moving, one in front of the other. Room two-eleven loomed in front of her, the door open. At least she wouldn't have to wonder if Ian was taking visitors.

She slowed as she arrived and peered into the room.

There was no one there, and sharp disappointment hooked through her at the same time a hint of relief soothed it.

"He's down in x-ray," a nurse said as she stepped past Nita. "You can come in. He won't be long."

"No?"

"Nope." She gave Nita a warm smile. "This one's popular. He's had people here with him all day." She started removing the sheets from the bed. "I'm just going to get him set up for the night." She kept working, and Nita felt stupid standing there watching her work in the tiny room. She put the food on the built-in desk that Ian could reach from the bed. A TV had been mounted to the wall above the door, and the world's tiniest recliner sat on the other side of the bed. Behind that, a slim window let in natural light and another door led into the bathroom.

The nurse finished making up his bed, and she bustled out of the room. Nita sighed as she sat down in the recliner, surprised she fit though she wasn't a very tall or very wide woman.

You're not here to see him, are you?

"Why can't I come see Ian?" she asked the empty hospital room. "Judd had. I'm no different than Judd."

She was, though, and she knew it. She wasn't here out of brotherly love for a fellow trainer. She wanted to see Ian so she could feel the sparks he sent through her whole body with a single look.

"Here you go," a man said, and a wheelchair came into the room, Ian riding in it. He wore the darkest look she'd ever seen on his face, and she immediately got to her feet, the fireworks going off like the Thunder Over Louisville, which was a massively huge fireworks show that kicked off the Derby season here in Kentucky.

"Looks like Shanda got the bed switched out," the man said, looking at Nita with a wide smile. "Let me lower the bed, and then we'll get it where you want it." He set about doing that, and Nita felt in the way in this microscopic room. She couldn't even imagine being trapped in here, with the door closed, with just her and Ian.

You won't be trapped, she told herself. *You want to be here.*

Ian hadn't said anything, and she fell out of his sight to make room for the nurse helping him get the bed as low as possible so he could just move over from the chair to the mattress. Working together, the two of them managed to get Ian into bed with only a slight groan.

"All set?" the man asked.

"Yes," Ian clipped out.

"They serve room service until ten," he said, bustling around the room to get out an extra blanket from the tiny closet in the corner Nita hadn't seen. "The menu is right there on the desk. You know how to call me or Shanda?"

"Yes," Ian said again.

"Anything you need right now?" He looked at Nita. "Either of you want water?"

"I'll take some water," Ian said, and Nita nodded to indicate she'd like some too.

The man smiled and nodded. "Be right back." He left, pulling the door closed behind him.

The moment it clicked closed, Nita flinched. It went well with Ian's sigh.

She wanted to offer to leave, but she couldn't bring herself to do it. "Sounds like you've had a busy day," she started with.

"Beyond." Ian leaned his head back and closed his eyes.

"Is the bed where you want it?"

"Not even close."

She reached for the remote. "I can do it. Higher? More laid back?"

"Higher for sure." He spoke with the timbre of wood mouse now—soft and meek and almost pleasant to listen to. "Then I can put my dinner on that tray right there."

"All right." She raised him up and rolled the tray into position. With her hands busy, she didn't feel so nervous. "I got barbecue ribs from Blue's. Mashed potatoes with country gravy for you. I got the sweet corn, because my momma taught me to always eat a vegetable with my barbecue and you didn't say what you wanted."

She told herself to stop talking, because she'd started to rush and ramble. She set the food in front of him.

"What did you get for yourself?" he asked, his eyes turning a touch softer as he looked at her.

"Ribs," she said. "Same as you." Panic streamed through her when she realized she'd have to eat like an animal in front of this man she could barely look at. "But I like the brown gravy, so I got baked beans instead of potatoes. There's cole slaw too, and that's technically a vegetable. Cabbage, you know."

A smile ghosted across his face, barely lifting his lips. "I know what cole slaw is made of."

Nita slicked her hands down the front of her jeans. "Okay."

He reached out and because the room was so dang small, he was able to reach her hand easily. She froze, every cell her body combusting, putting itself back together, and then re-exploding. Over and over.

His touch did things to her no man's had ever done before.

She had no idea what that meant. What she knew was that she'd drifted closer to him somehow, and that his other hand had reached up toward her face. She leaned down, and because the bed had been lifted so much, and she wasn't very tall, it wasn't that far of a dip to get close to him.

His hand curled along the back of her neck, and he whispered, "Thank you for making this dinner date happen. I've been looking forward to it." With that, he brought her mouth to his, his fingers insistent and yet soft at the same time, exactly like his kiss.

Nita hadn't been kissed in oh-so-long, and she hadn't expected to do this tonight either. She couldn't help sinking into his touch, and breathing in when he did, and sighing in pure bliss when he pulled back only a few seconds after the kiss had begun.

Wow, was the only thing she could think. *Wow, wow, wow.*

Someone knocked on the door, and she spun toward it

and then immediately away when Judd walked in. "Hey," he said. "I think I left my keys here somewhere..."

She hurried to the back window, wishing she could leap through it and disappear. Ian said something in a voice that didn't make it through the rushing in her ears, and Judd responded.

"See ya, Nita," he said.

She turned toward him. "Yep. 'Bye."

Their eyes met, and Judd narrowed his again. He knew too much about her, and she hated that. He also knew there was something going on here, and she wished he didn't. Instead of him blurting out the secrets she'd been keeping for years, he nodded curtly, said good-bye to Ian, and left.

"Sorry about that," Ian said.

"About what?" Nita asked.

"Didn't you hear him?"

"No."

"He asked if we were dating. I said no." Ian looked up at her, and Nita felt a knife go right through the fleshiest part of her heart.

She nodded and sat down in the recliner, though she'd left her food on his tray, out of her reach. "I guess that kiss was a mistake." She should've known better. Men like Ian Chappell weren't interested in women like her.

Familiar bitterness and fire flamed through her. "I'll just go."

"No, wait," Ian said, but Nita wasn't going to wait to be made a fool of again. She jumped up and pulled open the door, nearly ramming into the nurse who'd gone to get their water.

"Sorry," she mumbled and kept going. It wasn't until she'd made it into the silent elevator that she thought she'd heard Ian say, *It wasn't a mistake. Don't go.*

She couldn't go back now, though, and Nita let her humiliation and foolishness propel her out of the elevator car at full speed.

"Anita," a man said, holding up both hands as she nearly plowed into him.

She came to a halt, her chest heaving.

"Anita Powell?" He smiled, and she recognized him as the nurse who'd brought Ian back to the room. A woman burst out of the door to the left of the elevator.

Shanda. Ian's other nurse.

"Praise the heavens," she said panting. She pressed one hand to her pulse. "Can you imagine having to go back to his room if we hadn't caught her?" She looked at the male nurse, and Nita just kept volleying her gaze between them.

"Come on," the man said, his smile not slipping even a centimeter. "Ian asked us to come get you and escort you back to the room for dinner." He stepped to her side and linked his arm in hers.

"How did you get down here so fast?" Nita asked as Shanda pushed the button to call the elevator.

"We have secret passageways just for nurses," he said. "My name is Marty, and Shanda and I won't bother you or Ian for at least an hour." He glanced over to the other nurse as the elevator dinged. "Right, Shanda?"

"That's right." She led the way into the elevator. Nita wasn't sure if she'd entered an alternate reality or not. She knew Marty didn't release his grip on her arm at all, and Shanda's words echoed in her mind.

Can you imagine having to go back to his room if we hadn't caught her?

Ian *could* be a beast of a man. Nita knew that...and yet she still found herself smiling, her own pulse kicking out extra beats at the thought of dining with him—and maybe even kissing him again.

CHAPTER 3

Ian hated that he couldn't get out of bed. He'd wanted to jump to his feet and race after Nita as she'd fled the hospital room. His muscles twitched, even now, waiting with both eyes boring into the closed door. It had slammed shut after he'd asked Marty and Shanda to get Nita.

Maybe he'd barked the command at them. He wasn't entirely sure. He felt so far removed from his body, and he took a deep breath, trying to find somewhere inside himself that was calm and centered.

He closed his eyes and told himself to *Be quiet. Be still.*

The air felt right again, and Ian blew his breath out slowly. He raised his arms high above his head, because he could still move those. He could still press his palms together above his head and try to control his thoughts and emotions.

After his divorce, the only way Ian had made it through each day was through meditation. Morning and night. Sometimes at noon too. He'd taken up yoga for a while, but his shoulders were too boxy, and his hips didn't bend properly to do the moves. He settled for finding a quiet spot in the house or on the back deck, closing his eyes, and shutting out the world.

If he were being honest, he couldn't touch his hands above his head. Those broad shoulders and all. He simply didn't have that range of motion.

The door opened, and his eyes snapped open as he let his hands fall back to the bedrails.

"See, he's right there," Shanda said, as if Ian would've left. If he could have, he'd have been gone hours ago.

He met Nita's eyes, instant pleading streaming through him. His stomach grumbled, and he desperately wanted to say everything that came into his mind.

I'm so sorry.

That kiss was the most amazing thing I've experienced in years.

I'll talk to Judd and make sure he knows you're mine.

Maybe not that last thing, as Nita was as wild and free as a mustang, and he didn't think anyone would ever tame her. He certainly didn't want to, and he didn't want to categorize her as an object to be had or owned.

He stubbornly kept his lips pressed together. He couldn't say any of the things streaming through his mind, especially in front of the two nurses he'd been grumping at for hours.

"How's the pain?" Marty asked while Shanda handed Nita her cup of water. He looked up at the monitor and wrote something on the clipboard they left at the foot of his bed.

"Fine," Ian managed to say. "Thank you."

Marty glanced at him, so much said in a single second and without words. He dropped his chin for a moment, clearly saying, *You're welcome. No problem.*

Something beeped, and a voice came from somewhere over by Shanda. Ian couldn't make sense of it, but she said, "I'm on my way," and bustled out of the room without a backward look at Ian.

She was probably relieved to be called away to some emergency.

The clunking of the clipboard hitting the slot on the end of the bed made Ian flinch, and then Marty said, "I'll check in on you in a while. Call if you need anything." He too walked out without looking back at Ian.

Once again, the big, heavy, hospital door swung closed, but this time, it sealed Anita Powell in the room with him. Ian's chest rose and fell once before he looked over to her.

"I'm sorry," he blurted out. "Today has been very difficult and confusing for me."

She stood up from the narrow recliner, nodding. "I know the feeling." She moved the rolling tray back in front of him, but it was far too high for her to sit beside him and eat too. She turned away from him and opened the slim closet in the corner of the room. After taking out a folding chair, she set it up in the small space between his bed and the counter that ran along the wall on his right.

A quick smile graced her face while she took her Styrofoam container and started unwrapping her plastic silverware. He got busy doing the same thing, his mind firing things at him.

He'd been practicing his small talk with Conrad and Spur, the only two brothers who knew about this dinner date. He reminded himself that he and Nita had been texting a lot, and he knew things about her already.

Still, his mind flipped from topic to topic, unable to settle on one long enough to form words. Work, no. Raspberry fritters, no. Best barbecue restaurants, already done. Her training schedule, definitely not.

He thought of the expression on Judd's face when he'd walked in looking for his keys. The narrowed eyes as he'd asked if Ian was dating Nita, almost like he thought there was something nefarious at play if Ian said yes.

He'd spoken true—he and Nita weren't dating. They were on their first date—he wasn't counting the other meal at the hospital as a date. He was interested in her. He thought about her a lot. He liked talking to her. None of that actually constituted as dating.

Foolishness whispered through him, and he popped open the top of his container, his stomach growling instantly at the sight of Blue's barbecue ribs and the creamy mashed potatoes with that peppered, white gravy on top.

"Oh," he said with a sigh.

Nita started to laugh, and that brought his eyes to her face. Her smile could light whole rooms, and her laughter started low in her chest and came out in a feminine but not high-pitched sound. He grinned at her too and asked, "What?"

She giggled for another moment and then said, "I see what it takes to help you relax." She pointed her fork toward his food. "Country gravy and ribs."

He couldn't exactly deny it. "We all have weaknesses. One of mine is country gravy."

"Appropriate for breakfast, lunch, and dinner." She gave him a smile that did reach all the way into those gorgeous blue eyes, scooped up another bite of cole slaw, and ate it.

"I make a killer breakfast," he said.

"Yeah?" she asked. "Like what? Are we talking fancy, like eggs Benedict? Or protein waffles?"

Ian scoffed, as both suggestions were ridiculous. "No one actually likes protein waffles."

"I do," she said. "If there's enough buttermilk syrup." She grinned at him, and Ian found the return smile coming easily to his face.

"I'd eat cardboard with enough buttermilk syrup," he said. "That doesn't count." He reached for his meat and took a bite. He realized in that moment that he needed a stack of napkins and rifled through the plastic bag still on his tray to find one.

He wiped his mouth and took another bite while Nita asked, "So what would I get if you made me one of your 'killer breakfasts'?"

"Mm." He finished that rib and tossed the bone in the top of the Styrofoam container. "I'm real good with eggs, any style. Biscuits and gravy, of course. Chicken fried steak. That kind of stuff."

"So we're talking country breakfasts."

He gave her a grin and picked up another rib. "The best kind."

She nodded, something sparking on her face he didn't understand, and they fell silent for a few seconds while they ate. She ate her sides first, and Ian wondered if she didn't like meat. He didn't want to ask, but his mind misfired at him again.

"Conrad makes the best coffee," he said out of nowhere. "I'm pretty useless at that."

She nodded, her attention still on her food. "My mom makes the world's best coffee," she murmured.

"World's best?" Ian forced a chuckle out of his mouth, disliking how hard it was to do so. "I'd have to taste it to know."

Nita brought her eyes up then. She said nothing, but Ian felt like he should be able to read something in the depths of those baby blues. He couldn't, though. He was so far out of his league with this woman. He hadn't dated in way too long. He needed to text Conrad or Ry to find out what he should be saying, or what he could ask her.

He cleared his throat and kept eating, the weight of Nita's gaze on him for a few more seconds before she went back to her food. She closed the lid on her container without taking a single bite of meat, and Ian's chest started to storm. Maybe she didn't like Blue's. When she'd texted him to ask what to bring, he'd mentioned it. She hadn't argued or acted like she didn't like the food there, though everything was harder to know or judge through a text.

"Not hungry tonight?" he finally asked.

She shook her head and reached for her hospital cup of water. "I'm okay."

That wasn't entirely what he'd asked, but with such awkwardness streaming through the room now, he wasn't sure what to say next.

"How long did they say you'd be here?" she asked.

"They didn't," he said. "I guess there's an orthopedist who needs to come look at my leg. See if I need surgery or if they can cast it."

"It's not cast?"

"Temporarily," he said. "If I don't need surgery, they'll put a heavy-duty cast on it. Apparently, the tibia is a long bone, which is a bad break. And it's the bone that transfers weight from the femur to the foot, which is why I couldn't put any weight on my foot in the loft." His throat suddenly had sand in it, and he coughed as he reached for his drink too. After sucking down at least half of the water, he cleared his throat again.

He certainly wasn't helping the tension in the room, and Ian suddenly just wanted to be alone. "Depending on how the orthopedist feels, it could be months before I can really walk again."

"That's terrible," Nita said quietly. "I'm sorry, Ian."

The list of tasks he had to complete for the ranch, his horses, the upcoming training season, and the little wager he and Conrad had come up with streamed through his mind. He couldn't say it was okay, because it didn't feel okay.

It felt like someone had hollowed out the earth beneath his feet, and he was falling—hard and fast—into the dark.

"Yeah," he said, his voice made of sandpaper. "I guess this guy only comes here a couple of times a month, and they called him in specifically for tomorrow. Should be here by mid-morning, they said."

"So at least through tomorrow," she said.

"At least." Ian couldn't stand the thought of being in this microscopic room for another twenty-four hours, and his shoulders rose higher toward his ears as his muscles tightened. He had to consciously lower them and force the tightness out, but it didn't go far.

He drew in a breath and pushed it out, which drew Nita's attention again. Their eyes met, and hers held his so completely, he knew he'd remain in her gaze until she let him go. In that moment, he fought against his attraction to this woman, because he didn't want to allow anyone, ever, to have so much control over him.

"I should go," she said. "You look exhausted." She broke the spell she'd put on him by looking down and standing up, taking her container with her. "Did you get enough to eat?"

"Yes," he said, his voice once again getting put through a grinder. "Thank you, Nita."

"Sure," she said. "You'll let me know if you need anything else?"

He nodded, but he didn't feel her gaze on him. She packed up efficiently, and then there was just a few steps to the door. She didn't take them, and Ian got drawn back to her.

"I'm not sorry about the kiss," he blurted out, wishing he didn't feel so disjointed right now. He hated this weak, unsure feeling inside him, but he wanted her to know that.

She reached up and tucked that luxurious blonde hair behind her ear. "Okay," she said. "Then I won't be either." She moved toward him and leaned down, pressing her lips to his forehead as he allowed himself to trail his hand along her waist. She only stood there for a moment—a breath of time —and then she moved away again.

"We'll talk later," she said, already turning toward the door.

"Yeah," he said, and she walked out. The silence she left in her wake annoyed Ian, and he glanced around the hospital room. Without her, what did he have now? "You should've asked her about her family," he grumbled to himself, picking up the tiny plastic spoon. "Her horses. Her dog. Her house. The path she walks in the morning. *Some*thing."

Without her, he had a tiny, dark TV and a pile of mashed potatoes with country gravy. Sure, he liked them, but all he could think about while he finished eating and then put something on the TV that would hopefully lull him to sleep was how amazing it had felt to kiss Anita Powell.

* * *

"Yes, we'll get the medication," Spur said as he took the sheaf of papers the doctor extended toward him. He wore a frown between his eyes. "I'll make sure he knows what to take and when."

Ian was glad his eldest brother was there. He'd brought Daddy, Cayden, and Conrad, and they all seemed to have more mental awareness than Ian did.

The orthopedist had recommended surgery. That had happened three days ago. Ian had been in incredible pain for several hours after it, and even now, if he missed a pill by twenty minutes, agony bled through him softly and quietly until it screamed up his leg, into his hip, and down through his toes.

The nurses on all the shifts made him get out of bed and move every couple of hours, and his arms hurt from the crutches, and his left leg ached from bearing all of his weight without the help of his right leg. He sometimes stumbled over the smooth, tiled hallways in the wing where he'd been for the past five days, and he had no idea how he could navigate around Bluegrass.

His bedroom was on the second level at the corner house, and he knew he wouldn't be going up those stairs. He was pretty sure a doctor somewhere, at some time, had said to be very careful on stairs and not to use them if he didn't have to.

Ian wasn't sure anymore. The door to his room seemed to revolve with doctors and nurses, and he'd given up trying to remember who was who after the orthopedist had come. Spur, at some point, had told Ian that he was the best orthopedist in the South, and he'd done a fine job fixing up Ian's shinbone.

Great, Ian had said, probably before he'd fallen asleep. He seemed to do that a lot, and his life had been reduced to limping around the second floor, sleeping, taking painkillers, and eating whatever someone insisted he should.

Around him, the doctors and nurses talked to his family, and Ian let his eyes drift closed. When his mind wasn't so foggy, he'd figure things out. He could read a label on a pill bottle as good as anyone else, and he wouldn't have to manage things by himself in the beginning.

"All right," Conrad said, drawing Ian's eyes open again. "Wake up, brother. We're going."

"I'm awake," Ian said, but the words slurred. In his mind, he could move to the edge of the bed and stand by himself. He could stride down the hall to the elevator and on out to his truck. Of course he'd be able to drive back to the ranch and busy himself in the kitchen, making over-easy eggs and country fried steak, the way he'd done loads of times before.

In reality, he couldn't do any of those things, and with a start, he looked at the doctor. "What about driving?"

"Ian," Daddy said gently. "He talked about driving. It'll be a while."

"I've got you," Spur said, and he had to physically pull Ian to the edge of the bed. It took he and Conrad to get Ian to his feet, and the doctor positioned the crutches for him. When Ian felt like crying, he got angry, and he let the fury flow through him now without trying to tame it.

Every hobble-step, every inch of ground he covered from the second-floor room to Conrad's truck, he simply grew angrier and angrier.

Once they were alone in the truck, with Spur and Daddy in a vehicle in front of them, Conrad said, "Let it out, Ian."

Ian wanted to hold everything tight. He could control things if he kept them close, laced tightly inside his chest. He also knew the explosion that came after days and months of doing that wasn't pretty.

Conrad rolled down the windows and let in the hot, late-summer air, and Ian opened his mouth and yelled into the Kentucky sky.

CHAPTER 4

Nita wiped the dust cloth along the Venetian blinds, listening to her mother talk about her upcoming work party. "Yeah, you should take the extra whipped cream," she said, just to have something to contribute. Her mother was an excellent cook, and while she'd taught Nita a few things in the kitchen, Nita preferred doing something simple over something elaborate.

Knowing her mom, the fruit tray would really be a fully constructed farm scene made with strawberries, cantaloupe, watermelon, raspberries, grapes, and various other fruits. She'd take a picture from high above and post it on her social media, and she'd get featured in another magazine.

Nita smiled just thinking about that. Her mother deserved every good thing in the world after what she'd been through in the past few years, and she was glad her mom had found joy in creating centerpieces with food.

"Enough about me," Mama said. "What's new with

you? I heard someone got hurt at Bluegrass a couple of weeks ago."

Nita swallowed, her mouth suddenly full of saliva. She deliberately ran the cloth along another slat in the blinds. "Yeah," she said. "It was Ian Chappell." She hadn't told anyone about the semi-disaster that had been dinner in his room.

She'd eaten her ribs like a ravenous wolf, right in the front seat of her old pick-up truck, in the hospital parking lot. She hadn't been able to stand the thought of picking up the food and eating it in front of him, and he'd noticed.

He'd said a few things that made Nita's heartbeat pulse with excitement, but he hadn't called her since. He'd texted a few times, and she'd returned the messages, but they'd stopped talking about anything of consequence.

"I sense a story," Mama said, a singsongy quality to her voice. "Are you seeing this Ian Chappell?"

"Mama," Nita said with plenty of frustration in the tone. "You know who the Chappells are, right?"

"You've always been so concerned about status," Mama said. "I'm sure they're just people."

Nita thought of Ian Chappell. The man was not just any man, and any woman—no matter their age—who laid eyes on him knew it. She adored his dark hair and even darker eyes, and though she hadn't seen him smile very often, when he did, it made stars look dull.

"I haven't told anyone this." She wouldn't even know who she would tell. Her father? Nope. The elderly couple who lived down the road to her left? She doubted the

Finlay's would care—or know who the Chappells were. They'd moved in a year or so after Nita, and they entertained their grandchildren more than anyone else.

One other house sat on her road, and it was owned by a family of five. Mom, dad, three kids. The Billsons were kind and hospitable, but Nita wouldn't exactly call her and Ingrid Billson BFFs. Or even friends at all.

She could whisper to the horses at the stables about Ian, and they'd keep their mouths shut. Nita used to do that, but now she didn't trust that someone she didn't want to over-hear wouldn't be lurking just out of sight. The last thing she needed was for Judd Rake to find out more embarrassing things about her.

"Go on," Mama said.

Nita hesitated, then remembered that her mother didn't have any ties to any racing venues or people in Dreamsville. She lived in Lexington now, which wasn't that far away. "Ian asked me out," she said slowly, weighing the words in her mouth. "Our first date was the day he got hurt. I took him dinner in the hospital."

Mama said nothing, and Nita appreciated that. Sort of. It left space for her to continue, but Nita didn't know what to say next.

Finally, Mama said, "And?"

"And nothing. He hasn't asked again. He splintered his tibia. Had to have surgery. I haven't seen him around the ranch at all, and we text a little. He says he doesn't leave the house very often." She shrugged, though her mother couldn't see her. Nita finished with the blinds and positioned them so the sunlight could come inside.

She stood inside and looked out, watching the windmills slowly rotate in the fields beyond her backyard. They always calmed her, reminding her to breathe life into her lungs and take the day one moment at a time. Working with a horse helped her feel the same way, like she didn't have to solve all of life's issues and mysteries and misunderstandings before suppertime.

"Maybe you should call him," Mama said. "Stop by with dinner and see how he's doing."

"Maybe," Nita said.

"I can help you make something," she offered. "If you know what he likes."

"I know what he likes," Nita murmured, thinking of her mother's coffee. Could she really just stop by one morning with that, thrust the thermos toward him, and see how he reacted?

What if he frowned? What if he simply took the coffee, said thanks, and went back to pretending like they hadn't flirted for hundreds of texts and then agreed to go out?

You failed, she thought. She'd known Ian was fishing on the first date, and she obviously hadn't snagged his attention enough. On the other hand, Nita had the distinct thought that perhaps Ian was embarrassed. A man like him wouldn't want to have many people witness his weakness while he lay in a hospital bed.

He had kissed her, and he'd said he didn't regret doing so. Maybe she should stop by. Her phone beeped, and she glanced down at it on the windowsill. Glenn's name sat there, and Nita said, "I have to go, Mama. Love you."

"Let me know if I can help with Ian," she said, and Nita said she would before switching over to her father's call.

"Hey, Glenn," she said.

"Guess what I'm holding in my hand right now?" he asked, his voice full of laughter and joy.

Nita knew exactly what he was holding in his hand right now, no guessing needed. "I'm on my way."

"Yeah? You're not at the stables still?"

"I've been leaving early," she said. "Get there before dawn." She told herself it was to avoid the oppressive September heat that had been beating down on Kentucky, but really it was to be off the ranch before the afternoon grew too late, as Ian said a lot of his doctor's appointments were in the afternoon.

In the back of her mind, she'd wanted to be able to take him, should he need it. The thought was absolutely ridiculous, as the man had seven brothers who lived within a few miles of him who could take him. Two parents. A whole slew of trainers who admired him.

He didn't need her, that was for dang sure.

"Well, come by," Glenn said. "I think the contract looks great, and we can go over it and see if there's anything we need changed."

"The rollover is not happening until the New Year," Nita said. "That's in there, right?"

"It is," Glenn said. "We can make announcements once you sign, if you'd like. Or not. Up to you." Her dad had left a lot up to her, and Nita did appreciate that. At the same time, she sometimes just wanted someone to tell her what to do, and when.

Sometimes, the world and all its many decisions felt like too much for her to carry. Was Feathers For Brains ready to start training? Should she move her into the beginning stages to learn to race? What should she make for dinner? What time should she go to work? Which bill should she pay off this month? Could she trust herself to make the right decisions?

Should she text Ian Chappell?

"I think I want to wait on the announcement," she said. "Until right before the rollover. If that's okay."

"It's okay," he said. "And you'll start training a couple of horses right after that, so it'll be a great time."

"Yeah." Nita left the window and headed into the kitchen to put her dusting cloth back under the sink. "I'm thinking Feathers For Brains and Gone Fishing."

"That's who I would choose," he said. "Are you going to give Been There, Done That to someone?"

"Yeah," she said. "He just doesn't respond to me the way I think he needs to. He could be a great horse, but not with me as his trainer."

"They're finicky sometimes. You're smart for realizing it and not forcing it."

She remembered when he'd done that with a horse, and they'd both been frustrated. He'd spent far too much money for the equine not to have won major races, but their personalities just hadn't meshed. Training a horse was as much about matching them with someone they loved and wanted to please as it was giving them the right moves at the right time of their development.

"Okay," she said, "I'm finishing up a couple of chores, and I'll be over."

"Sounds good," he said. "Janet just put a meatloaf in the oven."

Oh, joy, Nita thought. Out loud, she said, "I ate a huge lunch, Dad. I might stay, but I won't eat much." That was her code for, *Please don't let her make a huge feast and then fuss over me not eating it.*

"I'll tell her," he said, and that was his dad-speak for, *I'll try, Jitterbug.*

Janet, his new wife, had a mind of her own, and while Nita didn't mind seeing her, she certainly wasn't her biggest fan either.

"I hear the ice cream truck," Glenn said, and Nita laughed as the call ended. Her father would buy a whole box of the cookies 'n cream ice cream sandwiches, and Nita would eat one of those with him while they sat on the back porch and went over the contract.

The contract. A new type of excitement built inside her. She'd been working with a lawyer for a few months now to get a contract that would transfer half of her father's stables —Glenn Marks—to her. It would be renamed Glenn Marks Powell, and Nita would have her own stable, her own business to build, and the recognition she'd been working for all these years.

"It's almost here, Sam," she said into the silence in her

small house. Sampson Powell didn't answer, of course, as he'd been laid to rest for several years now. Nita couldn't help talking to him sometimes, because they'd dreamed and planned for a whole life together.

It had been cut so short—they'd only gotten a year and a half together, with eight months of that as husband and wife —and sometimes the unfairness of life could drag Nita into the depths of longing and loneliness.

* * *

A couple of hours later, with a single slice of meatloaf and plenty of crispy Brussels sprouts in her stomach, Nita unwrapped her ice cream sandwich. The fan and mister Glenn had put on his back deck kept the heat at bay, and she smiled at her dad before she took her first bite.

His bite consumed half of the sandwich, and she shook her head as he smiled at her. They'd gone over the contract while Janet finished dinner, and everything had looked good to Nita. No changes needed in this round.

She still hadn't signed the papers yet, and Glenn had brought them out onto the deck with them. Nita loved spending time with him alone, and she always had. As the oldest of two kids in her family, she'd been toddling after Glenn for as long as she could remember.

"Your uncle would be happy about this rollover," her dad finally said, crumpling up his wrapper and tucking it into his pocket. "I think it's going to be amazing for you, for our brand, and for me. I won't have to worry so much about what happens on the track."

Nita looked at her dad. "Are you feeling old, Dad?" She grinned at him, clearly teasing, but he did look older than the man she held in her mind's eye. His hair had more gray in it than she'd ever seen, and as he chuckled and nodded, she realized that he probably was tired.

Horse training could be a twenty-four-seven job, as Nita well knew, and sometimes she felt bone-weary too.

She leaned her head against her dad's shoulder, feeling very much like a little girl beside him. A small toad in the shadow of a giant, the way she'd always been. He hadn't made her feel like that on purpose, and he likely didn't even know he did at all. She hoped with this rollover, that she'd be able to emerge as a beautiful butterfly, ready to fly and show the world her colors and spots.

"How are you doing, Nita?" he asked, his voice really soft. "For real? You still worried about being taken seriously?"

"Always," she said, her mind flowing toward Ian. If she was dating him, what would Judd think then? For someone like Judd to take her seriously, Ian would probably have to take lessons from Nita, not just take her to dinner. That would hardly matter to him, though he'd seemed perturbed that she'd been in Ian's hospital room weeks ago.

"What have you decided about a boyfriend?" he asked. "You mentioned that a while ago."

"I...I could probably stand to have a boyfriend again," Nita said. "Even though Karl was a disaster."

"You just go slow, sugarbaby. Not every love is like what you and Sam had."

"I know."

"Doesn't mean you can't find it again. Sometimes you just have to look harder, for longer."

"Yeah." She sighed as she sat up straight again. "Have you heard from Cal?"

Her dad shook his head. "Nothing yet. He said he'd call the moment Delaney went into labor." He offered Nita a wise smile. "Don't think I didn't notice you changing the subject lightning-fast just now."

Nita grinned at him. "What daughter wants to talk about boys with her dad?" She gave him a playful shove and got to her feet. "Besides, I already talked to mama about this today, and that's enough for one day."

"Oh?" Glenn rose too. "And what information did your mother get?"

Nita trusted her father, but she didn't want to lay out her cards for him just yet. He knew Ian Chappell really well —he knew Jefferson, Ian's father, and had for decades. She didn't want to see his approval or disapproval once she mentioned Ian's name, and her father wouldn't be able to hide it.

"No information," she said coolly. "I have to go rescue Goliath from Janet."

"She'll want to keep him," her dad said, following her back into the house. "She thinks French bulldogs are therapy animals."

"They are," Janet said as she turned from the kitchen

sink. She actually held the Frenchie in one arm while she loaded the dishwasher with the other. "He's so sweet. He calms me." She beamed at the dog and passed him back to Nita.

"I'll bring him this weekend," Nita said. "I'm going to Louisville for a couple of days for an auction, and he needs someone to babysit."

Janet's face lit up, and she actually bent forward to kiss Goliath on the snout. "Yes, anytime."

Glenn grinned at her and put his arm around her, the pair of them sinking into one another in a way that once again sent longing through Nita. She knew what it felt like to be one-half of a couple like that, and she did want that again. She knew that comfort, and she knew that acceptance, and she hadn't had it in far too long.

She hugged her father and step-mother and took her little French bulldog out to her grandfather's old truck. He'd left it to her in his will, and she'd been driving it for the past eight years. She waited for Goliath to settle down beside her, the big bench seat allowing him to curl right into her thigh.

"Ready?" she asked him. He didn't answer, but Nita pretended he did. She flipped the truck into reverse, her thoughts spinning around Ian Chappell the whole way home.

When she got there, she parked in her driveway and killed the engine. She let Goliath down to go run through the grass and take care of his business before they went into the house, and while he did that, she dialed her mother.

"Mama," she said. "When can you brew me some of the

best coffee you've ever made?" There would be questions, and Nita would have to explain. She'd have to rise early and get to Lexington and back with the coffee, hopefully before Ian left his ranch house for the day.

The task of showing up on his front porch with "the world's best coffee" felt insurmountable, but Nita answered her mother's questions, set the date, and hung up.

Ian claimed to make a killer breakfast, but Conrad made the coffee. How could she make sure she showed up at the right time?

Call Conrad, came into her mind, and while he wasn't exactly on her speed-dial, she wouldn't have any problem getting his number. A smile formed on her face as she held the front door open for Goliath. The two of them went into her silent, still house, and Nita paused to listen.

She didn't hear anything in her own soul or from heaven that she shouldn't take Ian Chappell some coffee, so she lifted her phone up and started working on getting in touch with Conrad. Though her nerves chased each other through her body, Nita squared her shoulders and kept texting.

If Ian truly didn't want to see her or talk to her anymore, he'd have to tell her straight to her face...over breakfast.

CHAPTER 5

Conrad's cuss came down the hall as Ian hobbled on his crutches toward the kitchen. "What's goin' on?" he called just as a terrible clatter filled the air. That didn't sound good. It sounded like glass and metal and more cursing.

Ian rounded the corner and found Conrad flipping on the kitchen sink, the scent of coffee filling his nose. Then he saw it all on the floor, a spreading, weeping stain that he'd normally jump to help clean up. He couldn't do that now, and that only made his jaw clench tightly. Not to mention that now he had no morning coffee.

"Sorry," Conrad said, as if he'd spilled the coffee on purpose. "I was on the phone with Spur, and I didn't get the pot all the way on the burner." He crouched to start soaking up the dark liquid with a towel.

"It's fine," Ian said.

"I'll make more." Conrad stood and held the towel under the running water.

"You don't have time." Ian crutched himself over to the fridge. "I'll be fine. Do we have any of those Baja Blast things?" Upon opening the door he saw that they did not.

"You have time to make a big breakfast," Conrad said. "Do that. You'll feel better." He finished cleaning up the spilled coffee about the time Ian spotted the chub of breakfast sausage. He could easily make biscuits and gravy this morning and still have time to spare.

That thought only put him in a worse mood, though he reached for the sausage, his mouth already watering for homemade buttermilk biscuits.

"I'm not going to have my truck for the vow renewal," Conrad said. "I got an appointment for that Friday."

"You can drive mine."

"You're coming, right?"

Ian sighed with plenty of heft, enough for Conrad to get the hint that he didn't want to talk about Duke and Lisa's vow renewal. "Of course I'm coming," Ian said, balancing on one leg and his crutch while he reached up to the pot rack to get down a frying pan. "I'd be skewered and left to dry in the sun if I don't show up."

"Mom wouldn't do that," Conrad said, though he chuckled.

"I just don't want to go alone."

"Then ask someone to go with you."

Ian rolled his whole head to go with his eyes. "Yeah, that's so easy to do."

"You talk to Anita still," Conrad said, wisely turning his back on Ian so he didn't get burned by Ian's icy stare. The date at the hospital hadn't been terrible, but it hadn't been good. Nita had stayed for maybe twenty minutes, and he'd been embarrassed and horrified at what she must think of him now.

Thankfully, he didn't have to see her out on the ranch. He didn't see anyone. He barely left the house. Thunder rolled through his soul, and the familiar dark cloud that had been his constant buddy for the past few weeks settled right on his shoulder.

"I bet she'd go," Conrad said. "That's all I'm saying."

"Right. So you'll drive me over to her house to pick her up. You and Ry. And we'll all drive the forty minutes to the stud farm, and everything will magically be okay?" He spoke with a level of sarcasm he hadn't achieved in a while.

"Ry's good with small talk."

"Making me look like an even bigger idiot," Ian said, shaking his head as he cut open the end of the sausage chub. "Thanks, but no. I've already humiliated myself in front of that woman."

He wished with all his might that he'd rescheduled their date. There was no reason she'd had to come that very night, other than to satisfy his own desires. If he thought hard enough, he could still feel the gentle pressure of her lips against his, and his head hurt before lunchtime for how much he thought about Nita and that kiss.

"So I'll see you at two?" Conrad asked, drawing Ian away from breakfast and his constantly looping thoughts of the blonde woman who wouldn't stop nagging at him. He'd spoken to Nita, of course. Texting counted as talking, in his opinion. They'd done plenty of flirting before the shin splintering, stifled supper, and surgery.

Even their texts were a little stilted now, and they both answered without expanding or asking anything in return. In all honesty, it had been a few days since he'd messaged her.

So you'll do it while the biscuits bake, he thought. He wondered if she'd come to the house for breakfast if he asked.

He immediately rejected the idea. He hadn't showered yet, as that took a great deal of time and energy, and because he didn't go out on the ranch all that much, he didn't need to bathe nearly as often as he once had. He didn't want to face Nita with a couple of weeks' worth of a beard, wearing yesterday's T-shirt, and a pair of basketball shorts that didn't hide his hideous cast.

All of his brothers and their wives and children had signed it, creating a big deal out of his coming home. Ian had appreciated it, and he thought of the party with fondness even now.

"Ian?" Conrad asked. "Two o'clock?"

"Yes, I'll be there," Ian barked, and Conrad stuffed his cowboy hat on his head and walked toward the front door. He may have muttered something about how grouchy Ian was when he didn't have coffee, and Ian wanted to ask him whose fault that was.

He sighed as the front door closed behind his brother, leaving him in the corner house alone. As one of eight boys in the family, Ian had often searched the ranch in an attempt to find somewhere he could be by himself. It hadn't happened very often, and he did crave solitude. Now, he'd had enough alone-time over the past five weeks to last a lifetime.

He wanted Conrad to talk to him the way he used to. He wanted Cayden to keep his focus on his face and not let his eyes drip down to his cast. He wanted Spur to stop by with pizza and soda to watch a game, not to check in on him and make sure he hadn't slept through taking his pills.

He put the sausage in the pan and started browning it. While that worked, he got out the dry ingredients for the biscuits and measured them all into a bowl. He let his mind go, which meant it wandered out to the stables. He went to see his cars and his horses every single day, because no one was going to stop him from doing that.

He'd been given Digging Your Grave for the training season, and despite his injury, he'd told Conrad he wanted to continue on with their friendly wager. As he mixed wet ingredients with dry and rolled out the thick biscuit dough, he had the idea to get himself a training partner.

Spur could probably do it. Trey would help if Ian asked. So would Lawrence, who could see strengths and weaknesses in a horse.

Ian wanted to ask Nita. He'd seen her work personally with horses, and she had the calm spirit and loving attitude they needed. If someone tried to give advice she didn't want, watch out, but she never lost her temper with the horses.

"You're being stupid," he muttered to himself. He

couldn't even talk to Nita about the weather. He was light years away from asking her to train with him. Conrad would never allow it anyway. He'd say that if Ian got a partner, he should get one too.

"Knock, knock," Spur said, entering the house. "Smells good in here."

"Biscuits and gravy in about twenty minutes," Ian said, placing the last biscuit on the tray. In a normal world, he'd spin and bend and slide the sheet pan into the oven, no problem. A breath and it would be done.

Nothing in his world was all that normal anymore. It took him a few seconds just to turn and get the oven open. Then he had to hobble back, get the tray, and turn again. Ages later, he got the tray into the hot oven and closed the door.

He set the timer for twenty minutes and stirred the nearly-done sausage. "What are you doin' here already?"

"Just dropping in."

"Conrad called you, didn't he?"

"I have spoken to him this morning," Spur said coolly. "He spilled coffee during the call, and I got an earful of expletives." He settled onto barstool at the island and grinned at Ian. "All-Out didn't mind the extra distance, and you have grass he hasn't smelled before."

Spur rode his horse to work each day, which was easy as he lived right next door to the ranch.

"How's Olli?" Ian asked, putting together the cornstarch and water that would thicken his cream and make the gravy.

Spur sighed something fierce. "She's...okay."

"When are you going to tell everyone about the baby?"

"At the vow renewal," Spur said, and when Ian glanced at him, more worry sat on his face. "We have a couple of announcements, actually."

Ian wasn't surprised. Spur had left a family activity in a hurry several weeks ago, and he'd been cagey about details since. He knew his brother's life wasn't one-hundred-percent perfect, though he had a beautiful wife and the cutest little boy on the planet.

"Listen," Ian said, keeping his back to his oldest brother. They didn't hide much from one another, and Spur had always been Ian's safe place. "I'm thinking about asking... someone to come to the vow renewal with me."

"Okay," Spur said evenly. No, *Wow, Ian, really?* Spur never judged. He let Ian talk, and he asked him questions that didn't feel invasive.

"It's just that everyone else will have someone, and it's this big, romantic thing, and I don't want to be leaning against the wall like it needs me to hold it up with my one good leg." He poured cream into the sausage and started stirring. The rhythmic motion and sound of the whisk calmed him.

Shisk, shisk, shisk, shisk. The little brown bits colored the milk and he added the salt and pepper, then the cornstarch slurry. When it boiled, it would all come together into meaty, salty, peppery goodness.

"You—it's a good idea," Spur said. "If you do, though, I'd make sure I texted everyone first."

"Yeah," Ian said dryly. "The last thing we need is Mom

fainting at the vow renewal because I show up with Anita Powell." He turned up the flame under the skillet and turned to face Spur. "I can ask her, right?"

"I don't see why not." Spur gave him a friendly, brotherly smile. "So what if one date was bad? You know? You're allowed one bad date, especially on the day you break your tibia."

Ian nodded in short little bursts of his head. "I know."

"So just call her and ask her. She clearly torments you."

Ian turned back to the stove so his gravy didn't over-boil. "Is it that obvious?"

"Only to those of us who can tell when you haven't been sleeping well."

"That could be because of the leg."

"Is it?" Spur challenged.

Ian couldn't say that it was, so he said nothing.

Spur's phone rang, and Ian knew the ringtone. Cayden. The brother who did a lot of administrative work for the ranch. Spur would answer, and sure enough he said, "I'll see you this afternoon, Ian. Chin up," before the barstool scraped the floor, his boots took him toward the door, and he answered with, "Yep, I'm on my way right now."

Ian got shut inside the house again, but this time there were almost-golden-brown biscuits and the scent of peppered sausage gravy to keep him company. He'd never admit it to anyone, but he'd also found a couple of game shows on TV that he liked to watch, and he could eat on the couch, in the air conditioning, and solve puzzles, and not a soul would know.

Or care, he thought, knowing that wasn't quite true. Conrad cared. Spur cared. All of his family cared.

Someone knocked on the front door again, which somehow annoyed Ian, and he yelled, "It's open." He certainly wasn't going to go answer the blasted door.

It swung open, and he bent to check the biscuits. "Breakfast is almost ready," he said, finding the tops of the biscuits brown and flaky. Perfect. He took out the tray and set it on the stovetop beside the pan holding the gravy.

Whoever had arrived hadn't spoken or moved further into the house. He turned toward the door in his awkward hobble-hop-step and froze.

Anita Powell stood there. Stunningly beautiful, blonde, blue-eyed, and smiling Anita Powell. She wore blue jeans that went down to cowgirl boots and a top the color of apricots with flared, sort of frilly sleeves.

His mouth turned dry, and Ian had to lean into the counter for fear his one good leg would give out on him at the mere sight of her.

She held up a thermos the size of his forearm and said, "Perfect. I brought my mother's coffee for you to try."

CHAPTER 6

Nita wasn't sure if she should continue into the house or not, and she told herself to simply take another step. She'd been up for hours, first to make sure every piece of hair and every eyelash sat in the right place. Then she'd driven to Lexington to get the coffee. Her mother had hugged her and told her to be brave and bold.

Two things Nita never really felt, at least outside the training ring.

She glanced along the island where Ian stood, looking for his coffee mug though she knew he wouldn't have one. Conrad had been waiting for her at the entrance to Bluegrass, and he'd leaned out of his window to tell her everything had gone exactly to plan. Spur was on his way to the corner house, and he'd only stay a few minutes.

Nita had parked beside Cayden while he called Spur, and they'd both seen him ride his horse away from the house.

With Chappell eyes on her, Nita had eased her ancient truck in front of the corner house, and she'd made the trek up the steps to the front door.

She'd come all this way, and she could go a little further. "I don't see any coffee here," she said, putting a mock frown on her face. "I thought you said Conrad made coffee every morning."

"He does," Ian said, pushing away from the counter.

Nita got moving too as he continued with, "He spilled it all this morning, though." A smile crawled across his face. "So this is perfect."

She returned his smile and set the thermos on the counter where he could reach it. "I think there's enough for both of us, though I was hoping to try Conrad's and compare it to my mom's."

Ian positioned his hands on his crutches and moved away from the delicious-looking food on the stove. "It's so great to see you."

She walked around the end of the island, and it was so easy and so natural to step into his arms, even with the crutches on the sides. "Same here," she said, holding onto those broad shoulders and chastising herself for waiting so long to do this.

"I'm so sorry," he whispered. "You must be so angry with me."

Nita didn't say she wasn't, though anger wasn't the right emotion. "I don't know what I am," she admitted. "I figured you needed some space." Which she was happy to give. Honestly, she was.

Ian stepped back and cleared his throat. "I haven't even showered today."

"I don't care," Nita said, her eyes dropping to his single sneakered foot. Surprise darted through her. "No cowboy boots." She met his eyes again. "Well, I'll be. As-cowboy-as-they-come Ian Chappell owns sneakers."

He laughed, the sound not very loud and dying quickly. "The boots slip too much, especially in the house. You're lucky I have shoes on at all." He started to turn around. "Do you really want to stay and eat? It's biscuits and gravy."

"I really do," Nita said, her first instinct to step past him and help him. She could dish everything up while he sat at the table. She resisted that urge, because Conrad had specifically told her Ian didn't want to be pitied or babied. He could do things, and he wanted to.

"Go ahead and sit then," he said. "I'll bring it over." He looked over his shoulder at her. "I'd prefer the dining room table. The bar is hard for me."

"Table it is," Nita said with a smile. "Can I get mugs or silverware?"

"Sure," Ian said. "The end drawer there has silverware. Mugs are in the cupboard right here between the stove and fridge."

Nita opened the drawer and got a couple of forks. She stepped past him, getting a noseful of that masculine scent that reminded her of spicy dryer sheets, and she may have moved a little too close to him to get the mugs out. He didn't seem to mind, and he even cut her a look out of the corner of his eye.

"Are you mad?" he asked.

"No," she said, reaching for two mugs. "You?"

"Not at you."

"At the world?" she guessed.

"Mostly," Ian admitted. "Everyone keeps telling me I'm going to heal, and I won't have the crutches forever, but it doesn't feel like it. Most days are filled with challenges I've never had to deal with."

Nita nodded and set the mugs on the slim counter between the fridge and stove. She shifted her weight so she leaned into Ian's side. "Has anyone ever told you that you don't have to deal with those challenges alone?"

His hand slid along her waist, sending shivers through her whole body. He had to feel that, and as he ducked his head toward her, Nita knew he did. Ian was a man, after all, and he'd certainly had girlfriends before.

He's been married, she reminded herself. *So have you.*

She knew how to talk to a man, and that reminder gave her another dose of courage. She looked up at him too, their faces only a few inches apart.

"I really am sorry," he murmured. "There's this level of embarrassment I'm dealing with. I just want to hide away until I'm all the way better. Then no one will get to see how pathetic I am."

"You're not pathetic," she whispered. Feeling reckless and out of control—about how she'd felt when she'd first met Sampson—she reached up and brushed Ian's longer hair off his forehead. "Handsome, yes. You're definitely that." She smiled at him as he grinned at her. She let her fingers trail down the side of his face. "A little scruffy with the beard, but I kinda like it."

"Hm," he said. "I seem to recall you throwing the word *scruffy* at me like it was an insult once."

"I will deny liking it until the day I die," she teased. "Besides, we all have bad days and things we're not proud of."

His eyebrows went up, and in the intimate space between them, Nita felt warm and appreciated. She hadn't felt like that in so long, and she wanted to stand at his side for a good long while. "Was that a bad day for you?"

"Not my finest moment," she admitted. "Marching over here and yelling at you? Yeah, I regret it."

Ian leaned closer and pressed his lips to her forehead. "I don't." With that, he shifted, and she moved a few inches away from him. Her mind cleared, and she took the silverware and mugs to the table. He followed with his clunk-step-shuffle and put the pan of gravy on the table too.

She returned to the bar to get the coffee, and then opened his fridge to find cream. At least three bottles sat on the top shelf, and she grabbed one. "Sugar?"

"Other side of the stove."

They performed a little dance so she could move around him, and she stepped slowly behind him as he took the biscuits to the table too. With everything there, Nita sat, not looking at Ian as he leaned his crutches against the wall and then hopped a couple of times to his seat.

He settled and looked at her, his eyes wide and open and

unassuming. "This is nice," he said. "Thank you for coming. I usually eat by myself on the couch."

"You just described every evening for me," she said. "Well, Goliath is right there, staring me in the face until I give him a little bite." She gave a light laugh and reached for a biscuit.

"You eat meat, right?" Ian asked, and Nita's eyebrows flew up.

"Yes," she said. "Why wouldn't I?"

"You didn't eat your ribs in the hospital." He glanced at her and went back to preparing his plate of food by splitting three biscuits and laying them open on his plate.

Nita had already spilled plenty of secrets, so she saw no point in keeping this one. "That's because I didn't want to eat like an animal in front of you," she said.

Ian paused, his gaze catching on hers and holding. The moment lengthened, and Nita allowed herself to blink. She would not look away, though. "You have nothing to be embarrassed of," she said. "Not when it comes to me."

She wasn't sure why she felt like she needed to convince him of that, but she did. The words were there, and she'd said them.

He gave her a short nod and ladled gravy over his biscuits. "Tell me about that truck you drive."

"It's my granddaddy's," she said, her nerves relaxing now that all the hard stuff had happened. "Well, it was. It's mine now. He willed it to me when he passed."

"I'm sorry. How long ago was that?"

"Eight or nine years," Nita said, taking some gravy too.

She cut into her biscuit and took a big bite. Saltiness, meatiness, and peppery goodness filled her mouth. "Wow," she said around the food. "This is amazing."

Ian laughed again, and it was so good to see him do that. She didn't think he had a whole lot to laugh about these days.

Nita chewed and swallowed, and said, "The whole reason I'm here: coffee." She reached for the thermos and poured him a mugful and then one for herself. The earthy, sharp scent of it made her sigh, and she reached for the sugar.

"I know you're a cream man," she said. "Do you put in sugar too?"

"Is coffee coffee without sugar?"

"No, siree," she said, grinning at him.

He doctored his up with plenty of cream but only a little sugar, while Nita did the opposite. Lots of sugar, only a splash of cream. She lifted her mug to her lips in sync with Ian, and she couldn't help staring at him.

He really was gorgeous, and the only reason he didn't have a wife and family was because he didn't want one. She needed to figure out why that was and if his stance on those things had changed. Every moment she spent with him caused her opinion to change, and she could easily see herself getting married again.

To Ian Chappell.

Slow down, she told herself. She didn't know him superwell yet, and she wasn't going to make the same mistakes she'd made in the past.

"This is fantastic," he said, lowering his mug. "Way better than Conrad's." He held his mug toward her, almost like a point. "Don't you dare tell him I said that."

Happiness exploded through Nita. "I would never. My mother will be thrilled." She set her mug back on the table too. "World's best, do you think?"

"Best I've had," he said. "So yes."

Nita nodded like that settled everything and cut into her biscuit again.

"Did you...I mean, what did you tell your mom?" Ian kept his eyes on his plate this time.

"Let's see," Nita said, flirting with him. "I told her there was this man I liked, and we'd tried to get together. But it was all...confusing, and he was in the hospital, and then he sort of stopped texting me. I sort of stopped texting him too, but I couldn't stop thinking about him."

She cleared her throat. "Plus, I wanted to make sure he was okay out in this house all by himself. I asked her if she'd make enough coffee for me to take him some, and well, here we are."

The weight of Ian's eyes rested on her, but Nita didn't dare look up. "She's expecting a full report afterward, and once you meet my mom, you'll get how terrifying that is." She tried to laugh, but it sounded too forced and she cut it off quickly.

"Am I going to meet her?"

"I would think so," Nita said. "If you...well, if you don't stop texting me this time." She lifted her head then, and the four feet between her and Ian felt like four inches. The man oozed intensity, and she knew he didn't do anything halfway, including relationships.

"I won't stop texting you," he said.

She nodded, and they ate for a couple of minutes. With her plate clean, she said, "All right, Ian Chappell. Tell me one thing about yourself that I don't know."

His eyes widened for a moment, and then his whole face relaxed into a smile. He had straight, white teeth and adorable crinkles around his eyes when he did that, and Nita's gut reaction was to smile back.

So she did.

"You love your granddaddy's truck," he said.

"Yes." She wasn't sure where this was going, and she folded her arms on the table in front of her, giving him her full attention.

"I own a few cars," he said.

Nita blinked, her heart skipping a couple of beats. "Define 'a few'."

"Come on." He got to his feet and while he hopped over to his crutches, Nita did too. She scooped his plate on top of hers and took them both to the kitchen sink before she followed him out onto the back deck.

He went all the way to the railing and indicated a massive warehouse-slash-shed. "Enough to fill that."

Nita stared at the light blue building, sure he was kidding. "Are you serious?"

Ian chuckled and nodded. "Maybe it's not full yet. But yeah. I have some pretty cool stuff out there."

Nita looked at him, and his smile slipped. "Do you drive all of them?"

"Sure," he said. "I go out there and visit them every day, especially now that I can't do as much on the ranch. That's pretty lame, right? My only friends are vehicles and horses."

"And your brothers," Nita said quickly. "And me." She stepped closer to him and put her arm around his back. "It's okay for the people we care about to see us at our worst." Her mouth filled with more words, and even when she tried to swallow them back, she couldn't.

"That's what my husband told me once," she said. "And he was right."

Beside her, Ian tensed. "Husband?"

Nita let the sadness wash over her, somewhat surprised at how quickly it dried up. "Yeah," she said. "Sampson died about six years ago now."

Ian's arms came around her then, and he held her against his chest. "I'm so sorry. I didn't know you'd been married."

Nita took a deep breath and let it all out. Then another. Standing in Ian's arms was like standing in the embrace of an angel, because he was so...*good*. So strong. In a lot of ways, he reminded her of Sampson. In others, he was completely different. She felt safe with him, though, and that was important to her.

"We only got a short time together," she murmured. "He was diagnosed with cancer a couple of months before our wedding. He tried to call it off, and he tried to break-up with me. He said he didn't want me to see him deteriorate, and he didn't want to make me suffer."

Ian's arms around her only tightened.

"What he didn't get was that I wanted to see all of that. I wanted to be right there with him, because I loved him. I only let him have a couple of days to himself, and then I showed up on his doorstep and said we were moving up the wedding date." Nita laughed, though it sounded more like a scoff or a sob. Maybe both. "We got eight months as husband and wife."

"You saw him at his worst," Ian said.

"His best, too," Nita said. "So please, don't be embarrassed in front of me, Ian. I'm a safe place for you."

"Thank you," he murmured, his lips pressing against her temple again. "Would you go to my brother's vow renewal with me? It's next weekend."

Hope and joy burst through Nita, and she said, "Yeah, sure. Of course."

"It's going to be a big deal."

She looked up at him, but his gaze was stuck out on the shed that housed all of his cars. "A vow renewal?"

Ian shook his head, a faraway look in his eye. "No, me showing up with you."

While Nita felt like she'd been the one revealing secrets and speaking truths, she heard the absolute meaning behind what he'd just said. "Why's that?" she asked.

Before he could answer, a dog barked, and Ian twisted back toward the house. Someone called, and he stepped away from her, balanced on his crutches, and started hobbling back that way. "Yeah," he called. "I'm out here."

Blaine Chappell appeared in the back door, and two

corgis trotted out onto the deck, happy little smiles on their faces and their tongues hanging out. They bypassed Ian and came toward her, and Nita crouched down, her own smile on her face for the pups.

"Sorry," Blaine said. "I didn't mean to interrupt something."

"You didn't," Ian said. "There's breakfast if you want some." Their voices faded as they went inside. Nita scrubbed down both corgis, hoping with everything inside her that Ian would keep his promise and text her this time. She had laid a lot on the line for him, and she didn't want him to kick it back into her face.

CHAPTER 7

Lisa Chappell sucked back the tears, as everything made her cry these days and she didn't know how to deal with it. The emotions that came with pregnancy weren't to be trifled with, she knew that.

Ian's text—a text from her brother-in-law—had made the feelings swirl this morning.

I've been advised I better let everyone know that I'm bringing a woman with me to the vow renewal. So I'm hereby letting you know.

"Holy cow," Duke, Lisa's husband, said from his side of the bed. "Did you see this text from Ian?"

"I just got it," she said, her back turned to him too. She rolled over at the same time as Duke. "Who is it?"

"I have no idea," Duke said, sitting up, his finger jabbing at the phone.

"He said he doesn't want questions."

"I'm not asking him." Duke continued to text, and Lisa went back to her phone.

Ian had said, *I would appreciate zero questions, zero staring, and plenty of support. She's great, and I think you'll like her too. Mom, do not make a big deal out of this. I just didn't want to be alone among so many of you who have someone at their side. It's nothing.*

Lisa didn't believe him for a second about that last part, and she smiled as Spur texted. All of the brothers would wait for him to say something, and she expected a flurry of responses now that he had.

It's not nothing, he'd said. *But I agree it's also not a big deal. I'm sure we Chappells know how to behave for Ian.*

I'm sure we do, Blaine said.

"How's he getting here?" Lisa asked as she rolled back to her side. She wasn't due until the end of March—another five months—but she felt huge already. She definitely had a baby belly, and she didn't carry much extra weight, so the ten pounds she'd gained with the infant felt like a lot.

"Conrad's driving him," Duke said, still distracted. "Spur's not talking."

"Leave it," Lisa said. "We'll find out when they get here." She got to her feet and added, "I'm going to go shower, and then we need to get those tables out."

"I got it, baby." Duke abandoned his phone then and took Lisa into his arms as she made to go past him and into the master bathroom. He grinned down at her, one hand moving to her baby bump. "How'd you sleep? Okay?" He bent to kiss her neck, and Lisa loved being loved by him.

"Yeah," she said. "Okay. You?"

"Just fine," he said. "I'll get breakfast going and the tables out while you get ready."

"Ginny and Mariah will be here in an hour."

"We'll be ready," Duke assured her, and Lisa decided to let him handle things today. They'd been over the schedule, and their phones had sounded an alarm at the exact same time. She went into the bathroom, and Duke stepped into a pair of jeans and left the bedroom.

Forty-five minutes later, Lisa emerged from the bedroom, fully dressed and ready for this family party. She'd invited both of her brothers and their families, her mother, and everyone who worked for Harvey's, the stud farm she'd inherited and now ran.

Duke stood in the kitchen, laughing with Bruce. They both looked at her as she went past the dining room table. "Hey," Bruce said, stepping into her and hugging her. "How are you?"

"Good," she said into his shoulder, her emotions once again rearing up at how tender and close their relationship was now. For a while there, before Daddy's death, and after it, she'd thought she'd lost everyone and everything. She and Bruce had been working hard over the past year to mend things between them, and she wasn't surprised to find him here early.

"Is Belinda on the way with the kids?"

"Yeah, she just texted."

"Kelly's outside," Duke said. "He's finishing with the chairs." He put a plate on the counter. "Come eat, baby."

"We're serving lunch in a few hours."

"That's at least three more hours *after* you need to eat." Duke gave her a look that said, *Please. A couple of bites.*

Lisa rarely ate breakfast as it was, but with the pregnancy, she'd been sicker on the mornings she didn't eat. She was through the first trimester now, though, but Duke didn't seem to care about that.

She picked up a wedge of watermelon and took a bite. "Thanks, baby," she said, because he did take extraordinarily good care of her. Duke turned back to the stove as Kelly came inside, and her other half-brother sat beside her at the bar and gave her a side hug.

"Morning," he said. "Are you two ready for this?"

"Why wouldn't we be ready for this?" Lisa asked as Duke turned from the stove and slid scrambled eggs onto her plate.

"It's a lot of people," Kelly said, exchanging a glance with Duke. "You don't like people."

"I like people just fine," Lisa said, shooting her husband a look. "Someone's been saying things they shouldn't."

"I just asked them to watch you and help you make an exit if you need to," Duke said, turning his back on her again. He didn't sound sorry either. "Eggs, Kelly?"

"If you're cooking 'em, yes," he said.

Duke cracked more eggs, and a few minutes later, the three of them sat down with Lisa to eat. They'd barely finished when the doorbell rang. Lisa had been served first, and had finished first, so she said, "I'll get it. You guys relax."

On the way to the front door, she prayed it would be

Darla. Her mother had RSVP'ed and said she'd come just for the day. Lisa didn't talk to her mom all that much, though she had tried to involve her more in her life since becoming pregnant.

Sure enough, Darla stood on the front step, wearing big, black, movie-star sunglasses though the day was a little overcast. She also wore a loud, flowery print that should've probably been worn in April or May, and a smile appeared when she saw Lisa.

"Hello, darling," she said, and Lisa refrained from rolling her eyes until she'd hugged her mom.

"Hey, Mom," she said. "How was the drive?"

"Oh, easy on a Saturday morning this early."

"It's not that early," Lisa said, as the clock almost read ten. She pulled away as more tires crunched over the gravel. Ginny and Mariah had arrived. "Remember, Mom, Ginny and Mariah are in charge. They'll put you to work, not the other way around."

"I remember," her mom said. "Now, where can I put these flowers?" She indicated a big, white bucket at her feet. "They're magnolias."

"I see that," Lisa said, admiring the white blooms. "Let's ask Ginny. I know she's in charge of decorations. Mariah is working with the food and facilities." Her two sisters-in-law were getting out of the SUV, with the back already lifted. "I'll go see if they need help bringing anything in."

"I've got it," Duke said, coming up behind her. "Good morning, Darla. How good to see you." Duke could charm a fence post, and he'd definitely won over her mother, once she'd realized who he really was.

He stepped into her mother and gripped her tight. Darla laughed as Duke lifted her off her feet, and he took her hand and said, "You come with me. I'm sure Ginny will have something for you to carry to the deck."

Lisa stood in the doorway and marveled at the blessings in her life, most of which stemmed from Duke.

From there, every time she tried to do something, Bruce, Kelly, or Duke would say, "I got it," and step in. She let them too, because she didn't have to be in charge, and it actually felt really good to let someone else run the show.

Ginny and Mariah had serious skills when it came to putting on parties, and no one would let Lisa out onto the back deck to see it. She stayed in the house, welcoming people as they started to show up just after noon.

The renewal was set to happen at twelve-thirty, and then they'd be serving lunch. The island and counters along the back wall held a lot of that food right now, and people lingered in the kitchen and living room.

"Congratulations," Olli said, drawing Lisa into a hug. She bore a baby bump too, though no official announcement had been made. Olli had told Lisa about her pregnancy privately a few weeks ago, at a lunch date she'd invited her to attend.

Lisa always felt so welcome with Olli, and she pressed her eyes against the tears trying to squeeze their way out. "To you too," she whispered, about all her voice could do against the emotions streaming through her.

She stepped over to Spur, who hugged her too, offering his congratulations. Lisa stood and talked to Beth and Trey for a few minutes. "When can she get the implants?" she asked, smiling at their baby girl, Fern.

"We're going to do them right after the Sweetheart Classic," Trey said, swiping his daughter's wispy hair to the right and smiling at her. "They say she's a good candidate."

"That's so great," Lisa said. "I hope she does well with them." Fern had been born without hardly any hearing, and Trey and Beth were going to get her cochlear implants once she turned a year old.

"Lisa," a woman said, and Lisa turned toward Duke's mother's voice.

"Hello, Julie." She smiled as she hugged the older woman. She'd been accommodating and welcoming to Lisa, and that had only been rivaled by her husband, Jefferson. Lisa hugged him too, and left them to talk to Trey and Beth while she said hello to Lawrence and Cayden, who'd just arrived together.

Right behind them came Blaine, Tam, and the twins, and Lisa immediately reached for Caroline. She was the fussier, whinier of the twins, but Lisa loved her with her whole heart. "Let's see if I can get you a strawberry," she said, smiling at Tam, who looked slightly lost without the little girl.

More cowboys and their wives arrived, and Lisa made sure she got around to all of them to say hello. She employed them, and they meant a great deal to her. Daddy had taught her to make sure they knew how much, and having dinners and parties was only one way she could show them she wanted them in her life, at the stud farm.

Finally, only a few minutes remained, and she had to relinquish Caroline to Julie and go down the hall. She reached for Duke's hand just as the front door opened again.

"It's got to be them," Duke said, jerking back toward the living room. "If it's not Conrad and Ian, I'm going to lose my mind." He hated being outside the family gossip, and living so far from Bluegrass Ranch had definitely caused some grief for him.

She went with him, and Conrad and his fiancée, Ry, stepped into the room first. They both wore wide smiles and started accepting hello hugs and handshakes. Ian, who would be on crutches for quite a while yet, was obviously slower, and even when Conrad stepped into Spur and gave him a hearty hug, she didn't see him.

A few seconds later, he made it to the end of the hall from the foyer, dressed to the nines just as Lisa would expect for a wedding vow renewal. He wore black slacks and a shiny shoe on his left foot. A light blue, short-sleeved dress shirt hugged his upper body, and a tie with plenty of white and blue and black stitching in the shape of paisleys sat around his throat. Every Chappell wore a dark cowboy hat, and Ian's was definitely the very blackest.

He reached the end of the hallway and glanced to his left, clearly looking for the woman he'd brought with him. A beautiful blonde stepped right to his side and slipped her hand into his waiting one. She had bright blue eyes and tan skin that made her light hair seem even whiter.

Lisa felt like she'd seen her before, somewhere, but she couldn't quite place it.

"Wow," Duke said. "It's Anita Powell."

"Who's she?" Lisa asked, putting her arm through Duke's.

"She's a trainer for Glenn Marks," he whispered back. "Let's go say hello first so we can go get dressed."

Lisa let him lead her across the room, where Ian had just stepped out of Blaine's arms.

"Hey," Duke said. "Thanks for coming." He hugged Ian too, and then looked at Anita.

"This is Anita Powell," Ian said. "Nita, this is Duke. He's the youngest." He smiled at Duke and then Lisa, who stepped into him to hug him too.

"How's your leg?" she asked.

"It's comin' along," he said, holding her tightly with one arm. She stepped back at the tail end of Duke's handshake with the pretty blonde. Lisa stepped in front of her husband and drew Anita into a hug.

If the other woman was surprised by the gesture, she didn't act like it. She had plenty of muscles in her arms and shoulders, and she too didn't carry hardly any extra weight on her petite frame. "Thanks for coming with Ian," Lisa said. "It's great to meet you."

"And you," she said. "What's your name?"

"Oh, sorry," Ian said. "This is Lisa, Duke's wife."

Lisa fell back to Duke's side as he added, "It's their vow renewal, since they kind of got married on the sly last year."

Anita glanced at Ian, surprise and questions in those eyes.

"We have to go get dressed," Duke said. "We just wanted to say hello and welcome real quick."

Lisa smiled and nodded, then she went with Duke while Mariah started calling for everyone to please find a seat on the deck.

In the privacy of their bedroom, Lisa quickly changed out of her jeans and blouse and into a pretty, peachy dress that felt like feathers and lace against her legs. Ry had designed and sewed it specifically for her and for this occasion, and Lisa almost lost her battle with her tears when she looked at herself in the mirror.

"Gorgeous," Duke murmured, holding up a necklace. "I got you this."

Lisa blinked at the diamond pendant, the silver chain, and the little charm near the gem.

"It's an L and a D," he said, stepping around her. Lisa lifted her hair so he could put the necklace on for her. "I had Ry help me with it, so it would match."

"It's beautiful," Lisa said, tears filling her eyes. "Thank you, Duke."

"I love you." He finished with the clasp and placed a kiss on the back of her neck.

She turned into him and kissed him square on the mouth, which helped her keep the tears from ruining her makeup. "I love you too."

Then they linked arms and left the bedroom together, the same way they were going to live the rest of their lives.

CHAPTER 8

Tan bore the weight of at least two dozen eyes, but he kept his smile in place. He loved his brothers. He loved their wives. He loved his parents, even if his mother stuck her nose into his business when she shouldn't.

"Hello, son," she said, hugging him.

"Hey, Mom," he said.

"We would've given you a ride," she said.

Yeah, so you could interrogate Anita, he thought. He said, "It was easy for Conrad. We live together, and Ry came out to Bluegrass and left her car there."

"Oh." His mom pulled away, searching his face the way only she could. "Where does Anita live? You didn't have to go back to town to get her?"

"No," he said, settling his weight onto his good leg and balancing with the crutches. Nita moved to his side and put her hand through his elbow. He looked at her, glad they'd fired up their texting game again, and beyond glad he'd asked her to give him space to hug everyone and then come back to his side.

She played the part almost a little too perfectly, and he wondered if it was a part for her today. It probably was, as she had a wide smile glued to her face too. He'd never known Nita to grin like that, though she didn't hold back with the smiles all that much.

"She lives over by the windmills," he said, swinging his head back to his mom. "It's like, ten minutes from the ranch, if that. Out by the river."

"Oh, that's wonderful," Mom said as if Ian and Anita would be married on her small plot of land the very next day.

Ian looked toward the open back door, and not just because Mariah had asked them all to move that way and find a seat. The rectangle letting in a patch of sunlight called to him, urging him to flee the confines of this house.

He reminded himself that he'd brought this upon himself by inviting Nita, and he had to admit he did like having her right at his side. She was ten times better than having Spur escort him outside.

"We better go get a seat," he said. "I want one on an end where my leg has room."

Nita's grip on his arm didn't slip, and she moved at his snail's pace through the kitchen, the same way she had from her front door to the truck, and then from the truck and into Duke's house.

Plenty of people had followed directions faster than

them, but Ian spotted two seats beside Olli and Spur—in the very front row. "Front, please," he murmured, and Nita kept them moving in that direction.

Thankfully, Mom peeled off on the second row with Daddy, and they sat beside Blaine and Tam to help with the babies. Ginny bustled around with Boone on her hip, the way Ian had seen her do for a few months now. Cayden had their seats saved, and he jumped to his feet whenever his wife even looked his way.

Ian did like watching his brothers interact with the women in their lives. He'd learned what a real relationship looked like, and as he sat down and let Nita take his crutches, which refused to bend the way the human body did, he realized that he might be able to recognize a true, living, breathing love again.

He glanced at Nita as she stepped past him, having leaned his crutches against the railing nearby. "Thanks," he said.

"Sure thing." She sat down and crossed her legs, tugging the black and white patterned skirt right to her knee. She'd paired that with a blouse the color of cantaloupe, and Ian reached over and took her hand in his.

She met his eye, a shy smile touching her face. He leaned toward her, the brim of his cowboy hat creating an intimate space between him. "You didn't have to buy a shirt to go with everyone."

She glanced around, and everywhere Ian looked, he saw shades of peach, apricot, and cantaloupe. "Can you imagine if I didn't?" she asked. "We'd stick out even more than we currently do."

He squeezed her hand, because she was probably right. "Is this okay?" He lifted their joined hands half an inch.

"It *is* a wedding," she said.

"Yeah, but—" he started, but everyone around him started to stand, and Ian twisted to look over his shoulder. Duke and Lisa stood in the doorway, and Ian wished he'd known he'd have to stand up again so soon after sitting down.

Beside him, Nita got to her feet and offered him her hand. "Just hold onto me," she whispered.

He wanted to yell that she was nowhere near strong enough to hold him, but he didn't want to cause a scene for Duke. Nita put both hands together, and Ian put one of his in both of hers. Her grip firmed up around his fingers, and the next thing he knew, he'd managed to get to his feet by pushing against her hands and putting his other hand on her waist and then her shoulder.

He hopped just once to find his position, and she slid her arm around him and pulled him into her side. He looped his arm around her too, and together, the two of them balanced easily on three legs.

Ian's heartbeat throbbed in his chest, moved up to his throat, and spread through his whole body. Nita was wiry and strong, and he'd underestimated her. He vowed it would be the last time he did that.

He met Duke's eye, who nodded, and then he and Lisa started down the aisle created by the rows of chairs. Maybe thirty or forty people had come to the vow renewal today, and Ian knew most of them, even the cowboys who worked here at Harvey's.

No one had looked at him with pity or condolences, and Ian appreciated that too. He told himself the day wasn't over yet, and Mom could say any number of things during lunch. Right now, though, he could just hold onto Nita and then enjoy watching Duke and Lisa renew their love for one another.

Once Duke and Lisa stood at the front of the crowd, Ian waited for Spur to step past Nita and balance him on his wounded, right side before he sank back into the chair. "Thanks," he said to his brother, who said nothing as he retook his seat and then took his baby from his wife.

Nita's hand migrated right back to Ian's, and he caught sight of a bit more skin on her legs as she crossed them again, this time without tugging the skirt down. Heat filled him from top to bottom, and his thoughts scattered.

This woman had him thinking things he hadn't allowed inside his mind in a decade, and he had no idea what to do about it.

"Thanks for coming," Duke said, dressed in a suit and tie. No tuxedo. Ian was surprised Duke had gone that far, as he usually talked about how casual he liked things. Beside him, Lisa wore a pretty dress in the renewal color of apricot, and Ian was sure Ry was behind that thing. It was gorgeous and definitely one-of-a-kind.

"We don't have a pastor or anything here, which I'm sure is a great disappointment to my mother." He grinned at her, because Duke had always been one of the more easy-going brothers. He had problems just like everyone else, and he'd been working hard on his classes and around the ranch. He still came at life with a glass-half-full mentality, and Ian did envy him that.

"Lisa and I just wanted to read our vows to each other and celebrate with y'all, because we didn't really get to do that the first time." He smiled at his wife, and there was simply something different about a man's smile when he gave it to the woman he loved. Ian could feel it way down deep in his chest, and in that moment of time, he wanted to smile at a woman like that again.

He had, once.

The cement he'd poured into his veins and had let fill his heart started to break up, especially when Lisa reached up with both hands and cradled Duke's face in her palms. "I love you, Duke Chappell, even when you make it hard to do that. Even when you track mud over my clean floors, and even when you say there's no space for Secondhand Lion at Bluegrass."

Duke chuckled, as did a few other men. He organized and scheduled a lot of their breeding, and he and Lisa had known each other for a while before they'd started seeing one another.

"There's no one else in the entire world I'd want to live this life with, and I can't wait to see if our baby has your nose or mine." She stretched up and kissed him, and Ian got another glimpse of what a woman in love actually looked like.

The kiss was short and chaste, and Lisa dropped her hands to her sides. Ian leaned toward Nita, who inclined her head toward him at the same time. "They have a box inside," he whispered. "We're supposed to put names in it for a boy or a girl."

"Do they know what they're having?"

"Not yet."

"Lisa," Duke said up front, and Ian shut his mouth. "I knew the moment I started thinking about you after I'd left work that I needed to ask you out. Even when you weren't very nice to me, and even when you wouldn't let me have King Arthur, even when my brother thought I was going to take a swing at you."

Lisa smiled and shook her head, and Ian hadn't heard this story. He did know that he'd been thinking about Nita for a while too, and he wondered if that was a good sign or not.

"So I thought about you. And thought about you. When you needed me, I showed up, even when you didn't want me there. I will always show up for you, because I love you. I'm thrilled to be yours, and I know we'll have plenty of happy, fun years together with our family."

"To Duke and Lisa," Spur yelled, as if he'd been instructed to, and several others joined in. Ian did not yell out, and he wondered if he would've had he been married already, or if he'd come alone.

He wasn't sure, so he just clapped along with everyone else as Duke and Lisa kissed again. He could whistle through his teeth, and he did that, which made Nita laugh. He grinned at her, thrilled they had this time together.

He'd seen her a few more times around the ranch since she'd shown up for breakfast last week, but he hadn't asked her out again. He probably should, but he didn't want to make her drive. He wasn't going to ask Conrad to do so again, as that had been ultra-embarrassing to hobble-walk up to Nita's front door while Conrad and Ry watched.

"We're going to exchange rings," Duke said as the whooping and hollering quieted down. He reached for the ring box Lawrence held out for him, and Lisa twisted to get a ring from one of her brothers.

"I got Lisa a new necklace," Duke said, his voice clear and loud. He loved being in the spotlight, and he had no problem with public speaking. Ian would rather have pins stuck in his eyes than do either of those. "This ring matches the diamond in the pendant, and it's got Chappell and Harvey engraved on the inside of the band."

He held up the ring like anyone in the crowd would be able to see it. Lisa's face shone like the sun, and she peered at the inside of the ring, pure delight streaming from her. Duke slid the ring on her finger, and then she held up his ring.

"I had this made from the ashes of one of Duke's breeding books. I know all of you here know what a control freak he is about the covering and the breeding at Bluegrass, and I convinced him to let me have one of his old notebooks from five years ago." She grinned at him. "Apparently, that was long enough ago that he doesn't need to leaf through it again."

"Hey," he said. "Those books are a lot of work."

She reached for his hand. "They can make rings out of ashes, and now you can wear that work with you every day. It'll be a reminder of who you are and what you do, but that we need to make sure we work on us too."

Duke nodded, not smiling for maybe the first time that day. Ian had watched Daddy work and work and work, and he'd witnessed Spur do the same thing. His oldest brother leaned over and put his arm around his wife, pressing a kiss to her temple.

This was a good reminder for everyone there—spouses needed attention too, and Ian could admit that the Chappell men knew how to do that for horses really well. Women... they needed to work on those relationships.

Duke looked at his ring, and then his wife, and they kissed again. Ginny got up and gestured with one hand. "We'll be serving lunch at the tables out in the garden. Cowboys, please help us move the chairs. If you're sitting in it, it needs to go." She grinned out at everyone, and the activity started.

Ian didn't move. He wanted to hold Nita's hand and smell the scent of her vanilla and rose perfume for the rest of the day. He let the others start to take their chairs down the steps to the tented area in the yard, and once Spur had a chair for him and Olli all set up, he came back onto the deck.

"I'll get yours," Spur said, and that caused Ian to get up. He took the crutches from Nita, who once again stayed by his side on the journey down to the tables.

He sat beside Conrad, who gave him a side-shoulder-squeeze, and Ian said, "Ry, her dress is fantastic."

"Thank you," Ry said, confirming his suspicions that she'd designed it. "She does look amazing in that color." She looked down at her own shirt, very nearly the same shade. "Unlike the rest of us."

"You look amazing," Conrad said, plenty of sincerity in his voice.

"This color washes me out," Ry said. "I'm not wearing it at our wedding." She gave Conrad a glare as if he'd suggested such a thing.

Ian couldn't hide his grin as Conrad held up both hands in surrender. "Absolutely not."

"All right," Ginny yelled from the long tables that had been set up near the head of the tents. "Spur and Olli have something to say, and then Cayden is going to pray. Then you can come get lunch. Everything is set up and ready."

Ian hadn't even seen anyone bring all the food that had been inside out, and he supposed there were a lot of helping, cowboy hands there. Normally, he'd have been some of them, and a twinge of guilt ate at him.

That quickly got replaced by a dose of worry as Spur cleared his throat and stood from the table only a couple of places away from Ian. All eyes moved to him, and he reached for Gus and then Olli, who stood with him.

"Olli's gonna have another baby," he said in a clear voice. "Round about April or so."

The congratulations and cheers started, and Mom even got out of her seat at the next table over to hug both Olli and

Spur. She loved being the center of attention too, and Ian found himself getting annoyed with his mother.

Things quieted again, but Spur didn't sit down. "She's got a few health problems that make the pregnancy high-risk. Namely, she's got a couple of blood clots we've been treating. She's been on a blood thinner for a little bit now—since her last fall—and one of the clots has broken up. Eventually, she'll need surgery to put in a filter to keep the clots from moving into her heart and lungs, where they can obviously kill a person."

No one moved. No one spoke. Ian couldn't have formed words even if he'd tried.

"I'm okay," Olli said into the void. "We're working with an amazing doctor, who coordinates with my OBGYN, and I'm going to be fine." Her voice cracked on the last word, and Spur tightened his arm around her shoulders.

"Some of her clots have pressed on her inner ear," he said, his own voice thick. "That's why she's been falling a little bit. But that's under control, and she's hired a new manager for her perfumery, and she's right. She's going to be fine."

He nodded, like the mighty Spur Chappell had spoken it, and therefore it would be true. "Cay?"

Cayden got to his feet and buttoned his jacket the way royalty would. He'd always been the most refined of the Chappell brothers, and Ian reached up to swipe his cowboy hat off his head as his brother did.

"Dear Lord," Cayden started. After a healthy pause, he added, "We're grateful for Lisa Harvey joining our family.

Bless her to be able to put up with all of us, and especially Duke, for a good, long while. Bless her as she carries their baby, and bless Spur and Olli with the health and strength they both need to endure their current situation."

He cleared his throat. "We're grateful we have each other, Lord, and we ask Thee to please help us to serve one another. Open our hearts to accept help from others, and to give it. Amen."

Ian looked up immediately while the others said, "Amen," too. He'd let Spur and Conrad help him, but not many others. Now that he knew how much Spur had been shouldering, extra guilt cut through him.

"You should've told me," he said to his brother. "I'd have had someone else come help me."

Spur gave him a dark-eyed look. "If you don't let me come over and help you, I don't know what I'll do."

"It's important to him," Olli said, reaching over and patting Ian's hand. "The man lives to mother others."

"Hey," Spur said, his voice wounded. "You say that like it's a bad thing."

Olli swung around to face him. "Not at all, baby. I like it when you take care of me." She grinned at him, and everything about Spur softened.

"Incoming," Ian muttered, because it seemed like half of the people had made a beeline for the buffet line, and the other half were headed toward their table. At least this time, Spur would have to handle all the questions and all the responses.

Ian pushed both hands against the table and stood.

"Help me through the line?" he asked Nita, and she jumped to her feet the way he'd seen Cayden do earlier. "We don't need to be caught up in this storm."

"No," she murmured as she handed him his crutches for the umpteenth time. "We do not."

CHAPTER 9

Nita listened to the rain hit the roof above her head, sinking into the sound with a sigh. She let her eyes drift closed again, glad the heatwave of October had finally ended. She didn't particularly enjoy working in the stables in the wet and muck, but she had knee-high boots she could pull on to keep her feet and jeans clean and dry.

She loved the rain—the scent of it, the sound of it, the way it cleansed everything in short bursts or longer deluges.

At the foot of the bed, Goliath whined, and Nita lifted her head. "All right," she said, and the bulldog came toward her. He burrowed onto her chest, his little face peeking through the blankets. She grinned at him and relaxed again, stroking his head and down his back.

She needed quiet moments like this sometimes, and this morning felt made of easiness and simplicity. Once she got up and got going, all of that would change. She'd obsess over her last text to Ian, which he still hadn't answered, or she'd worry that the rollover would hit the news before she was ready to face the press.

There would be press, Nita knew that. She needed to talk to her mother about the contract and that she'd signed it, and she also wanted to tell Ian. She hadn't mentioned it to anyone but her dad and Janet yet, so it was especially surprising that her mom didn't know.

She reached for her phone, realizing she hadn't turned on her furnace. The air conditioner had been needed yesterday, but the air definitely held a chill this morning. Her thumb and forefinger flew over the screen.

Wondering if you have time for lunch or something this week, Nita typed out. *You could even come for dinner. I have those cauliflower pizza doughs you like, and we can make our own pies.*

She sent the text to her mother and got up to get in the shower. After a detour down the hall to switch on the furnace, she got ready for the day, the sight and smell of her coffee reminding her of Ian.

Besides his brother's vow renewal, he hadn't asked her out after she'd shown up at his house with her mother's brew. They'd attended that last weekend, and she still didn't have a date with him on the horizon.

When they were together, he seemed interested in her. He held her hand. He spoke in a flirty tone sometimes, a real one other times, or remained quiet. He was a thoughtful man—more than anyone else Nita had dated.

"You're not dating him," she told herself as she filled a

thermos with coffee. She'd need it to stay warm today, and she looked up and out the window. Only damp grayness stared back at her, and the slight reflection of herself told her she hadn't lied.

Maybe she should ask him out. Her first thought was that he wouldn't go. Ian didn't want anyone to see him. His humiliation and embarrassment at being hurt kept him caged in that house in the corner of Bluegrass Ranch.

Her phone buzzed, and Nita pulled it from her back pocket. *Anytime this week*, her mom had said. *What's up?*

I want to talk to you about a couple of things, Nita said, keeping it vague for now. That way, if she didn't want to talk about the rollover, she wouldn't have to. She could easily substitute Ian in place of any topic, as she did need all the help she could get when it came to him.

Let's do tomorrow, your place, her mom said. *I'll bring that organic sauce you like.*

It was really her mom who liked the organic sauce. Nita would eat it too, and she wouldn't put up a fuss about it. Her mom liked it because it didn't have any added sugar, and she swore it tasted just like her nana's recipe.

Nita confirmed and said she'd have the oven hot around six-thirty, then she backed out to the main screen of her texts.

Ian's name sat right at the top, because she'd pinned it there. Probably pathetic, and even as she thought she should remove the pin, she knew she wouldn't. Her fingers seemed to have a mind of their own as they began flying over the screen again.

*If I came by your house this afternoon when I'm done with
my chores, would you come back to my place with me for
dinner?*

She read the sentence, then re-read it. Ian couldn't drive,
and he wouldn't want to ask Conrad for a ride. As if illuminated by a dozen spotlights, Nita realized why he hadn't
asked her out.

He couldn't take her himself. Perhaps he'd let her
take him.

*No restaurants. No one staring at you with the crutches.
Just me and you and Goliath, and maybe a movie on my tiny
TV. I have popcorn and caramel to go on it. I have frozen
pizza or I can make something real simple, like pulled pork
sandwiches.*

Nita stepped over to the freezer and opened it, sure she
had buns and a bag of leftover shredded pork from a month
or so ago. Sure enough, both appeared before her eyes, and
she got them out and set them on the stovetop. Hers wasn't
a fancy, gas-flame one like Ian's, but one of those flat-tops
that heated with electricity.

She hadn't sent the text, and Nita gritted her teeth,
searching for her bravery. She still hadn't quite found it
when she hit send. A little circle whirled next to the text, and
then it landed on Ian's phone.

She even knew he'd read it when the *delivered* changed
to *read.*

Her heart pounded, but she somehow heard the
scratching of claws on glass. Adrenaline spiked through her
body as she realized she'd left her Frenchie out in the rain,

and she darted over to the sliding glass door to let him in. "Sorry, Golly," she said. "Oh, you're soaked."

She tossed her phone on the dining room table and hurried into the kitchen to get a towel. She ran it over Goliath's smooth coat, though he'd shaken himself mostly dry already, and then smiled at him. "I'm so sorry, buddy."

Goliath didn't seem too concerned, and Nita went back to her phone. She shoved it in her back pocket, grabbed her rubber work boots, and headed out to her pick-up. Her rain gear sat in the back seat, and she started the truck to get the heat blowing.

Only then did she allow herself to look at her phone to see if Ian had answered.

Sure, he'd said. *You make the sandwiches, and I'll whip up something to go with them this afternoon.*

Her grin splintered her face, and she started typing again. *What kind of something?* she asked. *You said you couldn't cook much more than breakfast.*

My kitchen skills might be slightly better than I led you to believe.

"You sneak," she murmured as she typed the words and sent them. She added a couple of laughing-crying emojis, and Ian sent the same ones back to her.

It'll be a surprise, he said. *What time?*

Nita looked up and out the windshield. *With the rain? No idea. Maybe we can keep in touch throughout the day.*

Deal, Ian thought, and that was enough for Nita to put her truck in reverse and head for Bluegrass.

* * *

Hours later, Nita wanted to cancel on Ian. The horses at Glenn Marks had acted like they'd never seen a drop of water before, and every single one of them seemed to have pitched some sort of fit that day.

They were all diva-horses, as she and the other trainers had been telling them how outstanding they were since the day they'd been purchased. As she pushed against the rump of one particularly stubborn beast to get him out of the stall, though, Nita had had enough.

"Go on," she grumbled. "This sawdust is all wet, and I need to change it." She leaned into him even more and gave him a swat on his flank.

Gambling Big finally moved, making a ruckus about it as he did. At the front, the trainer leading him, Ben, chuckled as nothing seemed to rattle him.

Nita nearly fell flat on her face, and she was definitely rattled.

"He's too much horse for you," Judd said, and Nita turned to her left to find him and Rafe Rodrigo standing there. Judd wore a grin the size of Texas, and Nita wanted to smack it off his face.

"He thinks he owns the place," Nita said, turning away from the pair of them. She'd done a good job of avoiding them over the past several weeks, and she saw no reason to make today worse than it already was. She had no idea what time it was, but the sky was darkening fast, though she couldn't tell if with another storm or nightfall. It didn't really matter which.

She had to change out this stall and check on the next two before she could be done. She'd spent at least two hours on the roof of the rowhouse, fixing the leaks, and both Trey and Lawrence Chappell had been by to help her with it. Lawrence had assured her that the stable would get some money back on their rental for this month, and Nita had thanked him.

She understood things required maintenance, and Glenn had been renting this rowhouse from Bluegrass for years and years. It hadn't been empty for them to do the maintenance, and it had to be done as it came up.

"You should give him straw," Judd said, taking a step closer.

"He's on sawdust," Nita said.

"He's spoiled."

"Good thing you're not the one getting him to obey, then." Nita gave him a sharp look that she hoped told him to back off.

Judd did not back off; he never did. He advanced toward her, Rafe a step behind him. The man had no brain of his own, and he did whatever Judd did first.

Nita's heart began to throb in her chest, and she didn't want to turn her back on the two men. She did anyway, reaching for a shovel so she could clean out the stall.

"You're not getting him to obey either," Judd said. "I saw him a day or two ago. Still not changing that lead on the corner."

"He will," Nita said.

"He will, if Glenn gives him to me."

"You will *never* get Gambling Big," Nita said in a powerful voice. "Have you ever stopped to wonder why you don't get the big names, Judd? Or why I do?"

"I know why you do," he sneered.

Nita's chest collapsed on itself, but she still managed to say, "Because I've proven myself time and time again to be a certain type of trainer, and so have you."

"Exactly," he said, but he clearly didn't get that she'd insulted him.

Her phone rang, and she pulled it from her jacket pocket. Ian's name sat there, sending another round of panic through her. The last thing she wanted was for Judd to see him calling her.

Or did she want him to know?

She closed her eyes, a single moment of time holding so many thoughts. She'd once considered getting a boyfriend so these men would respect her. Ian Chappell would be the pinnacle of that...

She swiped on the call. "Hey," she barked into the phone.

"I don't want to step on your toes," he said in a rush. "But I can hear you and Judd, and I'm wondering if you need help."

Nita turned her back on Judd and Rafe again and leaned into the stall at her side. "You know what? Some help would be great."

"Be right there." He ended the call, and warmth and

relief rushed through Nita. She re-pocketed her phone and faced Judd again.

His eyes blazed with malice, and Nita realized that not only did he dislike her, he actually loathed her. She wasn't even sure what she'd done to make him feel like that.

"Listen," she said.

"No, you listen," Judd said, moving even closer. He held out his hand to keep Rafe back. "Just because you're Daddy's little pet doesn't mean I can't see right through you."

She stared up at him. "I am a good trainer. The last horse I took from beginning to end won The Gold Cup at the Royal Ascot," she said. "What have your horses won?" Her fists balled, and she told herself not to back up.

Don't move, she said over and over, though Judd had crowded her and true fear ran through her.

"There you are," Ian said, clearly out of breath.

Instantly, Judd fell back from the doorway of the stall, looking at Ian. The anger and unrest on his face smoothed away, but Nita saw it all.

"I was just coming to ask you something." Ian glanced at Judd and then Rafe, who'd closed in the circle too. Ian thumped one crutch against the cement. "I'm obviously a bit laid up, but Conrad and I have this wager."

He laughed, and it sounded normal and natural and wonderful in Nita's ears. "He said I can get a partner to help me train Digging Your Grave, and—" He ground his voice through his throat before finishing. "I thought about who

I'd want to be my co-trainer with him. Might you have time in your schedule, Nita?"

She gaped at him, sure all of those English words he'd just used had been put in the wrong order.

Ian shifted his good foot and ducked his head. "It's okay if you don't. I'm sure Powerplay is coming up on your schedule."

"Glenn hasn't made the assignments for next year yet," Judd said.

Ian looked at him, something fierce entering his gaze. "I'm sure Nita will get Powerplay, though. She's clearly the best trainer at Glenn Marks." He didn't say, *right?* but he might as well have.

Before Judd could argue, Ian looked back at Nita. "If you want to talk more about it—I realize this is right out of the blue—you can come by the house tomorrow morning. I know what you like for breakfast."

He gave her a dazzling smile full of stars and white teeth, nodded to Judd and Rafe, and started to turn around.

Nita could only stare at him as he hobble-walked away, sure the last five minutes had been a figment of her imagination.

CHAPTER 10

Ian made it to the corner of the rowhouse and turned left. His breath came in great gulps, and he pressed his back into the wood there, out of sight. If he could just calm his heart and his lungs, he'd be able to get out of the Glenn Marks stables and back to safety.

Where that was at the moment, he had no idea.

For someone on crutches and who'd missed their last dose of pain medication, crutching his way past a few stable doors had taken some effort. Unfortunately, he wasn't that far away from Judd, Rafe, and Nita.

Fortunately, he corrected himself, leaning his head back. That was how he'd heard them arguing in the first place.

He had wanted to talk to her about training with him. He had not mentioned it to Conrad yet, and his brother would likely pitch a fit.

"What was that?" Judd asked, and Ian's eyes snapped open again. "Are you seeing him?"

"So what if I am?" Nita asked, and Ian could just picture her lifting her chin as she said it. Though she couldn't be taller than five-foot-three, the woman held plenty of power in her shoulders and stance. She'd helped him to his feet at the vow renewal, and he had to outweigh her two-to-one.

"He said you weren't at the hospital," Judd said. "Does *he* know you have an insane crush on him?"

He knows, Ian said, glad when Nita said nothing. The last thing Ian needed was his relationship with Nita spreading around Bluegrass. He didn't want anyone to even be thinking about him right now. Once he was healed and back in full force, then he didn't mind if they talked about his horse and who might buy it.

"I don't have to explain anything to you," Nita said. "You better be on your best behavior, Judd. There are changes coming, and you won't know what hit you." Her footsteps came toward Ian, and he pushed away from the wall, not wanting to be caught there for some reason.

His mind screamed at him to go back and ask Nita what changes were coming. Instead, he kept going, reaching the other side of the rowhouse in only a couple of swift swings. The rain hit his cowboy hat and reminded him that he hadn't been planning to leave the house that day.

Something had urged him out of the corner house, though, and he'd just been walking around the ranch in his raincoat and gloves and cowboy hat. He'd overheard Nita, and he should probably acknowledge that he'd been led to the Marks stables.

Maybe it was the gravitational pull of Anita Powell that

had brought Ian to that part of the ranch. Whatever it was, he'd been able to help her, and he'd asked her to train with him, two things he wanted to do if he could.

His phone rang and he ducked out of the rain to answer Conrad's call. "What's goin' on?" he asked by way of hello.

"Howdy," Conrad said, and he sounded happy. "You left the house? I ran to town to see Ry for a minute, and she had calzones for her staff meeting. I brought one back for you."

His brother worked dang hard to see his very busy fiancée every single day. They had some sort of streak going on, and she came to the ranch or he went to her boutique or house every single day. Sometimes he was gone before dawn to take her earl gray tea or cookies, and Ian would only ever admit to himself that he found the gestures sweet.

He'd also been considering a similar tactic with Nita. He did like seeing her, and he was sure every day would be better for him if she was in it.

"Yeah, I just went for a walk," Ian said. "I'm headed back now, and I'll probably need to shower." Nita hadn't seemed near ready to be done for the day, and she'd been texting him throughout the day, so he knew about the leaking roof over their stalls.

He should probably let her know that if she wanted to cancel with him and spend her evening in a hot bath, she could. He wouldn't mind.

Yes, you would, he thought, but he could handle the disappointment if it made Nita happy.

"Probably," Conrad said. "There's so much mud out

there today. I'm surprised you left." He was clearly fishing for more information, and Ian decided to give it to him.

"I went to see Nita," he said. "I'm going to dinner at her house tonight. I think."

"You *think* you're going to dinner at her place tonight?"

"Yeah, she's not done working yet, and I can't help her get finished faster. She looked exhausted." He glanced over his shoulder toward the Marks stalls, but he didn't see anyone.

"I can head out and help her," Conrad offered.

"No," Ian said quickly. "She won't like that, and it'll be too obvious." What he really meant was that *he* didn't like that. *He* wanted to be the one to come to Nita's rescue, and his thoughts moved into a tailspin. "I'll be home in a bit. I'm on my way."

"Okay," Conrad said, but Ian almost didn't get the last part of the two-syllable word he hung up so fast.

Ian faced the rain right as it started to increase, and he didn't dare move a muscle. He couldn't be traipsing around the ranch in this, and he sighed as his options narrowed to only one or two. Call Conrad back and ask for a ride, or see if Nita had her decades-old pick-up truck nearby and could take him home.

He wanted to see Nita again, maybe hold her hand and flirt with her the way he seemed to be able to do when they were alone. He didn't want to make her any later, though, so he tapped to call his brother back.

"The rain sounds like it's going to come through the

roof," Conrad said, obviously already aware of what Ian needed. "I'm on my way. You're at Glenn Marks?"

"The one behind them," Ian said. "Take your time."

He watched the rain sluice through the sky, trying to untangle the knot in his mind. He wanted to see Nita every single day. He wanted to be the one to help her when she needed it. An hour didn't go by where he didn't think of her. She had a crush on him—and Ian knew it wasn't a crush.

She *was* as interested in him as he was in her, and a smile touched his face. "Maybe I'm ready," he said to the water in the air just before the sky erupted into a chorus of thunder. He laughed, because maybe that was the Lord telling him in a much louder voice that yes, he was ready to get out of his own way and see if this thing he had with Nita had real legs and could be nurtured into a real, lasting, meaningful relationship.

For the first time in a decade, he didn't push away the hope when it came.

* * *

A couple of hours later, he stood on the front porch of the corner house, watching the road leading away from him for any sign of Nita. The rain had drenched everything in Kentucky for a good thirty minutes, and then she'd moved on.

Nita had texted almost an hour ago to say she'd finished at the stables, but she wanted to go home and shower before she picked him up for dinner. *No problem*, he'd told her. The grumbling in his stomach told him there was indeed a problem. He'd ignored the calzone Conrad had brought home for him, claiming he'd eat it for lunch tomorrow.

He'd bathed too, and with a couple more weeks of practice, he could get ready by himself in less than an hour now. Something he used to be able to do in fifteen minutes or less.

Finally, her brown and white pick-up appeared, and he reached for the bowl of macaroni salad he'd made that afternoon. He wasn't a whiz in the kitchen, but he could boil water and cook noodles. He could open a bottle of mayo and drop in a couple of spoonfuls of sour cream. Salt and pepper and a bag of frozen peas and one of shredded carrots, and he had mac-salad for days.

His mom would be so proud.

He'd had to beat Conrad back with glares and threats, which had only made his brother laugh. Ian hadn't had time or the heart to bring up the fact that he'd asked Nita to help him with Digging Your Grave, and he told himself he had plenty of time still. They weren't even starting their training until January.

Nita's smile lit up the night, and Ian decided to wait until she came up to the porch to move. Then she could take the salad, and he could give his full focus to getting down the steps without killing himself.

"Howdy," she called as she got out. She wore black, rubber boots that went to her knees, jeans, and a bright red jacket that went real nicely with her white-blonde hair.

"Evening," he called down to her. She hurried toward

him and took the bowl. Ian wasn't sure what to say or do, but he found himself leaning toward her and brushing her cheek with his lips in a semi-awkward move.

Surprise colored her expression, and Ian leaned against the pillar on the porch, determined not to clear his throat. He could just talk. "Sorry today was hard. I said we could do this another night."

"We could," she said. "I want to do it tonight, if you're not too tired."

"I am not too tired," he said.

"Great." She wrapped her arm around the bowl of macaroni salad and tucked it into her side. With her other hand, she steadied him as he started down the steps.

"Thank you," he said. "I can get in vehicles pretty good now."

"Is that right?"

"Yeah." He cut a look at her out of the corner of his eye. "You sounded mad just then."

Nita dropped her hand from his arm. "I guess I'm just wondering if I'm going to have to be the one who does all the asking." She didn't look at him. To him, it sure seemed like she *couldn't* look at him. Her eyes flew all over the front yard, back to the porch, and then to her truck.

"If you don't want to see me, it's fine," she muttered. "I'll stop asking you to get together."

"I want to see you," he said, and that brought her gaze to his. "I'm just...wow, I'm really bad at this." He kept moving toward the truck and pulled open the passenger door. If he got in the truck, she couldn't drive away without him.

She didn't move to help him, thankfully, and once they were both in the truck, she asked, "Bad at what?"

"Dating," he said. "Talking to women. Being with someone I want to impress when I'm…" He gestured to his leg. "Like this."

"I already told you I don't care about the leg. It's just an accident." She put the truck in gear and started to back up, a little fast in his opinion.

Ian gripped the armrest and noted that he'd have to manually roll down the windows in this thing. "I also know that if I really want to be with you, I'm going to have to tell you things, and I automatically buck against that."

"What things?" Nita glanced at him.

"Things I don't talk about anymore." Ian folded his arms as she eased up on the angry driving and stared out the windshield. She'd told him about her marriage; he should be able to tell her about his.

At the same time, she and Sampson had been madly in love. His wife hadn't even liked him all that much. She sure had liked his bank account, which was just another thing he'd have to tell Nita about that he'd rather not.

"I get that," Nita said almost under her breath, and that helped Ian relax. She didn't say anything else as she drove them off the ranch and made a right when they got to the highway. She went that way, along the winding country roads for a few minutes, then made a left turn. Five minutes later, she made another left and drove around the corner to the street that ran perpendicular to the river.

She came to the second house and pulled past the trees

that stood sentinel out front. The first time he'd come here, he'd only been able to catch a glimpse of the house from the road, and there had been zero traffic. She'd told him later that only three houses existed on this lane, and hers was the second one down.

Past the trees, the house appeared, and she went right up the gravel driveway and parked in front of the garage. She put the truck in park, and they sat there. After only a breath, she turned all the way toward him.

"Start with something really easy," she said. "I'll even go first."

Ian nodded at her, not wanting to ruin this night with her. She'd already had a hard day.

"I can't park in my garage," she said, nodding toward it. "It's full of my grandfather's old stuff, or Sam's, and I can't bear to get rid of any of it yet." She shook her head, her eyebrows drawing down. "Pathetic, right? I mean, they've both been gone for *years*."

With that, she reached for the door handle and got out of the truck. Ian followed her, because he wanted to tell her it was okay to mourn for years. She walked around the front of the truck as he dropped to the ground on his good leg, and instead of twisting to reach for his crutches, he said, "I don't have a great relationship with my mother."

Nita froze at the corner of the hood, her eyes wide. "Really?"

"Really."

She took a tentative step toward him, and the word vomit started surging up his throat. "I want to ask you out,"

he said. "I don't know how. I can't drive. If I was well, I'd ask
you to go dancing with me. I'd take you to movies—the kind
with the recliners—and we'd share popcorn, and I'd think
about kissing you when I finally got you back to this porch."
He waved toward it.

Nita stopped moving again—everything except her
eyelids, which kept blinking.

"I'm not sure how you did it," he said. "But you're in my
brain, and I can't get you out. No woman has been in my
head for a decade."

Nita seemed to know she shouldn't approach, that he'd
become a terrified squirrel and one wrong move would send
him scampering back to the corner house. "Why's that?"

"That's when I got divorced," he forced out of his
mouth. "It wasn't a pleasant experience, and I vowed I'd
never get married again." He swallowed, knowing what that
sounded like to her. "But there you are, making me rethink
everything."

He commanded himself to stop talking, and stop talking
right now.

Nita said nothing, and that somehow prompted Ian to
start up again. "I guess what I'm saying is it's not pathetic to
not be able to get rid of a few things that meant something to
the people you loved. Sometimes things plague us for years."

His things were bad things, while hers were good, but
they seemed to have the same effect on the two of them.

"Okay," Nita said. "That's a lot of things, and they
certainly weren't easy."

"No," Ian said, hopping around the open door. "Nita, you make me want to make things easier. For you, and for me. Talking to you is easier for me than with anyone else."

"Oh, don't start lying now, Mister Chappell." She flashed him a smile. "Don't you dare take another hop either. I'm not delivering you back to Conrad with a second broken leg." She moved around him and got out his crutches. After passing them to him, she leaned in to get the mac-salad.

"I don't lie to you," Ian said.

"It's easier for you to talk to me than to Conrad? I don't believe that."

"Okay, maybe you're second," he said with a smile. "Fine, third. I can tell Spur anything."

"Anything?" Nita's eyebrows went up as she laced her hand through his arm again. This time, there was no anger and no tension between them. Ian marveled that he could feel things so clearly between the two of them.

"Most anything, yeah," Ian said, his throat dry. "He was the first one to know I'd been thinking about you and couldn't stop."

"Mm." She ducked her head again, a pretty flush filling her face.

"You like that? Tormenting me in my every waking moment?"

Nita looked up at him, joy streaming from her. "Yeah," she said. "I like that, cowboy."

He slowed, stopped, and leaned down. "I like two

things, Nita. One, when you call me cowboy. Two, thinking about you all day long."

"Yeah? What do you think about me?"

"How pretty you are. How talented. How I can get you to let me hold your hand again. If I should text you, and what. Then I pray the Lord will heal my leg faster so I can be the man you deserve. You know, stuff like that." He'd be eternally grateful he hadn't said anything about kissing.

His eyes dropped to her mouth, and while he'd lost his mind once and kissed her briefly, he wanted to do it again. He'd forgotten already how she tasted, and how soft her lips were.

The wind kicked up, and Nita got them moving again. "We need to talk about you asking me to train with you," she said.

"We do?"

She led him up the few steps to her porch. "I know that was a show for Judd."

"No," Ian said. "I'm going to need help come January, and I want you to do it. I've been meaning to ask you about it for a week or two." Probably three, but he'd revealed enough for one night.

He remembered the "changes" she'd spoken of, and he wondered if she'd even be available come January. "If you can't do it, that's fine. Conrad will want someone as equally as talented, and he'll probably ask for Spur."

Nita scoffed and then burst out laughing. "Please," she said as she opened the door and preceded him into her house. "I am not equivalent to Spur Chappell."

Ian swung himself over the threshold of her house and paused. "Nita," he said. "Of course you are. I've seen you work, and—oh, boy, here comes one more thing." He grinned at her, needing to start carrying a sock so he could stuff it in his mouth whenever he was about to say something embarrassing.

"I've had a lot of time at home, right? I maybe looked up some of the horses you've trained. They've gone on to win, and win big."

"You looked up my horses?"

"You're every bit as good as Spur, and don't you let Judd or Rafe think you're not for even a second." He nodded at her, swung past her, and left the front door for her to close. "Boy, it smells good in here. I don't think I'm the only one who's been a tad deceptive about their cooking skills."

CHAPTER 11

When Goliath barked, Nita looked up from her phone. The little dog held very still out by the pines on the edge of the grass, and in the country silence, his growl carried on the air. Nita watched for a moment, waiting to see if he'd spotted a raccoon or a bird or something.

Goliath relaxed, and Nita went back to her phone. Ian had messaged a couple more times, and she grinned before she'd even read them. Things between them had been going really well since the pulled pork dinner at her house.

Ian had asked her out three times, and they'd been on two more dates in the past ten days. He'd had pizza delivered to the field just off the road, and they'd had a great time talking and laughing. He'd held her hand as the sun had gone down, and Nita sure had enjoyed the silence, the golden light, and the handsome cowboy at her side.

Their second date had involved her driving them to a

pear orchard that had a late crop of pears, and he'd encouraged her from the ground while she climbed the ladder and attempted to drop the pears into the basket he held.

Afterward, she'd driven through a hamburger joint, and they'd eaten in her truck in the parking lot. Maybe not super romantic. Maybe not the typical dates Nita had been on before. She couldn't have cared any less, because she'd been with Ian, and he'd asked.

Not only that, but he'd come up with their simple dates, planned everything, and simply asked her to drive if necessary.

She liked everything about him, from the way he could blurt out deep truths at the drop of a hat and then sit in silence for a while and be completely comfortable. She liked his quiet strength and deep convictions. She liked the feel of his rough hand in hers, and the way he texted her until the moment he went to bed.

Their next date was set for tomorrow night, and Nita had a suspicion she'd get to do and see something not many people got to see and do. Ian had invited her for Chinese food and to "visit his cars with him."

He said he went out to the warehouse every single day, but he'd never said if he allowed others to go with him. Her guess was no, not many people—maybe Spur or Conrad— got through the door at the vehicle warehouse.

She wasn't sure what she'd find inside, and excitement poured through her at the picture Ian had sent. It showed part of a bright blue car, the kind that looked like it came from the future. The headlight was almost triangular, and

Nita had the feeling she better wear completely flat shoes tomorrow so she'd be able to boost herself out of the sports car.

Fancy, she sent back to him. *I like the blue.*

It's a manual transmission, he said. *I can't drive it. Can you drive a manual?*

I learned on one, she sent to him. *It's been a while, but I bet I could do it.* She reached over and patted Goliath as he arrived at her side. *Do you let other people drive your cars?*

Sure, he said. *The whole point of owning a car is to drive it.*

Interesting, she sent. Her phone rang, and Ian's name sat there. "Howdy, cowboy," she said, plenty of flirtiness in her voice.

"Howdy, cowgirl," he said on back. "Why is it surprising that I drive my cars?"

"I don't know," she said. "It just—you just seem like maybe someone who doesn't want a lot of people looking at them, and a rare, fancy car seems to draw a lot of eyes."

"Not all of the cars are fancy," he said. "Or rare. They're just cars."

"Oh," she said. "I guess I expected them to all be like that blue glimpse."

"Not all of them."

"Okay," she said. "You sound like you're offended I thought they were all sports cars."

"Maybe a little." Ian chuckled, and the deep, rich sound of it tickled Nita's eardrums. "All right, well, that was it."

"Mm, okay." Nita couldn't help smiling into the night.

Ian didn't love talking on the phone, and he did enjoy his silences. "See you tomorrow."

"Did you have something you wanted to talk about?"

"Not at all," she said.

"You think I'm funny because I don't like talking on the phone."

"It's a little...interesting," she said. "Where are you right now?"

"Conrad stuck me on the back deck and escaped upstairs to read his fantasy novel."

For some reason, that struck Nita as funny, and she started giggling. "Your brother reads fantasy novels?"

"Loves 'em." Ian chuckled.

"How'd you get stuck? Last time I checked, you could walk and get in trucks by yourself," she teased.

"He took my crutches," Ian said. "I think he's secretly talking to Ry, and he doesn't want me to overhear. I just wish he'd put me to bed."

"Like a baby," Nita said, and they both laughed. As she sobered, she added, "How do you—I mean, do you want kids, Ian?"

"Yeah, sure," he said easily, as if talking about tacos or the pizza they'd eaten last week. "What about you? Were kids on your radar with Sampson?"

"Yeah," she said. "We got married really young, so they were in the long plan."

"Good to know," he said.

"I'm older now," she said. "I think they should probably

be in the short plan if, you know, I meet the right cowboy and we get married."

"How old are you?" he asked. "Can I ask that?"

"Yeah," she said. "I'm thirty-three. You?"

"Thirty-seven."

"Small gap," she said.

"It's nothing," he said. "Oh, Conrad's back to rescue me. I better go."

"Yeah, go," Nita said, and the call ended. Ian didn't text again for several minutes, as he moved from the back deck to his bedroom. Then he sent, *Night, Nita. Sweet dreams. Can't wait to see you tomorrow.*

She lit up under the weight of his words, because she also adored how sweet Ian could be. She hardly ever dreamed, and if she did, she didn't remember anything. When she woke the next morning, she definitely felt a different charge in the air.

Goliath lay on the end of the bed, his eyes trained on the closed door. When she'd been married to Sampson, Nita used to sleep with the door open without a problem. Now, she had to close and lock it in order to give herself some sense of safety. Goliath barked at the slightest noise, and he hadn't made a yip yet.

"What's up, boy?" she asked, and the little dog turned and looked at her quickly. He refocused on the door again, his body tense and at attention. Nita got up and went to the door, taking a deep breath and then pulling it open.

Goliath barked then and leapt from the bed. He ran down the hall, and Nita followed him, scanning the part of the house she could see. Nothing seemed amiss inside, but Goliath went right toward the front door, not left toward the back, where she usually let him out in the morning.

She followed him, though all the blinds had been closed. Another thing Nita had to do now that she was single and lived alone. Not many people came down this road, so when someone did, they meant to be there. Or they shouldn't be there.

Nita sincerely hoped her mother had come for an early-morning visit or someone had delivered six dozen red roses. Her heart pounded as if either could come to pass, and she stepped over to the window and peeked through the slats in the blinds.

It wasn't her mother. No one had brought flowers.

A media van sat behind her truck, a satellite on top.

"No," she whispered.

Several people had gathered on her front lawn, every single one of them with microphones. Why did any of them care what her father did with his stables?

She reminded herself that they lived in Horse Country, where hundreds and thousands of people had dedicated their lives to raising horses, breeding them, training them, and racing them.

The fact that she was taking over half of Glenn Marks Stables—one of the bigger, more successful training operations in the Lexington area—was a big deal. The local media would definitely care, and she wondered who'd tipped them off.

It couldn't have been Glenn, and she stepped away from

the window and hurried back to the bedroom. She dialed her dad, knowing the man woke before the sun. He answered on the second ring, an easy-going, casual, "Mornin', sugarbaby."

"At least you didn't say it was a *good* morning," she snapped. Her bedroom sat in the back corner of the house, so she couldn't see the front yard.

"Why's that?"

"I have a media van here," she hissed. "Reporters on my lawn. They know."

A pause came through the line, and then Glenn said, "I'm on my way."

"No," Nita said quickly. "If you show up, then it'll really be a media storm."

"I'm coming," Glenn said, and all the sweetness in his usual *sugarbaby* endearment had vanished.

"Fine," Nita said. "I'll get dressed." She hung up and tossed her phone on her bed, moved over to the door, closed it, and locked it.

Thirty minutes later, a roar came from the front of the house, and Nita spun from the kitchen sink where she'd been rinsing out her cereal bowl. She jogged toward the door and unlocked it just as her dad's voice filled the air.

She opened the door, and the noise increased. She thought Dad would come in, but instead, he said, "Here she is. C'mon out, Nita."

How this was *handling it*, she didn't know, but she did what he said. Glenn had always been so good with the press, and he slung his arm around her as if they were old chums. "The new owner of half of Glenn Marks Stables, which will be rebranded as Glenn Marks Powell once the New Year comes."

He grinned out at everyone like this was the best news ever, and he'd been waiting for all of them to show up to make the announcement.

"Anita," a woman yelled. "How do you feel about this separation?"

"Anita," someone else yelled. "Are you going to take your father's horses, or buy your own?"

More questions flew her way, and she stood under her father's arm and smiled. That was about all she was capable of at the moment.

Glenn handed her a newspaper and held up his hand. "Thanks, folks. We don't have anything else to say right now." He herded her inside, and Anita let him close the door while she looked down at the newspaper.

Front page. Headline.

Daughter set to take half of Glenn Marks Stables.

A groan started way down in her stomach. Everyone would know who she really was now, and she told herself that this announcement would have been made in a little over two months anyway.

Her next thought landed on Ian, and she drew in a sharp breath. She hadn't told him about the rollover. She hadn't told her mother. She hadn't told anyone.

"Mom," she said, and her dad turned to look at her. "She doesn't know. I didn't tell her."

"You better call her," Glenn said, and Nita wanted to

throw the paper at him. She crumpled it in her fist and went into the kitchen to get her phone.

It rang before she could make the call to her mom, and her stomach sank all the way to the floor.

Ian's name sat on the screen.

CHAPTER 12

Ian glared at Conrad's back as Nita's phone rang. She wasn't going to pick up; his brother wasn't going to stop talking to the press, though he had no idea what he was even saying.

"Ian," Nita said, and she sounded a bit breathless.

He spun away from Conrad and hopped over to the far counter in the kitchen. "There are reporters on my front porch," he hissed into the phone. "They're asking all kinds of questions about whether or not we're going to merge our training operation with the new owner of Glenn Marks Powell." He paused to take a breath, wishing he and Nita stood in the same room together.

"I had no idea what they were talking about. Conrad took over."

"What's he saying?"

"I have no clue. I managed to gather that they think you're Glenn's daughter, and that you're starting your own stable. How they found out that I asked you to help me train one horse, I don't know."

Nita's sigh through the line weighed at least fifty pounds. "I have an idea."

"I didn't even know you were Glenn Howard's daughter," he said, his voice wounded and sounding like it. Betrayal ran hotly through him despite his attempts to cool it. "Is that true?"

"Yes," she whispered. "It's not something very many people know."

"How many people?" he asked.

"Four," she said. "Or five. Something like that."

"So I'm not in your elite circle."

"You are," she said. "I was going to tell you. The rollover isn't happening for a couple more months, and it was definitely on my list of things to talk to you about."

When she spoke in such a powerful tone, Ian believed her. In this case, he *wanted* to believe her, but he wasn't quite there in the first two seconds.

"Listen," she said, sounding tired again. "I have to call my mother. She doesn't know about the rollover, and I don't want her to get her feelings hurt."

A dozen more questions sprang to life in Ian's mind, but he simply said, "Okay."

"Don't say anything to the press," Nita said. "Or just deny any merging on our parts. We're *not* merging."

"Okay," he said again, when he wanted to tell her she wouldn't have time to help him train Digging Your Grave in

January if she was starting her own training facility and stables.

They'd talked very little about his ask for her to help him train, and maybe she thought he hadn't been serious. He *had* asked her as part of his attempt to help her with Judd...

"Judd," he said out loud, to which Nita said, "Yeah, my money's on him too. I'll call you later, okay?"

"Yeah," he said.

"Ian," Nita said. "I'm sorry. I should've told you. I *was* going to tell you."

"We'll talk about it later."

"Okay." She hung up, and Ian let his hand drop back to his side. He couldn't hear anyone talking, and he wasn't surprised when Conrad stepped in front of the sink and put their coffee mugs in it.

"What did she say?"

"She's Glenn Howard's daughter," Ian said, still staring out the window. "She is going to be starting her own stable and training unit in the New Year."

"Wow," Conrad said.

Ian looked at his brother, so much storming through him that he couldn't make sense of all of it. "What do I do here?"

"What do you mean?"

"I mean, she didn't tell me she's the daughter of one of the most successful horse trainers in the business."

That was a huge thing, and no wonder Conrad and Ian had reporters at their house too. Judd Rake knew Ian had asked

Nita to train with him. He'd overheard him ask Nita if they were dating. Ian had no idea if Judd knew Nita was Glenn's daughter or not, but if he did, Ian could see him tipping off a newspaper or magazine without considering his actions.

"It doesn't mean she's hiding a bunch of other stuff," Conrad said.

Ian nodded, but he didn't believe his brother either. When he'd finally started digging at Minnie, his ex-wife, there had been piles and piles of things to uncover. One secret usually meant there were more, especially when the secret-keeper knew how to keep their mouths closed.

Nita obviously knew how to do that, and do it well.

"I don't want to be with someone who won't talk to me," he said quietly.

"So tell her that," Conrad said. "She's been so good for you, Ian, and she's tried so hard."

Ian nodded, his throat so tight. "I know she has, and I haven't exactly made it easy."

"Seriously." Conrad grinned at him. "Coordinating that coffee breakfast almost took an act of Congress."

Ian had started to look away from his brother, but his attention snapped back to him. "What?"

Conrad's face paled, and that said a ton considering how much they both worked outside. "Uh, nothing. I have to go." He strode out of the kitchen, which was so unfair.

Ian couldn't follow him at that clip, so he just yelled, "Where are you going?"

"Mom's," Conrad said over his shoulder as he opened the front door to leave the house.

"That's not fair," Ian yelled, forgetting about the reporters who could probably hear him. The front door closed a moment later, leaving Ian in the corner house alone.

Conrad knew Ian wouldn't follow him to their mother's, even if he could drive or ride a horse.

His phone rang, and *Momma C* sat on the screen. Ian heaved a sigh and tapped to answer. "Hey, Mom."

"Ian," she said, her voice tight and set on warning mode already. "Someone just knocked on our door and asked your daddy if we're going to be partnering with the new Glenn Marks Powell operation."

"I know." Ian massaged his temple with his free hand and wondered if he could just go back to bed. He and Nita were supposed to get together that night for Chinese food and a tour of his vehicle warehouse, but he didn't think that would happen.

"They showed up here too. Conrad handled it. It's not true, obviously."

"I read this article online," Mom said anyway. "It said you'd asked Anita Powell to help you train an upcoming horse."

"I did," Ian said. "Because I can't walk, Mother. In no way is that a merger. There are tons of trainer collaborations where the trainers don't merge their operations. I didn't even know she had an operation to merge with."

He told himself not to say anything else. Mom couldn't help offering her advice, and Ian didn't want to hear it. Worse, her reassurances that he could trust himself when it came to women or that if he'd just try, he could find someone who would love him.

Not only that, but his mother had been against his divorce, and he hadn't been able to forgive her for that quite yet. She'd actually told him that if he stayed with Minnie and cared for her properly, that they could make their marriage work.

Ian had finally screamed at her that Minnie didn't love him and never had, and he didn't know how to "work with that."

He'd filed for divorce, and he'd gone to all the court hearings, and he'd fought for every penny he'd been able to keep. Every shred of dignity too, and every ounce of his heart he'd managed to preserve.

He didn't have to justify anything to anyone, and he'd stopped doing that a decade ago, about the same time he'd decided to live a female-free life.

Now that he'd allowed another one in, and she'd started to carve a place for herself in his heart and his life, he'd found out she hadn't been honest with him.

"I have to go," he said. "Just tell them 'no comment' and to get off the ranch."

His call waiting buzzed, and he saw Spur's name on the screen. "Spur's callin', Momma. I'll talk to you later."

"Daddy's going to send a text," she said. "Everyone seems to be getting questioned about this."

"Great," Ian said, half sarcastically and half sincere. "Tell him thank you." He quickly tapped to connect to Spur's call, already exhausted, and he'd had three conversations that morning.

"Hey," he said. "Sorry, I was on the phone with Mom."

"You're on speaker with me and Cayden. Tell me what's goin' on," Spur said in his no-nonsense tone. "I know what I'm hearing isn't right."

Ian appreciated that Spur hadn't believed anything and that he'd come straight to Ian to get the story. He took a deep breath and said, "All right. I'll tell you what I know."

He did, and he added, "And she's dealing with some stuff, and so am I, and so are Mom and Dad. Did you have people come to your house?"

"No," he said. "They were waiting outside our admin building. Cayden called me, and I came over."

"It's not a merger," Ian said. "She's my girlfriend, and I asked her to help me with Digging Your Grave come January, because I can't walk. That's it."

At least on his end, that was it.

Silence came through the line, and Ian rolled his neck. "I stunned you with the word *girlfriend*, didn't I?"

"I know it's why I can't speak," Cayden said. "Not sure about Spur." They laughed together, even Ian, and then he sighed.

"I know she's your girlfriend," Spur said. "I'm a little surprised *you're* calling her that."

"I haven't kissed her," Ian said, knowing that would be his brothers' next question. He wasn't counting that time in the hospital. Nothing that had happened that night counted, in his opinion.

He was the one initiating their dates now, and he could admit that made him feel better about himself. It made him feel more powerful, and like he was in control of his future with Nita.

That feeling had taken a big blow this morning, that was for sure, and Ian just wanted to get off the phone so he could analyze the fallout of the bomb that had been dropped into all of their laps that morning.

"I'm going to call a ranch meeting," Spur said. "I'll text it out."

"Daddy said he was going to text something too," Ian said, his guilt slicing through him. "I'm sorry, guys."

"This isn't your fault," Cayden said. "I've sent Ginny to get Mom and Daddy and bring them back to the homestead. We don't need Mom getting her feathers all riled up with every sound she hears today."

"I'm going to get Blaine, Trey, and Duke to get all the reporters off the ranch," Spur said. "Let's meet in about an hour, okay? I'll send it to the whole ranch. Ian, do you think Nita can be there?"

"I have no clue," Ian said. "It sounded like she had a situation on her hands at her house too."

"Does she need me to go get her?" Spur asked. "I could send Lawrence too. He's not to the ranch yet and will be coming from town."

"I don't know," Ian said. "Let me text her and see if she responds. Nita is pretty tough. She can handle herself."

"That she can," Spur said. "I'd love to have her there to say the truth. I can call her."

"I'll do it," Ian said. "I've already spoken to her once this morning."

"Let me know if another time works better," Spur said, and Ian said he would.

He hadn't left the house yet that day, and he already felt like he'd run a marathon. He wasn't done yet—he'd barely started—and he once again dialed Nita to find out if she could be at Bluegrass in an hour for a private meeting with everyone who worked and trained there.

She'd hate that, and Ian hated that he had to be the one to ask her. At the same time, he'd rather do it than let Spur or Cayden. This wasn't going to be her worst moment yet, and he should be the safe place for her that she'd been for him.

When she answered with, "Hey, Ian," in a weary voice, he said, "I want to come pick you up and bring you to Bluegrass. Would that be all right?"

"My dad's here," she said. "We're finishing up breakfast, and then we'll be on the way."

"Spur wants to have a ranch-wide meeting, and he'd love you to be there to give us the true details."

"Okay," she said with a sigh. "We'll be there soon."

"I'll be right at your side," he promised. "You don't have to do this alone."

"Thanks, Ian," she said. "I'll see you soon."

CHAPTER 13

Nita got out of Glenn's truck, faced the cameras and mob of people who'd been roped off, and turned when a man said her name.

Ian's face emerged among all of the other Chappell men, and relief hit her.

She wasn't completely sure what that said, but she did know she didn't want her relationship with him to end.

He swung toward her on his crutches, and Nita took a few steps toward him to close the distance between them.

"Hi." She stepped into his arms and steadied the two of them, sure everyone and their friends on social media were getting the whole show.

"You okay?" he asked, the kindness in his voice entering her ears at full force.

"Yes," she said, feeling the okay-ness all the way down in her toes. She stepped back and added, "You'll stand right by me, right?"

"Yep." He looked past her, and Nita turned to see her father had been one of their spectators. "Dad," she said. "This is Ian Chappell."

"I know who Ian Chappell is," Glenn said, a smile appearing on his face. "This must be the boyfriend." His eyebrows went up. "He is the boyfriend now, right?"

Nita wished he wouldn't talk, because now she'd have to tell Ian about how she'd once called him her boyfriend when he wasn't. "Yes," she said, giving her dad a piercing look. "We're dating."

Ian took her hand in his as he moved fully to her side, then extended his other one to Glenn. "It's great to meet you, sir, though I'm sure we've met before."

"I'm officially the girlfriend's father this time." Glenn chuckled, and to her surprise, Ian did too.

Glenn blew out his breath. "All right. Should we do this, Nita?"

"Yes," she said. "Do you see Spur?"

"He's up front," Ian said. "I'll take you." He released her hand, and she moved with him as they went past the crowd. It held cowboys, cowgirls, trainers, horse owners, and press.

Nita was going to throw up at any moment. This was exactly the kind of scene she'd wanted to avoid. In her mind, the new signs went up on the stables she still needed to talk to Lawrence Chappell about renting, and word would spread among those in the business. No interviews. No press conferences. Nothing.

She should've known better. Her father didn't have the

type of name or reputation to allow such a silly imagination to truly happen.

Spur caught her eye, and he lifted his hand as if anyone could miss him. He stood with Cayden and a couple of other Chappells, and she raised her hand in return.

She made it to Spur without throwing up, and she shook his hand, noting Ian's parents stood off to the side too. She went over to say hello to them too, as did her father.

Then they caught each other's gaze, and her dad nodded to the crowd.

Nita took one more steeling breath and pictured Sampson in her mind. He'd tell her this was what she wanted —her own stables. Her own training experience. Her own name.

They'd named their dog Goliath, because they were going to take on the world the way giants did.

"Hello," she said into the microphone Spur had handed to her in a moment she couldn't remember. Ian stood on her right and her father flanked her on the left.

"Thanks for coming, and I apologize for disrupting things at Bluegrass Ranch today. Julie and Jefferson Chappell are amazing, as are all of their sons for putting up with this."

She cleared her throat, because she didn't want to be rude to the media, but they'd caused this problem. *No,* she thought. *Judd Rake caused this problem,* and she searched the crowd for him.

Unsurprisingly, he stood right against the rope near the

front left corner. Her eyes met his, and she knew with that sly, devilish smile that he *had* caused this storm.

"My father and I have been talking about me taking over part of the training at Glenn Marks for over a year," she said. "The contracts were drawn up and signed this past fall, and come January first, Glenn Marks will still have a huge place in the race horse industry. I'm not taking any staff with me over to Glenn Marks Powell, which will be my training stables, which I'll run and manage independently of Glenn Marks."

She looked at her father and passed the mic to him.

"We expect the same excellence and tradition to come from Glenn Marks Powell under Anita's careful and masterful hand, as she's demonstrated outstanding training skills with our equines over the years. That's why she's keeping the name of Glenn Marks, which stands for top quality Thoroughbreds." He grinned like the professional he was, and held up his hand as a couple of people started to ask questions.

Nita took the mic again and held it up to her mouth. "Ian Chappell and I are seeing one another. It's a fairly new relationship, and I will not be answering any personal questions about it. Nor will he." She glanced at him without truly taking time to look fully. She hadn't talked to him about any of this, but she didn't think he'd object to not answering questions.

"He asked me to help him with the training of one of his horses for this upcoming season, simply because of his current health condition, which is improving every single day." She smiled at the crowd, finally feeling a little bit settled. "By January, he won't need my help at all, and he'll regret that he thought he needed anyone."

Ian's hand took hers in his, and Nita looked at him this time. "In no way am I merging my not-yet-operational training stables with Ian Chappell or anyone at Bluegrass Ranch. I'll simply rent stable space here, the way many racehorse operations do." She faced the crowd. "My father and I will be around for a few minutes to answer any other questions. Thank you."

She handed the mic back to Spur without letting go of Ian's hand, and as she faced the fray of people, a calmness stayed with her.

That had everything to do with the man at her side, and she kept Ian right with her as she accepted congratulations from other trainers and stable owners, answered a few questions from reporters, and then watched the crowd break up and disperse.

"Lunch at my place?" Ian asked, his mouth dipping close to her ear.

She nodded and let him lead her over to Conrad's truck. In the quiet cab, she breathed while he took a minute to talk to Cayden and Spur, then Conrad, and then get in the passenger seat, his crutches between them.

"You did great," he said.

"Thanks." She got the big truck moving down the dirt road and on toward privacy and the corner house. Ian didn't say anything on the way there, and several minutes later, Nita parked out front of the house.

"It wasn't anything nefarious," she said. "I just hadn't told you yet."

"I want to be with someone who tells me everything."

"I would've," she said, feeling defensive but also very small. She *should've* told him, but she had so very much to reveal to the man. She'd told him all about Sampson and the boxes of stuff in her garage.

She still didn't even know his ex-wife's name.

"It's not like you've told me everything," she said.

"No," he said. "I haven't, and there's a very good reason for that."

"Maybe I had a very good reason for not mentioning the rollover."

"What is it?"

"People—" She exhaled heavily. "People look at me differently when they know I'm Glenn's daughter. They make judgments or assumptions, and I *hate* it. I started separating myself from him when I was sixteen. I still learned, and I knew I wanted to do what he did. But I've spent half of my life trying to prove to others that I'm my own person. *I'm* a good trainer, regardless of my last name."

Her chest heaved, and she just wanted him to understand. No one ever understood.

"You're a Chappell," she said miserably. "Surely you get wanting to make your own name for yourself."

"I do," he said quietly.

"Not that you need to." She pushed her hair off her forehead. "Everyone's thought you were a god among trainers for your whole life."

"That's not true."

"Oh, it's true," Nita assured him. "I've known about you for years, Ian. *Everyone* knows who you are; you're that good."

"You're as good as me," he said.

"Now you're being ridiculous," she said with a smile. "Come on, I don't want to sit in the truck." She turned it off and pulled the key out.

He'd gotten out by the time she'd circled the front of the vehicle, and he looked at her. "You're an amazing trainer," he said. "I saw it before I knew who your dad was."

"You're one of the only ones," she said. "You've heard Judd and Rafe." They weren't the only ones who'd given her grief over the years.

"I know I need to be more open with you," he said. "I want that. It's just..."

"Hard," Nita said. "I want that too, Ian." She drew a big breath and looked out over the ranch and the road they'd just come in on. "Maybe we can just agree that right now, moving forward, we don't keep any more secrets."

"I'd like that," he said. "I want to trust you."

"You don't?"

"I have a very hard time trusting women," he said. "Or myself, especially when it comes to women."

"I'd love to hear that story," she said.

"I'd love to tell it." He swallowed visibly. "It's been quite the day already, though. What do you say we save it for another time?"

"I think that's fine." Nita moved toward him and helped

him get his crutches out. As she closed the door of Conrad's truck, she added, "Maybe you could just tell me the name of your ex-wife."

"Minnie," he said, and it sounded like a growl from the throat of a wolf.

Nita linked her arm through his and moved with him as he swung himself toward the steps.

He could get around pretty easily now, and up the stairs he went without an issue. Inside the house, he sighed and said, "Let's see. Ginny brought over some chicken and wild rice soup last night. Does that sound good?"

"Sounds amazing," Nita said, glad she'd been able to get through this morning. She followed Ian into the kitchen and penetrated his personal space.

She tipped up onto her toes and kissed his cheek. "Thank you for this morning. For being awesome about all of this." She knew it wasn't easy for him to be anywhere near the front of a crowd, and she knew him well enough to know he didn't want untruths spoken about him.

He put his arm around her waist and tucked her right against him, saying, "You're the one who's awesome."

* * *

The weeks passed without any more press showing up on her front porch or hassling anyone at Bluegrass Ranch. Nita showed up at her father's stables and did the work required of her.

In the few situations she'd run into Judd, he'd said

nothing to her, and she followed his lead. She wasn't sure what her father had done, but Judd worked an opposite shift than she did, or he'd been moved to other tasks, or something. She didn't ask him, and she didn't bring it up with Glenn.

Still planning on Thanksgiving afternoon at the corner house? Ian asked the week before the holiday.

Yes, Nita said. Her mother was planning a meal for one o'clock, and Nita had said she'd be there for that. Her brother was coming in from Miami, and then he'd go to Glenn and Janet's that afternoon.

Nita had told her dad she wanted to see Ian on Thanksgiving, and then she'd asked him when his mother served the turkey and mashed potatoes.

Noon, had been his answer. She'd suggested they get together at the corner house for pie and ice cream, and he'd seized that idea with both hands.

It had grown and morphed, especially once his sisters-in-law found out about it. Ginny and Olli were now planning a full pie buffet, and the last text Nita had gotten on the group text she'd been added to had been from Ry, exclaiming that she'd gotten her grandmother's hot fudge recipe and would bring it for the sundae bar they were planning too.

Nita had volunteered to bring a few gallons of ice cream, but she'd be buying her sweets at the grocery store. Her mom had said she'd donate a pecan pie for the occasion, and while Nita felt guilty taking it, she'd said she would.

She'd invited her mother to come to the dessert afternoon, but she'd declined, claiming she'd be exhausted after cooking and hosting dinner at her house.

Nita had let her get away with the excuse, as she wasn't particularly looking forward to an afternoon with twenty people, even if one of them was Ian.

And we're finally eating Chinese food and touring the warehouse tonight?

I will be there even if the world ends, Nita sent back to Ian. A couple of weeks had passed since the press incident, and their Chinese-food-vehicle-warehouse date had been canceled.

Great, he said. *I have something to show you.*

What is it?

A picture came in next, and it showed Ian standing there with only one crutch on his right side. He wore a bright smile that made Nita's pulse pick up speed.

The doctor cleared me to use one crutch, he said. *I can put partial weight on my leg now.*

She grinned like a fool as she typed out her response. *Amazing. I can't wait to see it—and you.*

He hadn't kissed her again, nor had he said a whole lot more about his previous marriage and wife. They'd been talking a lot about her stables, and she'd met with Lawrence about taking over the rent for half of her father's current rowhouses.

She'd met with him about the signs she could put up, and Ian had gone with her to order the new Glenn Marks Powell signs with her logo on them.

She had been learning more and more about him, but

not much to do with his mother or Minnie, and she'd determined not to push him. If he needed time to trust her, she could give it to him.

Can't wait to see you too, he said. *I might drop by your stables later this afternoon. Depends on how my prissy horse acts.*

She giggled at his adjective for Caped Heroine, a new horse his family had just bought. Ian had been tasked with easing her into the fold at Bluegrass, and Heroine hadn't done a great job of it.

Ian loved the horse, though, and Nita suspected she wouldn't see him until that evening. It was fine; she could wait. If he didn't kiss her tonight, though, Nita might have to take matters into her own hands. She'd done that before, and things had turned out pretty great so far, so she pushed aside her worries and fears and got back to work.

Then she'd have time to go home and get clean and made up for her date that night, and hopefully Ian would know with one look at her that she was ready to kiss him.

CHAPTER 14

Ian handed the man on his front porch a handful of bills and said, "Keep the change. Thanks for driving all the way out here."

"Sure thing, man." He looked down at the bills, and Ian backed up, hoping to get the door closed before the delivery driver could truly see the amount he'd been given. With his leg, even with the single crutch, he moved slower than he'd like.

"This is too—" the man started to say, but Ian kept the door swinging closed. He'd set the multiple containers of Chinese food on the side table, and he turned before picking up the bag and going into the kitchen.

Nita had said she'd drive herself over, as Ian still couldn't get behind the wheel of a car. He could, and he did, but he didn't drive. He did start up his favorite vehicles and just sit in them while they idled, usually the ones with bigger, more rumbly engines. He couldn't wait to drive one of his cars or trucks again, and a tremor of nervousness ran through him at opening the door to the vehicle warehouse and letting Nita inside.

He'd been letting her inside a lot of things in the past couple of weeks, and while he hadn't told her the whole disastrous story of Minnie yet, he was getting closer and closer to opening his mouth and having the whole sordid tale spill out.

They'd been sharing a lot about their lives, themselves, and what they wanted for the future. She'd told him about her grandfather and her previous husband, and other than that, she claimed her past was fairly uneventful.

Ian wished his was. Once he got the reason he distrusted women and himself out of the way, he wouldn't have much to say, he supposed.

"Maybe tonight," he told himself as the front door opened. Since Nita probably wouldn't just walk in, he expected to find Conrad when he turned around.

Instead, he found Lawrence walking in. "Howdy, Ian," he said, plenty of joviality in his voice. "Nita said she'd be here tonight." His eyes swept the house, but Nita wasn't there.

"She will be," Ian said, dropping his gaze to what Lawrence carried. "Are those her signs?" Excitement filled him, because Nita had shown him the new logo for Glenn Marks Powell, and he'd helped her find a supplier who could get her the signs quickly.

"Yep," Lawrence said. "They arrived at the office while I

was there just now. I texted her to let her know I'd bring them here."

"Have you seen them?"

"No," he said. "I was just talking to Cay about our yearling sale when the delivery showed up." He put the three tubes on the dining room table and turned toward Ian. "You're moving really well."

"Thanks." Ian lifted his crutch a few inches off the ground. "I'm feeling better and better every day."

Lawrence grinned at him and stepped over to hug Ian. "Does Nita have anything to do with that?"

"Yeah, I'm sure she does." Ian didn't mind the question, because Lawrence never asked in order to tease later. "I sure do like her, and I'm trying to figure out...things."

"Ex-wife things?"

"Mostly, yeah," Ian said.

The doorbell rang, and they both turned toward it. "I'll let her in," Lawrence said. "Can I stay to see the signs? She said they fit our guidelines, but she wouldn't let me see them. I told her if they didn't, I couldn't let her put them up." He looked concerned that he'd have to enforce something he didn't want to with Nita.

"I went over them with her," Ian said. "They'll be fine."

Lawrence started toward the door and opened it. "Come in," he said.

"Oh," Nita said. "Ian's here, right?"

"Yeah," Lawrence and Ian said at the same time. "He said I could stay to see the signs."

"Sure." Nita stepped past him, and Ian got a few seconds

of watching the gorgeous blonde walk toward him. She'd obviously been home, because her skin glowed with makeup, and her smile shone with glossy lips. She wore a black and white skirt, and he'd really like to see her climb on his Indian motorcycle in *that*.

She wore a bright purple blouse with the skirt, flat shoes —smart on her part—and she'd actually curled her hair.

Ian couldn't drink in her beauty fast enough, and he couldn't swallow or speak.

"Evening, Ian," she said, stepping into him and placing both hands against his chest. He steadied himself as she brushed her lips against his cheek.

"Evening," ground through his throat.

"The signs came early," she said, meeting his eyes for a moment, plenty dancing there. Ian couldn't quite read it all before she turned toward the table. "Let's open them."

"I'll get the scissors." Lawrence did exactly that, and he handed them to Nita. She snipped and sliced, and the plastic ends of the cardboard tubes got removed.

She looked at Ian, pure playfulness in her gaze. "I'm so excited."

"You look like you might throw up," he teased.

"A little nervous," she admitted. "It's like, this is...real."

"It's real, all right," Lawrence said. "Let's see these." He gave her an encouraging smile, and Nita pulled the first couple of canvas banners out of the tube. She spread them out with a snap and laid them on the table.

The letters GMP sat inside an oval that filled the middle of the banner. The tops of the letters rounded with the oval, and the words "Glenn Marks Powell" sat below the shape, curved along the bottom edge.

Three horses done in black silhouette grazed beneath that, with "champions since 1975" along the very bottom of the banner. Everything was done in black ink except for the P, which stood for Powell.

That had been done in blue, and it was the only color on the banner, making it stand out and call attention.

"It's stunning," Lawrence said. "Fits the parameters too. Nice job, Nita."

"Thanks," she said, pulling the bottom banner on top of the first. They were the same, but she needed more than one. Some owners hung banners across the front of their champions' stalls, and they all had them over the rowhouses they rented.

"We'll hang them right after the New Year," Nita said, rolling them back up to put away. "You'll help me, right?" She stuffed them back into the tube and looked at Ian.

"Of course I will," he said. "I'm going to be climbing ladders again real soon."

"Yes, you are." She grinned at him, her eyes dripping down to his single sneaker. "Look at you with only one crutch."

"I can get to the front door in eight seconds," he said, so proud of himself. "It used to take me about twenty, and I was in the foulest mood by then." He chuckled, and Nita giggled with him.

"I'll see y'all later," Lawrence said, and Nita flinched when she realized he was still there.

"'Bye," Ian said without looking away from Nita. Once the front door closed, he added, "The food's here. Are you ready for this?"

"I think you're the one who needs to be asking yourself that," she said.

"I'm ready," Ian said, and he meant for more than showing her the cars, trucks, and bikes he had in the vehicle warehouse. "Will you carry the food? It's on the counter there."

"Yep." Nita picked it up, and Ian moved to the back door. She came out onto the deck with him, and he liked how she'd always moved at his pace. When he was at his healthiest, he'd be able to walk far faster than her, and he told himself to never do such a thing. He always wanted her to be able to keep pace with him.

Another part of his heart healed, and he glanced at Nita as he reached the top of the steps. "Minnie and I were only married for six months," he said, his memories of this event absolutely clear. "She didn't love me, and I didn't see it. We dated for a year, and I didn't see it."

Nita went down the steps with him, one by painful one. "I don't get it," she said. "Why'd she marry you then?"

"I have a lot of money," he said, and it was far easier than he'd anticipated. He didn't look at her as he started across the grass toward the warehouse. "She thought if she put up with me long enough, she'd get a bunch of it."

"You have got to be kidding."

"I wish I was." He focused on the light gray door in the blue warehouse, refusing to look anywhere but at it. "I had no idea, and I felt like such a fool. I still do, sometimes."

"I'm so sorry, Ian," she said. "I don't understand how people can be so cruel."

"Money does strange things to people," Ian said. He took one step and then another. "Do you care about my money, Nita?"

"Yeah, of course," she said. "I think most women would like a really nice car to drive or a really big diamond from the man they love." The weight of her eyes on his face couldn't make him look at her. "Other than that, no. I know how much money the Chappells have."

"Do you?"

"You've been in the racehorse business for decades," she said. "You're putting on your own races now. Everyone within this industry knows how much money you have."

"Not the exact number," Ian said.

"No," Nita said. "And I don't need to know that either." Her grip on his arm tightened. "I don't like you because of your money, Ian."

"Why do you like me?"

"Fishing?"

"No," he said, only a few steps to go to the door. "Wondering. Curious."

She came to a stop and turned toward him. "I adore you, because you're quiet when it's time to be quiet. You say what needs to be said and no more. You're really good at making breakfast, and you're not afraid to be yourself."

Ian searched her face, trying to find an ounce of dishonesty or untrustworthiness there. He couldn't. *That doesn't mean it's not there*, he thought, but he pressed against the idea. He had to learn how to trust himself again, and he had to learn how to take what Nita said and believe it.

He reached up and brushed his fingers along one of her curls. "You did your hair real nice."

"Mm."

He looked into her eyes again. "So making breakfast is one reason you like me?"

"I have fond memories of our breakfast here," she said. "It showed me how you interact with your home environment. You're clean, and you like food full of flavor. There was more to it than just cooking."

"You like how I just blurt things out," he said.

Nita grinned and brought her hand to his face. "And this scruffy beard."

Ian ducked his head, though that caused her to drop her hand. "Okay, you've fed my ego enough. Thank you." He reached to open the door, which wasn't locked. The scent of metal and motor oil met his nose, and he took a deep breath of it.

"All right," he said. "We can look at all of them first or eat first. My vote is going to be eat first, and I have one of my favorite trucks picked out for that."

"I knew we'd be eating in a car." She waited for him to enter the warehouse first. "I should've worn pants."

"It's a normal truck," Ian said with a smile. He moved past her and into the warehouse, snapping on the overhead lights. They buzzed as they burst to life, and one of his safe havens came into view. "I have several cars and trucks. Three motorcycles. We'll be over here in this shiny red one to start."

"I don't know where to look first," Nita said.

"This is a 1978 Dodge 'Lil Red Express truck," Ian said. "It's been restored, but it's got all original parts. Some reupholstery. It runs great still." He ran his hand along the straight hood, admiring the bulging metal that came out over the tires, with the pipe running up behind the passenger door and the bed of the truck.

"At the time, they were the fastest American-made vehicle."

"Wow," Nita said. "It's stunning. It runs?"

"Sure," Ian said. "I drive it sometimes, usually when I want to load something in the back. Straw, hay, big bushels of peaches for my mom." He smiled at the truck and then Nita. "It has a smaller bed, with the wooden accents, and we can sit on the tailgate. I've been sitting there, and I'm good."

"Your wish is my command," Nita said, and she followed him to the back of the truck. He lowered the tailgate and hopped up while Nita set down the bag of Chinese food. Ian extended his hand to help her get up, and the moment her fingers touched his, his entire plan for the evening changed.

He normally didn't like to plan how he'd kiss a woman anyway, and it had been such a long time since he'd even wanted to. He'd been hoping he might be able to taste Nita's lips tonight, but he'd been thinking it would happen later, after dinner and after the warehouse tour.

Nita got on the tailgate beside him and arranged her skirt so it fell properly. She turned and looked at Ian, and he reached out and cradled her face in both of his hands. He seemed to be able to ask if he could kiss her with just his eyes, because hers glinted back at him with the word, *yes. Yes, yes, yes, please kiss me.*

Ian did.

She tasted like mint and cherries, and he wanted more from the very first hint of it. The kiss in the hospital had been unplanned and quick, almost like a mistake or an afterthought. Or something he hadn't thought about at all.

This was so much more, and with every stroke of his mouth against hers, Ian felt something new. Acceptance. Happiness. Loyalty. Love.

Nita kissed him back, matching his passion with her own, and Ian was absolutely sure he'd never been kissed like this, not even by the woman he'd once called his wife.

He never wanted it to end, so he breathed in through his nose and kept kissing Nita.

CHAPTER 15

Nita pushed Ian's cowboy hat off his head in order to get her fingers through his hair. He had cut that, and she knew his "scruffy beard" was a choice. One he'd made deliberately. One she really liked.

As she kissed him back with as much as he gave her, she moved her fingers to curl around his ears and then down over that soft, handsome beard. It had been a while since Nita had kissed a man, and as Ian deepened the kiss with a growl in his throat, she realized she'd never been kissed the way he was currently kissing her.

He was more than a man, and more than a cowboy. He was a god among trainers, and he was a champion among cowboys.

Her heartbeat raced around her body, and finally, Ian caught control of himself and broke the kiss. Nita kept her eyes closed and her fingers curled into the hair on the back of his head. She just needed one more moment to commit all of this to memory, and then she'd open her eyes and make sure this wasn't a dream.

For she had dreamt of kissing Ian a time or two. She finally opened her eyes and found that Ian had not pulled away very far. The dark depths of his eyes glinted with desire, and Nita wanted to dive right into them again.

He cradled her face with just one hand now, almost like he wanted to hold her in place so she didn't get too far away. She wasn't complaining, and they breathed in together, no laughter or giggling in sight.

The moment was pure, real, and sober, and when he did put a few more inches between them, he reached up and ran his hand through his hair. He twisted and picked up his cowboy hat. "I hope that was okay. You didn't seem to not want me to kiss you."

"I've been waiting for you to do that for a while." Nita untied the handles on the plastic bag and lifted out the first container of Chinese food. "What did you get?"

"A while?"

"A couple of weeks." She opened the flaps on the white container. "This one looks like Mongolian beef." She set it on the tailgate between them, which was saying something as they sat nearly thigh-to-thigh.

She continued to unbox the Chinese food, finally opening a pair of chopsticks and picking up the orange chicken while Ian selected the Mongolian beef. He hadn't said anything else, and Nita certainly didn't know what to say after a kiss like that.

"Where did you and Minnie live?" she asked.

"A little house on the outskirts of town," he said. "You and Sam?" He held his beef in his chopsticks and waited for her to answer.

"We had an apartment close to the hospital," Nita said. "He had to go all the time for chemo and radiation treatments, and because we lived so close, I could still go to work. His sister or his mom would help get him home. Sometimes my parents."

Talking about Sam had become easier the more she did it, and she hoped the same would be true for Ian when it came to Minnie.

"I see myself just staying in the corner house now," Ian said. "Conrad's getting married in the spring, and we've already talked about the living situation."

"And?"

Ian blew out his breath and pinched up another bite of beef. "I think I'm going to move in with Ginny and Cayden for a little bit. Conrad and Ry are looking to build a house halfway between town and the ranch, since she has her boutique, and he obviously works here."

Anita nodded, her mind going down paths it probably shouldn't. "What if Conrad and Ry just lived in the corner house and you moved in with your new wife?"

"Sounds ideal," he said. "If not months and months away."

"I do live only ten minutes from Bluegrass," she said. "I've got five acres of land. There's only three people on the street."

"I could put a warehouse in the back corner of the yard for the cars."

Nita smiled and set down her container of chicken. She picked up the lo mein and twirled her chopsticks in the noodles. "Horses in the back. I think it's probably time I cleaned out the garage."

"I can help you with that," he said quietly.

"I can help you move in with Ginny and Cayden," she said.

They ate for another couple of minutes, and then Ian asked, "Did we really just talk about getting married?"

"I think so."

"Right after the first kiss," he said with a chuckle. "Wow."

"Yeah," Nita said, grinning as she put the noodles in her mouth. *Wow* was a pretty good way to sum up her feelings for Ian—and the way he'd kissed her.

* * *

"Yes, okay," Nita said, holding out her hand. "Pass me the sweet potato casserole."

"If you don't want any, that's fine," Mom said, but it obviously wasn't. She'd been pushing the stuff on Nita for the entire Thanksgiving meal, which was almost over.

The house had been too hot the moment she'd arrived,

and when Nita's brother, Calvin, had arrived, the tension in the house had only escalated. Mom had been acting weird since the news of Glenn Marks Powell had come out, and Nita couldn't blame her for that.

The jagged line between Glenn and her mom often found Nita swimming from one side to the other, trying to climb the ragged cliffs, and make sure both of them stayed happy. Such a feat was impossible, and yet, Nita kept trying.

She loved her father, even if she didn't love what he'd done to her mother. They still worked together, and Nita wanted and needed his guidance and support as the date when she'd be taking over her own training unit came ever closer.

"I do want some," Nita said. "I'll just have a little bit."

"It's the marshmallows," Cal said. "Nita doesn't like marshmallows."

The entire top of the sweet potato casserole bore browned marshmallows, but her mom passed her the dish anyway. Nita took a spoonful from under the sticky whiteness and put it on her plate. She smiled at her mom. "Thanks."

"They have a candied pecan layer," she said, a line she'd said at least three times already. "You do like pecans."

"I love them," Nita said, keeping her smile hitched in place. She'd already seen the pecan pie Mom had made for the dessert-fest at Ian's in a few hours, and it was the most beautiful thing she'd ever laid eyes on.

Every nut had been placed with care, and the crust had been browned to perfection. Nita had wanted to eat a slice right then and there, but she'd wait until later, because part of her wanted to show off the pie to all of Ian's brothers and sisters-in-law.

Calvin's baby, a four-month-old named Chloe, started to fuss, and both he and his wife, Delaney, stopped eating to attend to her. Nita had spent the morning either tiptoeing or whispering, because Chloe had been asleep down the hall, in another room, with the door closed.

Her head ached, and while she loved her family, there was a reason she didn't see them all that often.

She didn't want to hurt her mother with the rollover, and she'd spent plenty of time talking to her about the business. She'd always come before the horses, and her relationship with her mom was very important to her.

Important enough to eat the sweet potato casserole she didn't want. She took a bite, her mom's eyes boring into her. More sweetness than Nita liked exploded through her mouth, but she smiled. "It's great, Mom."

"It's Chloe's favorite thing," Cal added, and Nita gave him a grateful glance. They'd already talked about their mother's job, and Cal's, and how Delaney wasn't going to go back to her job teaching preschool.

They'd talked about Chloe cutting her first tooth so early and everyone's Christmas plans. Nita had spoken of the horses she'd take with her over to Glenn Marks Powell, and there only remained one thing she hadn't told everyone yet.

"So," she said. "I'm seeing someone. It's getting quite serious." She and Ian had talked about marriage and where they might live last week, and she'd seen him and kissed him every single day since then.

Whenever she saw him limping toward her, giddiness galloped through her, and she sure had enjoyed sneaking off with him for a few minutes, talking, laughing, and kissing him. He seemed to be a completely different man—happier, more carefree—but at the same time, the quiet, dark-eyed man with a quick temper still lived just beneath the surface of all of Ian's smiling.

"You are?" Delaney asked, so much incredulity in her voice that Nita gave her a withering look. "Sorry," she added. "It's just..." She looked at Cal for help, and Nita cocked her eyebrow at her brother.

"Who is it?" Cal asked.

"Ian Chappell," Nita said at the same time as her mother.

Cal's eyes bulged, and he blinked rapidly several times. "I guess he won't need a place to live. Or a few bucks for groceries."

Nita shook her head. "No, he doesn't need either of those things."

"He's one of the best trainers in the industry," Cal said to Delaney. "You must've met him at the stables." He swung his attention back to Nita. "Yeah?"

"Yeah," she said. "I mean, I've known him for years. Known of him. About him. Whatever."

"So how did this all happen?" Cal asked.

"I don't know," Nita said. "I chewed him out for talking to Powerplay, and he kind of...got in my head after that. It took a few months, but we've been seeing each other for a few months now."

"Wow," Delaney said. "The Chappells are the men on that billboard we passed on the way in." She looked up from her phone. "This says they're one of the premier horse breeding, training, and racing ranches in the area."

Nita nodded. "They are. Glenn's been boarding there for a decade. I'm going to keep my horses there too." She glanced at her mother, just to see how talk of the horses affected her. She seemed to glow with the thought of wedding bells in Nita's future.

"How serious?" she asked.

Nita shrugged. "I don't know, Mom. He doesn't have a diamond or anything."

"Are you thinking big or small?"

"He's a Chappell, Mom," Cal said. "That means a big wedding, probably right on their ranch." He met Nita's eye. "Right?"

"I don't know," she said. "We haven't talked about those specifics." She put the last bite of sweet potato casserole in her mouth and told herself to stop eating. She had plenty of dessert in her future.

She picked up her plate and stood. "Anyway, I thought you'd all like to know. It's not going to be super soon or anything, but I do like him."

"You like him, or you're falling in love with him?" Mom asked, getting up too.

Nita thought about the question, her mind racing from thought to thought. "Maybe both?" She looked at her mom.

"You're friends with your spouse, right? You like them, *and* you love them."

"Usually, yes," Mom said.

"Yes," Cal said behind her. Dishes clacked together, and his wife chastised him when the noise scared Chloe. Nita rolled her eyes, glad she was facing away from her brother and his wife. Her mom put the plate she carried in the sink and leaned in close.

"Heaven forbid that baby feel bad or scared for even a moment."

Stunned, Nita stared at her mother. Then they both burst out laughing. She stayed to help her mom clean up, and she even took Chloe and held her while Cal and Mom played cribbage, something they'd done so often around the holidays as Nita and Cal had grown up.

"Nita," Mom said. "You better get your pie and go."

She looked up, half drowsy from the warm baby and the big turkey dinner. "What time is it?"

"Almost three," Mom said, and that got Nita to jerk all the way awake.

She got to her feet and passed Chloe back to her mother. "Sorry," she said. "I have to go."

Delaney took her baby and smiled at Nita. "Good luck."

Nita hurried into the kitchen and picked up the pecan pie. When she turned, her mom stood there. She put both hands on Nita's shoulders. "You're going to have fun."

"His whole family is going to be there."

"But so is he," Mom said. "He won't leave your side, and it's going to be fun. Just focus on Ian, and you'll be fine."

Nita nodded and hugged her mother. "Thank you so much, Mom. I love you."

"I love you too, sweetie. Have fun." She stepped back, and Nita headed for the front door, almost as nervous to drive to the corner house today as she'd been when she'd had a thermos of her mom's coffee with her.

CHAPTER 16

Spur Chappell liked to stay out of the way during the big family parties. He could observe the family and see where he needed to be more easily if he let everyone arrive, group off with those they felt most comfortable with, and watch where the cards fell.

Today, he and Olli arrived a bit after several others, which was fine with him. Anything dealing with all seven of his brothers and their significant others, plus his parents, and that was eighteen adults. With children, the family was definitely growing.

Olli carried Gus on her hip, but Mom took him almost the moment they stepped in the door at the corner house. Ian and Conrad took good care of the place, and he liked coming here. His brothers always acted glad to see him, and he gave Conrad a smile as he let the front door close behind him.

"I'm going to go help Ginny," Olli said.

"If you feel tired," Spur said, and he didn't finish the sentence. He didn't need to. Olli nodded at him, concern in her eyes. She'd take care of herself, though Spur couldn't help worrying about her. He'd decided that worry was part of his love for his wife, and he'd given up on trying not to do it.

"Spur," Trey said, and he turned toward his brother.

"Howdy, Trey." He enveloped Trey in a hug, his eyes on Daddy, who stood talking to Ian and Conrad. Ian clearly was thinking about something else, or looking for someone else, though he was trying to participate with Daddy.

It made sense, as Spur didn't see Nita anywhere. Ginny, Mariah, Beth, and Olli all worked in the kitchen, setting pie plates and bowls on the island. Tam sat on the floor in the living room with her twins, as well as Mom, Gus, Boone, and Fern.

TJ ran by the sliding glass door with the corgis, and Spur didn't see Duke or Lisa, nor Ry.

"What's up?" Spur asked Trey as he stepped back.

"Beth and I wanted to ask if you and Olli would take TJ when we take Fern in for her surgery."

"I'm sure we can," Spur said. "Did you get it scheduled?"

"We're doing the preliminary appointments," he said. "We'll know the surgery date in mid-January, and I'll let you know."

"If Olli's feeling good, we'd love to have TJ," Spur said, noting mentally that he'd need to talk to his wife about having the six-year-old come to stay with them. She loved TJ, though, so it shouldn't be a problem.

She would be eight months pregnant, and Spur was perhaps a little overprotective of her, so he didn't want to commit one-hundred-percent.

"If you can't, I can ask Ginny and Cay," Trey said.

"It's hard to say," Spur said. "Sorry, Trey."

"No, don't be," he said. "I get it. I'll talk to Ginny and Cayden and make sure it's okay for them."

The door opened behind him, and Spur edged out of the way as Duke and Lisa arrived. Ian actually took a step toward the door and then fell back. Conrad's eyes flickered in this direction too, but he kept talking to Daddy.

Spur's heart went out to Ian. Nita had suggested a pie afternoon for the two of them today, and Ian had made a mistake by mentioning it at one of their after-church luncheons at the homestead a few weeks ago. Ginny and Olli could be like hurricane-style wind and rain when they got their teeth into something, and Mariah literally planned events like this for a living.

Lisa and Duke went into the living room instead of the kitchen, and Spur smiled at how Lisa chose to sit next to Mom. She didn't have a great relationship with her own mother, and Spur wondered if his mother knew how much Lisa needed her.

If she didn't, Spur wasn't going to tell her. Then his mother would go overboard in the wrong direction, and that was the last thing anyone needed.

Cayden migrated toward him, bringing Lawrence in his

wake. The two of them worked together a lot, and Spur joined them quite a bit too. He wanted to be in-the-know when it came to the administrative side of the ranch. He just didn't want to spend every waking moment of his time trapped behind a desk.

In Spur's opinion, there was nothing worse than desk work. He craved the open air, being on a horse, and watching them do what they were born and bred to do: run.

"You got new boots," Cayden said, and Spur looked down at his feet.

"Yeah, Olli got them for me." Spur smiled at Cay and Lawrence. "What's new with you guys?"

Duke usually hung out with Conrad and Ian, while Lawrence could be at-ease with Spur and Cayden or with Ian and Conrad. Trey was somewhat of an outlier, as he'd always marched to the beat of his own drum. He had no problem being alone, and he didn't do a whole lot on the administrative side of Bluegrass.

Blaine was Spur's very best friend in the world, but they spent most of their time together with just the two of them. Blaine also could be found with Duke, as he was now, the two of them laughing at something Duke had on his phone.

"Nothing," Cayden said. "Ian looks like he's about to scratch off his own face." He raised his can of cola to his mouth as he turned to look at Ian.

"Cut him some slack," Lawrence said. "So much has changed for him in a short amount of time."

"I wasn't giving him any flack."

"Conrad doesn't look perfectly calm either," Spur said. "What's with him?"

"I think Ry might not be coming," Trey said quietly. "That was the rumor I heard a few minutes ago. He's not super happy to be at this alone."

"It happens," Spur said. "He'll be okay." Spur would stick by his side if Ry didn't show up. "Where is she?"

"I guess they're opening their boutique for a huge sale for two hours tonight," Trey said. "Six to eight or something like that."

"It's not even three yet."

"I don't understand retail either," Cayden said. "I guess it's a thing."

The doorbell rang, and that meant Nita, in Spur's opinion. Both Ian and Conrad started for the door, Conrad in the middle of saying something. Since he didn't have a crutch, he moved faster, but Spur and three other men literally stood a few feet from the front door.

Cayden was the one to take the steps and open the door. Nita stood there, her arms and hands full of desserts. "I gotcha," Cayden said, taking one of the plastic bags containing a couple of quarts of ice cream. "Trey."

"Right behind you."

Cayden passed him the ice cream and twisted to get more. When Nita was left holding a pie, Ian arrived.

"Hey," he said, his smile as real and as wide as Spur had ever seen it. He took a step away from the door and toward the kitchen, drawing the others with him. If he were Ian, he'd want some privacy, and Spur could give that to his brother.

Nita said something Spur didn't catch, as her voice registered too low in his ears. "What do you ladies need?" he asked when he arrived at the island. He smiled at Ginny and then his wife. "We look set up."

"Nita's ice cream," Cayden said, and Ginny took it and put it with a couple of other containers of the dessert.

"We're ready," Olli said. "She's got a pecan pie too, so we'll need to cut that. Could you get it from her, baby?" His wife looked past him, and Spur turned too. "It looks like Ian's going to take her outside."

"Yeah, he wants to kiss her," Trey said, plenty of dryness in his voice.

"Like you never did that," Cayden said, and they both chuckled.

Spur did what his wife said and walked back toward the front door, where yes, Ian had it open and waiting for Nita to walk back onto the porch. "I'll just take the pie," he said. "Then you two can take your time."

"Thanks," Nita said, passing him the baked good.

The scent of sugar and flaky pie crust filled his nose, and Spur definitely wanted some of this. There was nothing better than Kentucky bourbon pecan pie. He took the pie over to Olli and Ginny, but it was Mariah who collected it from him and began to slice it into pieces. She didn't go across and then across again, creating triangular wedges.

Instead, she made straight cuts that ran parallel to each other across the circular pie, making squares out of it, some with rounded corners on one side. "Ready," she announced. "Lawrence?"

Before Spur could comprehend what she'd said, an ear-splitting whistle filled the air. He flinched away from the sound, and when Lawrence finally finished, one of the baby Chappells had started crying.

"Goodness," Ginny said, though she had to be expecting that. Lawrence whistled to get everyone's attention at most major family events. Most of those were outdoors though, and the shrill noise had definitely been louder in the house.

"We're ready," Mariah called into the quiet. Tam had managed to soothe Caroline, which was easier than breathing. Yes, the girl got upset by a lot, but she could be calmed as quickly.

"It's not rocket science," Mariah said. "There are five or six different types of pies. There's plenty of ice cream and toppings. Conrad, where can we eat?"

"Anywhere," he said. "Table, bar, couches, out on the deck. We don't care."

"Not up in the loft," Ian said, having come back inside. He filled the doorway, his hand linked in Nita's, who waited behind him. "There's a pink couch up there where Con reads his fantasy novels. He wants that spot." He grinned at Conrad, who just rolled his eyes and shook his head.

"Giddy-up," Cayden yelled, and that got people moving to pick up paper plates and plastic bowls to get their Thanksgiving Day desserts. Since Spur stood in front of the bar, he simply edged down a little bit to get a plate. With the pies cut into bite-sized squares, he could take one of each and not feel bad.

He did just that and offered the plate to Olli. She took it and put a bowl on the empty space. "What kind do you want?" she asked.

"Tennessee Trailrider," he said. It had a butter pecan base, with plenty of sweetness and caramel, but then someone had had the genius idea to substitute fudge-filled horses in place of the nuts. A ripple of fudge ran through the ice cream too, and Spur didn't need toppings after that. "You keep that one, love. I'll get another plate of bites."

He picked up another plate and used the serving utensils to get his pie, only turning when he heard Conrad whoop. Ian and Nita grinned from ear to ear, and when they moved, they revealed Ry standing in the doorway.

Conrad rushed at her and lifted her right up off her feet. Anyone could see how much in love they were, and it warmed Spur's whole heart.

"Take those to your mother," Olli said. "She's got all the babies over there."

"Yes, ma'am," Spur said, turning to leave the island. He snagged a fork as he went. He approached Mom and extended the plate toward her. "What ice cream do you want, Mom?"

"This is fine for now," she said, smiling at him. "Thank you, baby."

"You okay over here?" Spur grinned at his son as Gus toddled closer to his grandmother. "He's gonna want some."

"I'll give him a bite." Mom forked off the corner on her

apple pie bite and held it out for Gus. The boy eagerly ate it, and Spur wondered if his mother would eat any of the pie he'd given her. Knowing her and how much she loved the grandchildren, probably not.

He turned back to get a treat for himself, but others had thronged the counter, including Nita and Ian. Spur fell back a foot or two, accepted the bowl of Tennessee Trailrider Olli handed him, and was content to watch for now.

He sure did love his big, loud family, and really the only way to make getting together better with them was to serve pie and ice cream. In that moment, he realized what a genius Anita Powell was.

His eyes migrated to her, and she tucked a piece of her hair behind her ear and held a plate in front of her as she loaded it with the mountainberry pie Ginny had become Chappell-famous for.

Even Spur liked it, and he didn't like many berry-based pies. Ian said something to Nita that caused her to look at him in surprise. She asked him something with only her eyes, and he grinned and nodded.

A foot or two down the line, Nita picked up the carafe of cold cream and poured it over her mountain-berry pie bites. She looked at Ian, clearly asking him if she'd done it right.

He nodded, handed her a spoon, and nodded toward the other side of the living room. They went that way, and as Spur took another bite of his ice cream, he watched them climb the steps slowly.

Ry and Conrad didn't go up to the second-floor landing

where the pink couch was. That spot had clearly been taken by Ian and Nita, and Spur chuckled as he smiled to himself.

"What?" Olli asked.

"Nothing," he said. "Why are we standing up to eat pie? Let's find somewhere to sit." He led her over to the couch in the living room where Gus and the other babies were playing, returned to the kitchen to get his pie, and then joined his wife on the soft furniture.

Ry and Conrad had escaped the confines of the house too, as had Duke and Lisa. The others stayed inside, most of them ending up in the living room with him and Olli, and such contentment filled Spur. Even three years ago, he never would've been able to imagine a scenario like this, and as joy filled his heart, and on this Thanksgiving Day, he thanked the Lord for all the good men and women in his life.

CHAPTER 17

"It's not going to be a big deal," Olivia Chappell said. "It's dinner with your family, and a cake that will probably take Gus four seconds to blow out." She knew, because she'd been having her one-year-old practice blowing out candles. Spur didn't know that, though, and he didn't need to know.

"I'm just saying," Spur said. "You're tired, and it's been a long week."

"I ordered the food," Olli said. "I'm not too tired to sit on a chair and have you bring me something to eat. You'll do that anyway." She didn't want to cancel the dinner party. Their son was the oldest biological grandchild, and she wanted to have a first-year birthday party for him.

The week had been long, her husband was right about that. It had rained and snowed in Dreamsville, which meant mud and sludge and sleet. Everything Spur left the house in came back caked in grime and soggy, and she'd seen him come home at lunch to shower and change before going out again.

Olli's warehouse manager had also put in her two weeks' notice, and Olli had started to look for someone to replace her. That caused quite a bit of stress in Olli's life, and she wasn't supposed to allow herself to get too worked up.

Her blood clots were all gone now, the medication she'd been taking for a few months now doing its job. Both her obstetrician and her cardiologist were happy with her health for the moment. She hadn't had another fainting spell since going to the doctor and getting the MRI, and Spur had absolutely nothing to complain about.

"They're loud," Spur said, turning off the kitchen sink where he'd been scrubbing his hands. "I'm not sure I'm in the mood to have them all here."

"Then go in the bedroom when you get overwhelmed," she said. Spur would never do that, and she knew it.

He dried his hands, his eyes trained on her. Olli kept cubing the cheese she'd been cutting up for lunch. Gus already sat in his highchair, and he banged both hands down on the tray and yelled.

"Hey, bud," Spur said. "You don't get food any faster when you do that, trust me. I've tried."

Olli kept her head down despite the smile that curved her lips.

"You can't yell at Momma like that either. She's getting you the cheese."

"He wants the noodles," she said, moving over to the microwave and opening it. "They should be ready." She took out the bowl of elbow macaroni and Alfredo sauce and handed it to Spur. "I make him try with a spoon first."

"Okay." Spur collected one from the drawer and went to sit in front of their son. Olli had to admit she liked it when he came home for lunch, muddy or not. He helped out for a few minutes, and just seeing him in the middle of the day made her happy.

Gus managed a few bites of noodles with the spoon before he grew frustrated and started using his fingers. Half the time he couldn't hit the target with his hands either, and the creamy, white sauce started to spread across his face.

She put a few cubes of cheese on his tray and kept the rest for herself. The baby she was carrying now adored dairy, and she'd eat cheese for every meal if she could. She trailed her fingers along her husband's shoulders. "I'll send someone to pick up the food if that'll make you feel better."

Spur looked up at her. "It's fine, Olli. I'm just tired right now, but I think I'll stay home this afternoon and take a nap with you and Gus."

"Yeah?" She grinned down at him. "How do you know we take an afternoon nap?" She was teasing, because she texted him every afternoon when she was lying down. Then he didn't freak out when he tried to get in touch with her and she didn't respond.

"Can I crash your nap party?" he asked.

"I wish you would every day." Olli leaned down and kissed him, adoring the way he put his hand on her belly as he kissed her back.

Hours later, after all of them had gotten their naps and a

quick snack, Olli opened the door for the caterer she'd hired. She'd called in during lunch and asked for a delivery instead of a pick-up, and they were right on time.

"Thank you," she gushed at them. "Right in here." She didn't care that the house was a little messy. She'd never been the greatest of housekeepers, and with the Christmas holidays almost upon them, there seemed to be a bauble or a knick-knack on every surface.

Stockings over the fireplace, the Christmas tree with ornaments only two-thirds of the way down it, and of course, candles everywhere. The scent of pine mingled with chocolate, and to Olli, she needed to bottle that and make it one of her holiday candles.

The woman entered, followed by a man with another tray. She went over the food, Olli signed a receipt, and they left. Not sixty seconds later, the Chappells started to arrive. Cayden and Ginny arrived first, and Olli's energy rebounded at the sight of her very best friend in the world carrying the most adorable baby boy.

Boone had all the same dark features as Ginny, and no one would ever know he wasn't her biological son. Olli took the boy from Ginny and said, "There's food in the kitchen. Help yourself. We're doing cake in forty-five minutes."

That was the pinnacle of the party, and Olli wasn't going to serve a fancy dinner. She didn't even care if they all ate at the same time. Her house wasn't overly large the way the homestead was, and the lot of them didn't gather here that often.

She left the front door open as she saw Trey and Beth

walking up the sidewalk, and she repeated herself to them. From that point on, she stood on the front step and said hello to everyone as they arrived. Behind her in the house, chatter and laughter filled the air, and Olli realized how much energy had been added to her life.

Finally, everyone had arrived, and Olli took Boone back inside. People had found places to sit to eat and talk, and while it wasn't the fanciest party, or even the most organized, Olli loved the casual, low-key atmosphere of it.

After a few more minutes, it was time for the cake, and she passed Boone to his father to go get it ready. Gus loved all food it seemed, but he especially loved a layer cake Olli had learned to make from her grandmother.

It had a layer of yellow cake on the bottom, plenty of vanilla pudding, and then a chocolate cake on top. Chocolate frosting covered the whole thing, and Olli had then crushed up Oreos and covered the cake with that to make it look like a cookie.

A giant Cookie Monster rose out of the cake as if he'd been down inside the cookie, munching away. He held a single candle, and Olli fitted it into his muppety hands before she lit it.

"Lights, Spur," she said, and her husband got up from the table and flipped off the lights. That worked as well as Lawrence's ultra-loud whistle, and a hush fell over the family.

Gus's face was lit by the single flame, and his little feet kicked in the highchair. Olli loved him more than anything else in the world—except for Spur. "It's your birthday, buddy," she said to him. "Let's sing for him, and then he can blow out the candle."

All of their voices combined together as they sang *Happy Birthday*, and tears filled Olli's eyes about halfway through. She'd once lived in this house alone, and she'd thought she'd been happy. Just her, her flowers, and her perfumery. The Chappells next door had never bothered her, and she'd never seen a reason to go knocking on their door either.

Somehow, Spur had been brought into her life at precisely the right time, and she leaned into his love and strength as the song finished.

"Okay," she said, sliding the cake onto the tray in front of Gus. "Blow it out."

Her son leaned forward, and just like they'd practiced, he extinguished the flame with a single blow. The family erupted in cheers and applause, Olli included, her pride swelling when she heard someone say. "I've never seen a one-year-old do that so well."

Gus had already started to reach for the cake with his chubby fist, and right in he went. She giggled as Spur groaned, but he wouldn't have to clean up that night.

"Don't worry," she said to him. "I have more cake."

"Thank goodness," Spur said. "No one wants to eat what a baby has spat on." He grinned at her, and Olli tipped up to kiss him. "Love you, Olls."

"Love you too, Spur." She stepped away from him to get out the other cakes, saying, "Okay, everyone. Cake down here."

CHAPTER 18

Ian answered the door without a crutch, his heartbeat already racing through his whole body. Nita stood on the porch wearing a bright green dress with so much sparkle, his breath caught in the bottom of his lungs.

"Howdy," she said, but Ian had no words.

He stepped into her personal space and drew her into his arms despite the weakness in his leg. The doctor said it would take some time for the muscles he hadn't used in over three months to rejuvenate and strengthen.

"I have missed you terribly," he whispered just before kissing her. He couldn't help himself. Now that the physical barrier between them had been broken, he wanted to hold her hand and kiss her every chance he got.

He had, too, and he didn't feel bad about it.

He loved kissing her, and Nita sure seemed to like it too. She pressed her fingers up the side of his face, through his beard, and along his sideburns. She pulled away minimally and murmured, "You're going to ruin my makeup."

"That's why you came early, right?" He grinned at her, his smile still on his lips when he pressed them to Nita's again. She giggled but quickly matched her mouth to his again. It was New Year's Eve, and Ian could kiss her all he wanted.

Never mind that midnight sat hours from now, and he'd probably be in a foul mood by the time the clock struck twelve. If he could kiss her at the top of every hour, he would. Her mother had invited them to a New Year's Eve party, and Ian would be meeting Kathy Howard for the first time that evening.

Nita said they only had to stay for an hour or two, and then Ian had a reservation for a ten p.m. dessert and coffee table at Bourboned Sugar. They'd get coffee, drinks, and sweets for an hour, and then there was a dance for the last sixty minutes before midnight.

Ian still had to use the crutch, despite his ability to stand there and kiss Nita, but he was planning to dance tonight. Nothing was going to stop him from welcoming this New Year into his life the right way. He wasn't taking any of the negativity from his injury with him. He only wanted happiness, health, and maybe a really good woman to spend his life with.

He pulled away from Nita, and she was this amazingly good woman in his life. He took her face in his hands and opened his eyes. "Nita," he whispered. "I'm falling in love with you."

Her eyes snapped open, and the normally warm, bright depths of them filled with tears. "You think so?"

"Yeah," he said. "I think so."

She touched her lips to his again, hers trembling now, in a chaste, closed-lipped kiss. "Let's go celebrate," she said. "Trust me when I say we don't want to be late to one of my mom's parties."

Ian grinned and grinned, wondering if he'd ever stop. "Why's that?"

"She hands out tickets at the beginning," Nita said. "If you get there first, you get more."

"Why didn't you say so?" Ian asked, limping backward to grab his crutch. "We should've been on the road ages ago."

Nita burst out laughing, and Ian loved the sound of her giggles. He wanted to hear them every single day, and that told him a lot about how he felt about this woman.

He got in Nita's truck while she made to start it. The engine wouldn't turn over, and she cranked the key again. Ian watched her while trying not to let her know he was watching. It took four tries before the engine stuttered over itself, and Nita gave it some gas to get it growling properly.

"Should I be afraid that we'll get stranded at your mom's?" he asked. "We can take my truck."

"You can't drive," Nita said. "I'm not going against what the doctor said."

"I'm not either," Ian said, facing the front again. "You can drive my truck."

"It's twice as big as this."

"Are you saying you can't drive a truck because it's big?" Ian laughed and shook his head. "It's all the same thing."

"We won't get stranded," she said, flipping the ancient pick-up into reverse.

"If you're sure." Ian was used to riding in the passenger seat now, though he hoped the doctor would approve him to drive at his appointment in a couple of weeks. Conrad had been taking him to all of his appointments, and he did have one coming up where he expected the doctor to clear him of his crutch and to drive.

Ian could hardly wait, and his excitement felt happy instead of frustrated. "What do you want for this year?" he asked Nita, leaning back against the headrest and looking at her.

She glanced at him. "I don't know."

"What do you mean you don't know?"

"Tell me what you want for this year," she said, giving him a dry, somewhat dirty look.

"I want this year to be amazing," he said. "I'm going to walk for most of it. I want to prove to Conrad that I'm a better trainer than him by winning our training wager. I think there's going to be a whole bunch of other changes, but I think they'll be good for me."

"When are you going to move in with Ginny and Cayden?"

"Not until Conrad gets married," he said. "That's April. A couple of babies around then too."

Nita didn't say anything as she navigated them off the ranch. "My mother is going to grill you," she said, actually shifting in her seat. "She'll want to know if you're going to ask me to marry you and how many kids you want. Stuff like that."

"She will?"

"Yeah," Nita said with a sigh. "I usually introduce her to my boyfriends very last, because she's a little intense." She looked at him with nerves in her expression. "I've told her not to, but she still will."

"I can handle it," Ian said. "Minnie's mom was pretty intense too. She wanted us to have a baby in the first nine months of our marriage, and let me tell you, I'm relieved and beyond happy that didn't happen."

"Sam and I wanted kids, but when we found out he was sick, we decided we better not have any for a while. He didn't want me to be left alone to raise them."

Ian couldn't even imagine all of the things Nita and Sampson had dealt with, and as Nita's old, old truck trundled down the road, he felt deeply that lots of people went through very difficult things in their lives. His situation with Minnie had been terrible for him, yes, but he wasn't the only person who'd ever suffered through something hard.

"I want you to have happiness this year," Ian said. "If that's with your stable, or with cleaning out your garage, or with me, it doesn't matter. I just want you to be happy."

"Thank you, Ian," she said. "I want you to be happy too."

"I'm going to work hard with my horses," he said. "I'm going to be happy about wherever I'm living. I'm going to try not being so intense."

"You can be a little intense," she said.

"I know. I'm working on it." He looked out his window, noting that the sun had already started to go down and make everything dark. "I need to go talk to my mom too. Clear the air between us and forgive her."

"My brother could stand to do that with my dad," Nita said. "I guess I could too. Things have been rough between us since he cheated on my mom and left her."

"You still get along with him."

"I do," Nita said. "Mostly because of the stables. After a while, I figured he had a life to live, and so did I, and I didn't have to agree with everything he did." She gave half a shrug. "It's a work in progress most days."

"I feel like everything is," he said.

"Here we are," Nita said, pulling into a driveway at a house where light shone through every single window.

"How many people did she invite?" The house looked like it might be full of people, and Ian didn't particularly want to hang out with a bunch of people he didn't know.

"She said a few friends from work," Nita said, peering at the house. "She joked about how they wouldn't even stay until midnight."

Ian thought it was a good thing they hadn't committed to staying for very long, and he reached to unbuckle his seatbelt.

"Oh, that's Joanie," Nita said. "Okay, we're good."

"Yeah, except she's going to get all the winning tickets." Ian grinned at Nita and got out of her truck. He stayed right beside her as they went up the sidewalk and then the steps to the door. She didn't knock or ring the doorbell but just went inside.

Music played from a speaker somewhere, and a few older ladies milled about. Ladies his mother's age, and Ian realized quickly that he and Nita would be the only ones in their generation at this shindig.

"This is insane," Nita said, pausing in the doorway. Glitter, gold, and silver hung from every available surface—the beams in the ceiling, the barstools, the blinds, all of it. A huge *Happy New Year!* banner hung across the kitchen, and a table had been set up underneath it that seemed like it might buckle from the amount of food that had been placed on it.

Ian's stomach grumbled, because he hadn't eaten dinner yet, and the sliders he spied sure looked delicious.

"Nita," a woman said, and Nita's hand in Ian's tightened.

"There you are," Nita said. "How long did it take you to decorate?"

"Oh, an hour or so." Her mother hugged Nita, but her eyes didn't leave Ian.

"I don't believe that," Nita said with a laugh. She stepped away from her mom and indicated Ian. "Mom, this is Ian Chappell. Ian, my mother, Kathy."

"Wonderful to meet you, ma'am," Ian said, reaching up to tip his hat at the woman. "Anita has told me a lot about you." He extended his hand for her to shake, which she did. "I think the place looks great. Smells great too." He smiled at Kathy, and she grinned on back.

"She's told me a fair few things about you too."

"I'm sure none of them are true." Ian brought Nita back to his side, and they faced her mom together. "Nita tends to have a higher opinion of me than she should."

"Yeah, like how much he follows his stomach." Nita patted his stomach, which surprised Ian. "Come on. I know what you need before we do any more talking to my mother." She led him into the kitchen, where no less than three other women her mother's age waited with more questions.

How long have you been dating?

Oh, are you getting serious?

If you're serious, why haven't you asked her to marry you?

It was like meeting six or seven mothers at the same time, and Ian could admit he was completely out of his element at this New Year's Eve party.

Nita handed him a plate with three sliders on it and plenty of macaroni salad, and things got a little brighter.

* * *

Hours later, Ian had eaten far too much for one day. The coffee mugs had been cleared, and the dessert plates were getting picked up at that very moment.

"You ready to dance?" he asked Nita once the waitress walked away.

"I was born ready," she said, and Ian slid to the edge of the booth. He used the table and the side of the booth to stand, and then he steadied himself on his crutch. Nita stepped right into his arms, and they swayed right there at the end of their booth.

Ian had held her before, but this was more intimate. This was slow and sensual, and he wanted to spend hours just like this. "Mm, this is nice."

"Do you want to go out a little further onto the dance floor?"

"Maybe in a minute." Here, he could stay in the semi-darkness. He didn't have to be under the bright spotlights, with the big disco ball spraying gems of light everywhere.

He brought Nita closer to his body, both hands on her lower back and holding her right where he wanted to keep her. "I think this is going to be a good way to bring in the New Year," he whispered.

"I think so too," she said. "You make me happy, Ian."

"Do I?"

"Mm hm," Nita hummed into his chest, and Ian felt himself slipping right down into love with her, no matter how hard he tried to dig in his feet and stop himself.

He couldn't help wondering if he'd gone slow enough with Nita. Did he know her well enough to know if she was telling him the truth or not?

You make me happy, Ian. The words ran through his head, and they sounded real and true...and he believed her when she said them.

CHAPTER 19

Nita's back ached at her to slow down, and her steps did stop moving at such a rapid clip. She told herself she didn't have to have everything set up in less than an hour. Such a feat was impossible anyway, and there wouldn't be anyone there to see the new stables once she did finish setting them up.

Ian waited for her, still holding the corner of her new sign while his brother Lawrence stood up on the ladder, his end of the signage already almost in position.

"Okay," she said. "Sorry, I forgot Dave had given me this hardware." She'd had to go back to her house to get it, and she hoped they hadn't been frozen like that for the past twenty minutes.

The smaller signs that went on each stable door had been affixed to the wood, so they'd been busy. Ian gave her a smile and said, "It's fine. Mariah brought scotcheroos, so we've been fine."

"What is a scotcheroo?" Nita asked, pausing in handing him the nuts and bolts they needed to hang the new Glenn Marks Powell banners above her stable.

"It's like a rice crispy treat, but made with butterscotch chips in the marshmallow," Lawrence said. "And with Chex instead of rice crispies."

"With chocolate on top," Ian added, and Nita knew the man had at least one weakness. Chocolate. He also loved good coffee, horses, and dogs. Nita was sure he didn't have many other weaknesses, and his strength made her feel stronger.

"Wow," she said as her stomach grumbled. "That does sound amazing."

"I saved you a couple," Ian said. "They're in the fridge in your office."

Warmth filled her. She stepped closer to him and kissed his cheek. "Thank you, cowboy."

She'd taken over five stables, but she only had three horses she'd be working with this year. Only one was old enough to be training for next year's racing season, and she'd joined Conrad and Ian's bet to see who could produce the best horse.

Conrad had flat-out refused to let Ian have a helper, especially now that his cast was off and he was back to walking normally. Nita had stepped right in and volunteered to be in their bet too. Her, training a horse named Gone Fishing. Conrad, training Rolling Thunder, who Ian claimed was the Chappell's prize horse. Ian, training Digging Your Grave.

CONVINCING THE COWBOY BILLIONAIRE   201

He said Conrad had a huge advantage, and the two of them could still collaborate if they wanted. *What Conrad doesn't know won't hurt him*, Ian had said.

Nita climbed the ladder, glad Ian hadn't argued with her again or volunteered to do it, and he stepped back to give her and Lawrence directions for who needed to go higher and who should lower until the sign was exactly even.

She reached down for the hardware, and Ian passed it up. She got it hooked into the wood of the stable and slipped the grommets over the screw. Then she secured it all down so it wouldn't flap around in the winter wind that had come to Kentucky this week.

"There," she said, moving back down the ladder. Ian's hand slid along her hip, guiding her to the ground and right into his arms.

They moved back to see the stables from a further position, and Nita leaned into Ian's side, beyond pleased with how everything had come together.

"This is a dream come true," she whispered. "I've worked and waited so long for this."

Ian kneaded her closer. "I know you have." He stepped away for a moment to clap his brother on the back. "Thank you, Lawrence."

"Yes, thank you," Nita said. "I meet all the requirements?"

"Yes." Lawrence gave her a smile and a hat-tip, and he took down the ladder and carried it with him as he left.

"The last man I dated," Nita said as Ian came back to her side. "He stole a lot of money from me, so I couldn't do this a year ago. I had to work two jobs last summer to pay off all the debts he racked up."

Ian turned his head and looked at her. "You didn't tell me that."

"I just did," she said.

"Who was that?"

"This guy named Karlton," she said. "We broke up a while ago. I didn't even know about the debt until I started getting calls from collectors. Then I had to figure out how to get caught up. That's when I got the job with the Parks Department."

"You won't have to do that this year."

"Nope," she said, bumping him with her hip. "I'm going to spend my summer with Gone Fishing, and we're going to blow you and Conrad out of the water."

She grinned at Ian, who chuckled, though she really hoped what she'd just said would come true. She needed to turn out winning horses if she wanted to be competitive in the industry—and if she wanted to be taken seriously.

"Okay." Nita took a deep breath. "Now we just need to get the horses over." She hadn't set up her office either, but she could do that while Ian went back to his own work.

"I can help," he said.

"I'm fine," Nita said. "I can move a horse from one stable to another."

"Yeah, but it's almost lunchtime, and I've got those frozen cheeseburgers you like." Ian grinned at her, his dark eyes sparkling with something she couldn't quite name.

She liked that he knew her well enough to know of her

obsession with the frozen White Castle burgers. If she ate two or three, they could become a meal, and if she peeled a banana or sliced up an apple, she didn't feel so bad for eating convenience foods.

"All right," she said with a laugh. "Come help me with Powerplay and Gone Fishing."

She started toward her father's stables, and Ian followed her.

At Powerplay's stall, he asked, "You've got three horses, don't you?"

"Yes," she said. "But I'm not getting the other one until next weekend."

He nodded, and they each took a horse over to the new GMP stables. Nita didn't want to leave quite yet, and she wanted a few minutes to herself in her new role of a stable owner and the main trainer of her own business. She'd imagined what this moment would feel like, but now that it was here, she hadn't been able to imagine it properly.

Ian seemed to pick up on the fact that she needed a minute to herself, because he wrapped her in a hug and said, "Take your time. I'll go get lunch started."

She nodded, her voice suddenly folded somewhere inside her throat. Once Ian's footsteps had receded and she stood in silence in front of the rowhouse, Nita let the tears touch her eyes.

"I did it, Sam," she whispered. She hugged herself inside her rain slicker and then pulled out her phone.

She'd started new social media accounts for GMP, and she needed a few inaugural pictures to kick things off. She took them from the far view, from a slanted one, where all three stall signs could be seen, and a couple of closeups of each horse as they stood in the doorways of their stables.

She could post them while she sat at the table with Ian, and Nita turned away from her new venture, happier than she'd ever been.

* * *

The following weekend, Nita pulled her grandfather's truck with an attached horse trailer down the dirt road to the farm where she was picking up her third and final horse for GMP.

The gray roan stood out in front of the barn, obviously freshly washed and ready for transport.

Nita smiled at the animal though she had no idea why she was there. She'd met her before, when she'd come to look at her several weeks ago. Most owners named their horses, but Nita would rename her. When she ran the racing circuit, she'd likely go by something else entirely too.

The gray horse with white and black spots along her back legs reminded Nita of her very first horse, and her heart expanded with love for the animal. They'd get along just fine, and Nita couldn't wait to start training her.

Paul Jessop, the horse's owner—at least for the next ten minutes—came out of the barn, a smile on his face when he saw Nita.

She parked her truck and got out, leaving the door open for Goliath to jump down and come with her.

"Howdy," Paul said, striding toward her.

"Morning." Nita extended her hand to shake Paul's. "She looks really good."

"All clean." Paul turned and admired the horse. "She's going to be a great horse for you. I hate to give her up."

Nita's pulse pounced through her throat, but Paul Jessop wasn't known for backing out of deals. "I've got the rest of the money," she said, reaching into her back pocket to get out the check she'd picked up at the bank that morning.

Paul took it and looked at it, smiled, and tucked it in his back pocket. "Let's get 'er loaded. I can't wait to see what you do with her."

Nita hadn't paid three-quarters of a million dollars for her as her father had for Powerplay, but one-hundred-fifty thousand sure was a lot of money.

Money she'd have to pay back to the bank a little bit at a time, every single month.

She pushed aside the nervousness and moved to help Paul get the gray horse out of the paddock and into the truck.

She went willingly, and Nita stroked her neck through the window. "All right, girl," she said. "It's just a short ride, and then you'll be at your new home."

After another handshake, Nita whistled for Goliath, and then got behind the wheel of her truck and headed to Bluegrass Ranch. She sang along with the radio, her little French bulldog panting over on the passenger side.

She backed up to her rowhouse, using her big rearview mirrors that poked way out on the sides, and once again got out of the truck.

"We're here," she said to the horse, and she'd just gotten her all the way out when Ian arrived.

He whistled appreciatively, his eyes scanning the gray horse from head to hoof. "She's a good-lookin' horse." He reached for her, and of course, the equine leaned into Ian's touch. They seemed to simply understand him on a level humans didn't.

Nita smiled at the two of them. "I hope she's great," she said. "I paid a lot for her, and she's my very first solo purchase."

"She's got great legs," Ian said. "She'll grow into those real nicely."

"I hope so," Nita said again. "She'll be ready later this year, but she came up for sale, and I wanted her."

"I would too." Ian smiled at Nita. "What are you going to name her?"

Nita bent and picked up the horse's rope. "Sampson's Girl." She led the horse away from the trailer and toward the third stall she and Ian had prepared when they'd set up the stables.

With the horse inside, Nita turned back to Ian. He still stood beside the back of the trailer, a frown drawing down his eyebrows.

"What's on your mind?" Nita asked.

"Sampson's Girl?" Ian repeated, and Nita froze, hearing the name she'd chosen in his voice.

Ian erased the emotion from his face, but that didn't make Nita happy. He took a couple of steps toward her. "Just tell me one thing, Nita," he said, his voice low and on the outer edge of dangerous. "You're in a place where you can let Sampson go, right?"

He lifted his eyes to hers, searching her face. "You're not still in love with him or anything? You *want* to...I don't know. Move forward without him, don't you?"

Nita opened her mouth to say of course she did. She wasn't hung up on her husband, who'd died years ago.

No words came out.

CHAPTER 20

Ian's blood popped through his veins. Nita's silence, her hanging mouth, and the way the shock paraded through her eyes didn't bring him any comfort.

He sighed when she said nothing, his eyes releasing hers and going back to the gray horse. "She's real pretty." With that, he stepped past her and started walking along the trailer and her truck.

Part of him wanted her to call him back and reassure him that she was ready to move forward into the future—with him. Another part wanted her to have the space and time she needed to be truthful with herself and with him.

They'd been seeing each other for a few months now, and he'd never felt like she was hung up on Sampson Powell. She'd spoken of him without crying, though she'd definitely shown some sadness.

"She has that whole garage full of his stuff," Ian muttered to himself, thinking of Ryanne. She'd cleaned out her house, which had been stuffed with her deceased sister's belongings. Nita hadn't done that purge yet, and Ian told himself that everyone healed differently. Perhaps Ry needed to get rid of everything and Nita didn't.

"Ian," Nita said from behind him, and his first instinct was to turn and face her. He did, and she hurried toward him, panic on her face. "Wait."

He waited, his hands shoved down into his pockets.

She paused an arm's length from him. "I'm over Sam."

"Okay," he said, but he didn't believe her.

"I just thought..." She exhaled and pressed her palms together. "Sam and I used to lay in bed at night and talk about the stable." Tears filled her eyes. "He wasn't a horse trainer, but he was excellent at supporting and encouraging me in my dreams."

Ian hung his head, plenty of guilt and confusion pumping through him. How could he compete with this man she'd obviously loved so much? It wasn't like Sam had left her. They hadn't fallen out of love and gotten divorced. There'd been no fights; nothing bad to remember about him.

No, she'd *lost* him when she'd wanted to keep him.

"He sounds amazing," Ian finally said when Nita remained quiet. He drew in a breath and lifted his head again. "I can't compete with him, Nita. I know you loved him, and I don't want to take that from you."

He shook his head, not sure how to navigate this maze. "It's okay. Forget I said anything. She's a great horse, and you can name her whatever you want." He turned and started walking again.

Nita caught him and moved into stride with him. Her hand touched his, and Ian slid his fingers through hers.

"He doesn't change how I feel about you," she said. "He wanted me to move on and find someone else to love. I've been trying, especially with you, and I just thought the first horse I got would be a nice tribute to him. It doesn't mean I'm still hung up on him. You don't have to compete with him."

"Okay," Ian said again, though he still felt like he *was* in a competition with someone he'd never met and couldn't see.

"We're still going to dinner tonight, right?" Nita asked.

"Sure," Ian said as cheerfully as he could. "I'll come pick you up at seven."

"Okay." She released his hand, and Ian slowed his step. He faced Nita again, and she reached for him. She took his face in her hands and said, "Tell me we're okay."

"We're okay," he whispered.

She kissed him, and Ian sure did like the way she kept it real and slow, without letting too much passion creep in and make things too rushed or too hormonal.

When she pulled away, Ian kept his head ducked, his own embarrassment making it hard to hold it up. "See you tonight."

"I'm looking forward to it."

Ian walked away, and after only about five or six strides,

he realized he'd learned something from the past fifteen minutes with Nita.

He knew when she told him the truth and when she didn't. She had been telling him the truth when she'd said he made her happy and when she said he didn't have to compete with her husband.

She wasn't completely ready to move into the future without Sampson, though.

"Would you be?" Ian asked himself as he got behind the wheel of his truck. He didn't want to propose and get married next week or anything. He could give Nita the time she needed, and with that thought in his head, he got back to work.

* * *

He pulled up to the house where his mother and father lived, the early morning sunshine barely lighting the day. The air held a crispness to it that left frost on the grass and the promise of snow if the weather turned, and Ian hunched into the collar of his coat as he sat in his truck.

He was the one who'd asked Mom to meet him for breakfast, and while he wasn't late yet, if he sat here for much longer he would be.

Ian thought through the past couple of weeks since Nita had set up her stable and brought home her first solo-purchased horse.

Sampson's Girl.

They'd been out several times, as usual. He saw her

almost every single day, and he definitely spoke to her or texted her daily. He hadn't allowed himself to let go of the very last handhold keeping himself from falling in love with her, because since she'd brought the gray roan to Bluegrass, things between them had been different.

Something came along with them on their dates, though Ian couldn't name what it was. A level of tension and awkwardness he'd thought they'd already gotten past. The ground beneath his feet felt like it might disappear if he stepped too hard, so he'd been tiptoeing around for a couple of weeks now.

He slipped from the truck the way a sigh wisped between his lips, and he made his way up the sidewalk to the front door. He knocked and went in immediately afterward, saying, "It's me, Mom."

"Good morning, Ian," she said, groaning as she rose from the recliner in the living room to his right. She removed her reading glasses and set them on the end table, turning to him with a smile.

She looked tired and older than Ian remembered. "How are you?" she asked, coming toward him and opening her arms to embrace him.

Ian had always known his mother loved him. She may have said cruel and insensitive things sometimes, but she'd lived and perfected the role of the taskmaster in their family for so long, he supposed he couldn't blame her.

He hugged her back, feeling parts of himself heal with the action. "I'm good," he said. "How are you? You look a little tired."

"Oh, we need a new bed," she said. "The one we've got now hurts my back, and I didn't sleep great last night." She stepped away from him, and Ian caught the exhaustion in her eyes. "There's coffee, though. Your dad put the breakfast casserole in the oven and went to shower. He'll be out soon."

Ian nodded and followed his mother into the kitchen. "I wanted to talk to you for a minute anyway."

He took a seat at the bar while Mom got down coffee mugs and started setting out cream and sugar to go with it.

He cleared his throat once, then twice, and when Mom finally settled at the bar too, he said, "I've never wanted your advice, and you drove me away with it once."

"I know," she said. "I'm sorry. I've said nothing about you and Nita."

"I appreciate it," Ian said. "I'm here for advice about her, believe it or not."

"You are?" The level of surprise in her voice screamed through Ian's ears.

"I don't want you to start in before I explain a few things," he said. "That's what you did wrong last time, Mom. You had no idea what was going on with me and Minnie, and yet you acted like you did." He looked at her, opening up the part of himself where he'd boxed away all of his hurt feelings. "You said such horrible things, I swore I'd never talk to you again."

Tears filled her eyes, and she nodded. "I don't do that anymore, I swear. I was still learning how to parent adult children, and many of your brothers have been helping me the past few years."

She fiddled with her spoon, her nerves plain as day. "I'll listen, and I'll try to understand before I say anything."

Ian nodded and poured some cream into his coffee. "Nita's been married before too," he said, wondering how to give the backstory without saying too much. He was so used to making sure his mother stayed in the dark and didn't know details, that he wasn't even sure how to talk to her anymore.

"Her husband died," he said. "Only eight months in. They knew he was sick before they got married." He stared at the dark depths of his coffee, watching it lighten with the addition of the cream. "It's been a few years now. Five or six. I'm not one-hundred-percent sure she's over him, and maybe she never will be. I don't know if that's a deal-breaker for me or not."

"Why would it be?" Mom asked.

"She loves him," Ian said, looking at her and feeling like he'd just cut open his chest and exposed his heart. "I don't know how to let go and fall for her when she loves someone else."

Mom took a sip of her coffee and gazed out the windows beyond the island and above the kitchen sink. She set her mug down and studied it as if the words she wanted to say simply wouldn't come.

"Will you break up with her if she can't stop loving him?" Mom asked.

"I don't know," Ian said. "I don't have to be...I mean, that makes me sound like a complete jerk. Like, I'm this huge egomaniac who feels threatened that his girlfriend has ever liked another man."

Mom didn't smile or immediately contradict him. "You have valid concerns, Ian," she said. "You want a woman who loves you unconditionally. You want to be number one in her life, because you had a horrible situation where you thought you were all that to someone, and you weren't."

"Yes," he said. "Is it wrong to want to be number one for your spouse?"

"No, baby." His mom shook her head again. "It's not wrong."

"I feel like I'll always be second." He would literally be Nita's second husband, but at the same time, she'd be his second wife.

Mom reached over and patted his hand. "One thing I know about having eight babies," she said. "The human heart has an unlimited capacity to love. It's my belief that she can love him *and* you. It's not a competition at all."

"That's what she said. That it wasn't a competition."

"Do you trust her?"

Ian drew in a breath. "You know what? I do, yeah."

"Then if she says it's not a competition, she means it. Nita doesn't seem like the type of woman to play games and say things she doesn't really mean."

"She's not," Ian said quietly. He lifted his coffee to his lips and took a sip. It was good, but nowhere near as good as what Nita had brought to his house in that thermos all those months ago.

"I'm so close to being in love with her, and I'm scared," he finally whispered.

"Is this the part where you want advice?" Mom asked.

Ian looked at her, embraced his fear, and nodded.

"It's time, son," she said, reaching over and cradling his face in her palm. "You've held onto this hurt and this pain for long enough. You've punished yourself for ten long years. It's enough. Release it all, and let yourself love again."

Ian closed his eyes and pressed his face into his mom's hand. The timer on the oven went off, and his eyes snapped open again.

"The casserole is done," Daddy said, appearing in the kitchen almost instantly. "Oh, Ian's already here. Morning, son." He paused and looked from Ian to Mom. "Everything okay?"

"Ian's in love with Nita Powell," Mom said, causing Ian to sigh. "Oops. He probably wanted to tell you that." She gave him a grin and got up from the barstool.

"Is that right?" Daddy asked. "Maybe Conrad and Ry would do a double wedding."

"No," Ian said quickly. "We're not going to be ready that fast. I'm not in love with Nita."

"Yet," Mom said knowingly, and Ian glared at her.

"You're doing it again, Mom," he said.

"Sorry," she said quickly. "Let's eat and talk about something else."

Daddy met Ian's eyes, and Ian nodded at him. "You'll know what to do, son," Daddy said. "You've always had such a good head on your shoulders, and I have never doubted you."

"Thank you, Daddy," Ian said, somehow getting the exact dose of confidence he needed in only a single sentence from his father.

He'd needed to hear his mother's words too, and Ian let them rotate through his mind while his dad served the French toast and sausage breakfast casserole and they talked about how the breaking of Digging Your Grave was going.

CHAPTER 21

Nita checked the beef roast in her slow cooker, turned the dial to low, and reseated the lid. Ian would be at her house for dinner in a couple of hours for shredded tacos, and on this rare afternoon she'd taken off, she took a moment to breathe in the scent of garlic powder, cumin, browned meat, and silence.

It had been snowing for a couple of days, and everyone around Dreamsville and Lexington were all up in arms about it. Apparently, the organizers might call off the Sweetheart Classic, which traditionally took place over the weekend following or leading up to Valentine's Day.

The arena had been covered and preserved from the snow, but everything beyond that—the stalls, the training stables, the parking—would have to be done in the mud.

Nita wasn't sure what to pray for. Sunshine to melt the snow so the Sweetheart Classic could continue or more snow so they wouldn't have a drought come summertime? It felt like the media was constantly talking about a drought, though, and Nita had yet to see a horse farm without luscious green grass and the trademark white fences.

She faced her open garage door and let the music she'd started out there reach her ears. She'd set her Internet radio to classic rock, as she'd grown up with the bands and ballads currently filling her garage.

Sampson hadn't loved her choice of music, but it reminded her of easier times with her mom and dad, when they'd all gone out to the pastures to check their horses. When they played games at night, or when they took road trips to visit her grandmother in Tennessee.

Nita filled the doorway and looked at the stacks in the garage. She'd told herself to simply start with something easy, and she'd gone through a couple of her grandfather's boxes.

Ian had said he'd come help her, and Nita honestly didn't want to do much more without him. He'd be able to infuse some reason into the contents of the boxes, and she wouldn't be able to rely so much on her emotions.

She'd found a box of little coils of wires she had no idea why her granddad had kept, so she'd thrown those away. She'd found a box filled with old tea towels, and it looked like moths or some other bug had gotten to them. They too had gone in the trash.

Nita hadn't kept anything yet, and she could admit she felt lighter. She needed something to keep her spirits buoyed, because the weather and the way her training had been going with Gone Fishing weren't helping.

Her relationship with Ian strained along the edges too, despite their continued dates and conversations.

Nita had been in enough relationships to know when something wasn't quite right. She'd asked Ian if they were okay, and he'd said they were. She hadn't brought anything up with him, but she had a feeling she better. Soon.

She simply didn't want to lose him and his calming presence in her life. She'd hired two cowboys to help her keep her stalls and stable functional without her having to work twenty hours a day, seven days a week, and the last one had spoken highly of Ian, as if Nita had any way to connect the two of them. Perhaps he thought Ian's knowledge and skill with a horse would absorb into her through osmosis or something.

She hadn't told him about it, and Jameson was a good cowboy who always showed up on time.

Nita exhaled as she went down the few steps from the house to the floor of the garage, and she reached for the next box of her grandfather's. She and her dad had packed most of his things into apple boxes, as he'd lived on an apple orchard for the last five years of his life.

The lid came off easily, and Nita peered into the box. Old, dusty afghans sat there, the scent of dirt the strongest smell.

Even if she used afghans, which she didn't, Nita didn't think these would wash and come out well.

She ran her fingertip along the edge of one of the flowers, remembering her grandmother's weathered hands moving the crochet needles at the speed of light while Nita told her about the 4-H project or the rodeo she'd been to.

A smile touched her soul, and Nita cherished memories like this. She didn't need a blanket to conjure them up, and she replaced the lid on the apple box and lifted to move it somewhere else.

What she needed was a Dumpster she could fill and then have picked up. Glenn would know who to call for that, and Nita went back into the house to call her father. She first washed the grime from her hands and then dialed him.

He gave her the name and number of a clean-up service who would bring her a Dumpster and leave it in the driveway while she filled it.

"Are you going through my dad's things?" Glenn asked.

"Yeah," Nita said. "It's time, and I feel good about it."

"Good," Glenn said. "Let me know if you need any help." Her dad had already gone through everything and taken what he wanted. Uncle Mark had taken some things, as had her aunt Phyllis.

"I will," she said, and the call ended. She called to get a Dumpster reserved, and she was confirming that it would be delivered the following Wednesday when her doorbell pealed.

Goliath burst into a howling bark, and Nita got off the phone quickly. "It's just Ian, Golly." She gave him a quick smile that came with a frown and hurried toward the door.

"It's just me," Ian said as he opened the door and walked inside.

"Howdy, cowboy," she said, still rushing to meet him.

She wanted his arms around her right now, because today was a weird day.

"Hey," he said, taking her into an embrace. "Are you okay?"

"I am now," she whispered. She could feel him looking around the space behind her, and she didn't want to hide anything from him.

She drew in a breath of his steadiness and stepped back. "I hope you're ready to get your hands dirty. The boxes out there are disgusting."

"You said come for dinner," he said, and Nita couldn't tell if he was teasing or not.

"I said I needed help with a project," she said, trying to meet his eye. He kept looking around her house as if he'd never been here before.

She stepped away from him and went into the kitchen. "The roast is ready to shred," she said. "We can eat right now."

"I was teasing, Nita," Ian said, but Nita didn't turn to look at him. She caught movement out of her peripheral vision, and she turned to find him leaning into the garage, looking.

"You've started going through the boxes." He turned to face her.

She nodded. "Yes. I told myself to just start with the easy stuff. The boxes closest to the steps are my grandfather's stuff, and it's all garbage."

"Is it?"

"All of it," she said. "I went through it once with my

parents. I didn't get any of it out to put in the house, so I really think we can just start putting whole boxes in the trash." She indicated her phone sitting on the counter. "I just called the clean-up boys to bring me a Dumpster."

Ian's emotions stormed across his face. "That's great, Nita."

Her first instinct was to smile and nod, get out plates, and serve dinner. She still needed to make the cole slaw and slice the buns, and she told herself to do that.

She didn't move as words piled beneath her tongue. She finally said, "Tell me what's wrong."

"Are you going to go through Sampson's stuff?" Ian asked.

"Yes." She didn't know how much she'd get rid of, but she could probably pare things down enough to the point where she could park in the garage instead of having to clear her truck of snow every morning.

"I was hoping you'd help me," she said, feeling one second away from collapse. "You're so strong, and you can help me see reason when it comes to what I might want to keep."

Ian started shaking his head before she'd finished speaking. "I don't know if I can."

"Why not?" she asked. She wanted to beg him to just *tell her* what the problem was.

"I'm not that strong," he said. "I'm not sure I can see how blissfully happy you were with Sampson."

"Ian," she said. "You're the one who wanted everything out in the open between us. No secrets, remember?"

He pinched his fingers across his forehead as if having a really taxing conversation with a child. "I know."

"He's part of my past. A good part. Maybe you just wanted all the bad stuff." She folded her arms, tired of this game. "If you don't want to be with me because my husband died six years ago, just say so."

"I'm not going to say that," he said. "It's not true."

"You've been distant since I got that horse," she said. "Admit it."

His eyes blazed with anger. "I can admit that."

"You told me we were okay."

"We are."

"You're not."

"No," he said. "*I'm* not, but that is not your problem. I need some time to go through things in my head and make them all line up." He took a step toward her. "I'm still asking you out. I'm still calling you. I still want to be with you."

Nita's chest pinched, and she swallowed back all the other accusations piling up inside her mouth. "Okay." It sounded like she choked the word, but she couldn't fix her tone now.

"Okay," Ian said. "Plus, you probably need some time too."

"For what, Ian?"

He pressed his teeth together, making his jaw jump. "Forget it."

"No, say it." Nita's tears pressed against the backs of her eyes, and she just wanted him to leave so she could break down and cry.

"I think you need some time to really learn if you can love another man the way you loved Sampson," Ian said, lifting his chin on her husband's name. "I want to be number one in your life. I'm not sure you can put me there. That's what I'm working through. I think you have things to work through when it comes to Sampson too."

"I did already," Nita said. "I've been dating for years, Ian. You're not special."

He blinked, his eyes widening.

"I mean—that's not what I meant," she said.

"I know what you meant," he said, his tone as dark as his eyes and hair now.

"No, you don't," she said. "I just meant that you're not the first man I've been serious with since Sam died. I know how I feel, and I'm not stuck in the past. I'm not."

Ian didn't fire anything back at her. His eyes glittered with that burning fire she'd seen before when they'd argued. When she'd shown up at his house and told him to leave her prized horse alone. When she'd called him scruffy.

He still had the long hair and facial hair, and Nita actually loved it on him. It suited him perfectly.

"I don't want to fight," she said wearily. "I was looking forward to you coming over tonight, because we *don't* fight. Because everything is easier with you around."

The lines on Ian's face softened. "Do you really mean that?"

"Yes." She turned her back on him and brushed at her eyes. "Can we just eat? Then we can put on a movie and close the garage door, and it'll just be me and you." A sob gathered in her throat. "The world can't get to us when it's just me and you."

Her voice broke, and Ian's boots made noise as he came closer. He gathered her into his arms and held her tight while she cried into his chest.

"Just me and you," he whispered. "Shh, it's okay, Nita. It's just me, and I'm right here, okay? I'm not going anywhere."

"You're special to me," she said, lifting her head and letting him see all the tears, all the things she felt. "I didn't mean it the way it sounded."

"I know." He smoothed her hair off her forehead and placed a tender kiss there. "I know, sweetheart. I know."

CHAPTER 22

Ginny Chappell turned from the stove, her hand shaking with the weight of the cast iron skillet. "It's ready," she said, and her husband, Cayden, twisted toward her. Their son, Boone, yelled with his father's attention somewhere else and not on feeding him more of the mashed bananas and peanut butter Ginny had dusted with cinnamon.

"Thanks, sweetheart." Cayden left Boone in his high chair and came into the kitchen to get breakfast. "I *love* these sandwiches." He pressed a kiss to her temple, and Ginny leaned into the touch.

She didn't normally make a big breakfast, and Cayden didn't usually linger in the mornings to feed their son. Ginny adored being home with him, though she still had to go over to Sweet Rose Whiskey most days. She'd worked for decades for her family company, and she didn't want to lose that either.

She'd fought hard to keep it, and she either loaded Boone into her SUV and took him with her, or she dropped him off at Beth's for a few hours. Trey and Beth had been such a big help to her with watching the boy, as had her best friend, Olli.

A few years ago, Ginny would not have put herself living in a homestead on a huge horse ranch, but she wouldn't trade the life she had now for anything in the world. She loved her cowboy husband with her whole heart, and while it had taken them a little bit of time to get a baby, Boone really was the blessing in her life he'd been named for.

Still, a sigh moved through her body as Cayden took a couple of sandwiches and put them on a plate. "Can Booney eat eggs?" he asked.

"He loves eggs," Ginny said, and she loaded a plate with two sandwiches too. She'd pick at one and feed the other to the baby, all while she mentally went through her checklist for the day.

Armed with a fork and at the table, she sat and gave her son a bright smile. "Here you go, baby." She put a chunk of scrambled egg on his tray and let the eight-month-old try to get his chubby fingers around it. "I'm expecting the bed this morning," she told Cayden.

He nodded and hastened to finish chewing his sandwich. "I'll be here. Spur's gonna come, and we'll get it all set up for your mom." He gave her a warm smile, and Ginny reminded herself that they'd been over and over her mother coming to live with them.

Mother had lived her whole life as a queen, and Ginny

had known her health had taken a serious slide when she'd agreed to first see a doctor, and second, to consider not living on her own. She could certainly afford an assisted living facility or a sixty-five-plus community, but she hadn't wanted either.

Ginny had met with her brothers at their usual table at Old Ember's, and they'd gone through other options. Every single one could've taken in Mother, but as Ginny was the oldest and the only girl, she'd offered first.

Mother had said she'd love to come live with Ginny and Cayden if they'd have her. She'd changed her tune about Cayden's worthiness to be Ginny's husband, especially after she'd seen the Summer Smash a couple of years ago.

Ginny didn't like thinking that wealth was all that impressed her mother, but money really did go a long way with her. She'd also learned from Cayden to talk more about how she felt. If she got everything out into the open, it could breathe—and then heal.

"The bathroom is ready," Ginny said. "So is the rest of the bedroom. We just need that bed."

"It'll be here when you two get home tonight," he said. "You're still taking the afternoon off to go get her loaded up, right?" He reached for his second sandwich. "Are you sure you don't need a truck?"

"I'm absolutely sure we will need a truck," Ginny said. "But I don't want one. With just my car, Mother will be forced to bring only what's absolutely necessary. She'll see she doesn't need her myriad of tea cozies." She grinned and shook her head. "I'm not going to let her turn this place into her house."

"She can pretty up her kettles in her own room," Cayden said with a grin. "We can put a hot plate in there."

"No." Ginny shook her head even as she smiled back at him. "She's far too old and sick to be trusted with anything that can start a fire. She can come out here to make her tea." She looked toward the doorway that led into the bedroom she and Cayden had cleaned and decided to give to Mother.

It sat down a short hallway, with a bathroom right next door. The two weren't connected, but no one else ever went that way. Another half-bath sat off the kitchen, and when Cayden's family came to the homestead, most of them used that bathroom.

The bedroom took up the left front part of the house, with the formal living room on the right. Both branched off the front door, which again, hardly anyone used. All the men and women who came to eat Sabbath Day meals used the garage entrance or came up the steps to the back deck and then in the back door.

Ginny didn't anticipate Mother going anywhere alone, and she could get her outside easily and down the front steps to her SUV without too many issues. The bedroom would be quiet, as Cayden and Ginny's room sat behind the stairs, with Boone's next to theirs. No one lived upstairs anymore, so there'd be no cowboy boots overhead.

"Ian asked about moving in still," Cayden said as he dusted his fingers together. "I said I'd talk to you."

Ginny put another chunk of egg on Boone's tray, and

the baby boy's eyes brightened. "I think it'll be fine," she said. "There are four bedrooms upstairs. Mother won't go up there."

"He's worried he'll be too loud."

"We can put him over us or the kitchen," she said. "Mother won't even hear him. Besides, I'm going to stop and get one of those white noise machines today before I go to work. She'll be fine."

Ginny wanted to help her mother. When she'd first learned of her heart disease, she'd run out of the homestead without a second thought. She'd cried in her husband's arms at night. She'd worried about what would happen with Sweet Rose, the family whiskey company that had been in her family for generations.

Since then, though, she'd seen all the legal documents, and she had nothing to worry about. Mother had a trust that poured over seamlessly to Ginny and her brothers, with the majority of Sweet Rose belonging to her. She'd been to appointments with her mother, and she'd learned more about her condition.

Her mother was over eighty years old now, and with her diagnosis, she'd grown weaker and older in only a few months. Right before Ginny's eyes, she'd shrunk to half the powerful presence she'd always been. She'd skipped all the holiday parties, and Ginny and Cayden had dressed to the nines and been the public face of Sweet Rose.

Ginny had come to terms with losing her mother. People passed away, and Mother had lived a long, good life. Ginny wanted her to be comfortable and cared for, but she wasn't going to tell Ian he couldn't stay at the homestead when they had four empty bedrooms because it might disturb her mom.

"She'll have the whole front suite," Ginny said. "Especially if you hang that barn door like we talked about."

"It'll be here in a couple of weeks," Cayden said. "I'll get Ian to come help me with it." He gave Ginny a smile and pinched off a corner of his sweet roll for Boone. "He'll probably want to move in pretty soon. Conrad's getting married at the beginning of April, and that's only a few weeks from now."

Six, but Ginny didn't say anything. She simply nodded, because she knew how things got around Bluegrass come racing season.

Intense, crazy, and vibrant, that was how.

"Fern's having her surgery," Cayden said. "Two babies right around the wedding. Then the wedding..." He got up and took his empty plate into the kitchen. "Then the Derby is right after that. He'll want to be settled before all of that."

"Before Fern's surgery?"

"He's thinking the first or second week of March," Cayden said, getting another sandwich. "If it's not okay, I need to tell him."

"I think it's okay," Ginny said, glancing up as he returned to the table with more sandwiches. "Mother will be fine. Ian will too. Anyone can use the kitchen. I'm used to having things in the fridge someone eats without asking."

Cayden smiled, but his eyes remained somewhat serious.

His lips straightened, and he'd always been able to get to the core of an issue incredibly well. "Are you okay?" he asked.

"Yes," she said. "I don't cook every night. I warned Mother of that. We should make sure we tell Ian."

"He knows," Cayden said. "He's lived a bachelor life for a while. He can find food." He continued to gaze at Ginny. "You sure you don't want me to come help this afternoon? Anyone can be here to get the bed and set it up."

Ginny looked down at her breakfast, her emotions parading through her. "I think...I think I can do it." She met his gaze again. "But thank you." She leaned toward him and he toward her, meeting her halfway for a sweet kiss.

Boone squawked, clearly not happy with the kissing and wanting more eggs.

"All right," Cayden said, grinning at him. "Hold your horses."

* * *

Later that afternoon, Ginny pulled into the driveway of her mother's mansion and drove around to the back of the house. Mother lived on the first floor now, thank the heavens, but getting her out of here wasn't going to be easy.

Harvey's truck sat there, and Ginny groaned. Of course her brothers would come help. Everyone in the Winters family knew Mother was moving out of the mansion she'd been living in for decades and in with Ginny that day.

As she came to a stop, her brother stepped out of the back door. He lifted his hand in greeting, and Ginny smiled at him. She got out of the car as the sound of another vehicle approaching met her ears.

Elliot's hulking SUV came down the lane, and he pulled in beside Ginny, their youngest brother in the passenger seat.

"It's a family reunion," Ginny said, smiling at Drake.

Harvey chuckled as he embraced her. "How are you holding up? Are you sure you can do this?"

"I'm good," Ginny said, wishing everyone would stop asking her that. She was a strong woman who'd run their family company for a long, long time. She could handle Mother.

"All right," Elliot said, joining them. He put his arm around Ginny and squeezed her shoulders. "Is everything set at the homestead? Should Drake and I go help there?"

"Everything is set," Ginny confirmed. "Cay sent me some pictures of the bed and everything. He's even picked up dinner."

"I'm so glad I came to help, because maybe I'll get fed." Elliot laughed, and Ginny giggled a little too.

"I don't want anything packed into your cars," she told her brothers. "I've told Mother over and over and over that she can only take what'll fit in my SUV." Hers was far smaller than Elliot's, even with the seats down. "She doesn't need everything she has here. We have a fully stocked kitchen and bathroom and bedroom at the homestead. All she really needs is clothes, a few personal things, and her toiletries."

"It's like she's going on vacation," Drake said.

"With her family photo albums and legal documents," Harvey added.

Ginny looked around at her three brothers, her heart swelling with love for them. "Yes, it's kind of like that," she said. "Except all of the legal documents are housed in my office at Sweet Rose, and have any of you ever seen a photo album?"

They looked at one another, and it took a couple of seconds for the four of them to burst out laughing. Ginny shook her head and sobered first. "All right," she said. "As long as we're all on the same page."

"We are," Harvey said.

"Let's do this." Elliot straightened his polo and reached for the doorknob first. Ginny followed him inside and past the formal kitchen on the left. Mother lived in a couple of rooms just past that, and Ginny had been at the mansion every day for the past week helping her mother pack.

"You've got to be kidding me," Drake said under his breath, his footsteps slowing.

Ginny continued on, pressing into his side and peering past him to see what had prompted his disgust-filled statement. The boxes she and Mother had packed earlier were all open. Some still had things in them, but some had been emptied.

"Mother," Ginny said, easing past Drake and finding her mother stooped over a box. "What are you doing? We were just loading today. Everything was ready."

Mother looked up from the box, a half-burnt candle in her hand. "I wanted to find my tea set. I thought I'd make tea for y'all this afternoon, and I couldn't find it."

Mother owned at least a dozen tea sets, and Ginny didn't

know which one she had in her mind. "Mom," she said as gently as possible. "We didn't pack any of the tea sets. It's probably upstairs." She met Drake's eye, and he stepped into the room too.

"Which one, Mother? I'll go get it."

"The white one with all the birds on it," Mother said, straightening her back to her full height. She was still commanding and powerful, but in a more personable way, if that was even possible.

"Be right back."

"I'm putting this stuff back in the boxes," Harvey said. "And taping them up. Then we'll get them out to Ginny's car." He met Ginny's eye, the message in his expression clear.

There's no way all of this is fitting...

Ginny just shook her head and went to help him start putting the things back into the boxes that she'd already packed.

CHAPTER 23

Trey Chappell pulled a shirt over his head, walked into the kitchen, and came to a complete stop at the sight in front of him. "Hey, ho," he said, trying to take in the mud, slush, and clothes on the floor. It honestly looked like a scene from a horror movie if blood was made into mud.

"What in the world happened?" He found his son TJ standing at the kitchen sink, scrubbing his hands and then his arms. Today was supposed to be an easy day for them all. No school for TJ. No work for Beth or Trey.

He supposed that sitting at the hospital wasn't exactly easy, especially when he and Beth would be passing over their one-year-old baby for surgery. TJ was set to spend the day with his grandparents, though, and all he'd had to do while Trey showered was go feed the dogs.

"It's a mess out there," he drawled, and Trey thought for a moment he'd recorded himself talking. He'd said those exact words so many times in the past month, as Mother Nature had not been particularly kind to Kentucky this February.

The Sweetheart Classic had been canceled, and Trey had been secretly happy about it. He hadn't had to stress or worry about his horse, his jockey, or getting anywhere on time. Since he and Beth were already operating from a place of stress with Fern, it was nice to remove something from his plate.

"I tried to get everything off at the door," TJ said, glancing over to Trey again. "Stupid Barney knocked me down, and I was covered."

"Are you okay?" Trey asked, finally able to get himself to move again. "He knocked you down?"

"He's just a puppy," TJ said, shaking his head. "He acts like he hasn't been fed in a year."

Trey chuckled, because Barney, the new German shepherd pup they'd gotten a couple of months ago, did act like that. He plucked the towel from the stove and held it under the water as TJ continued to wash. "You'll need to shower again. This isn't going to be enough."

The floor beneath TJ's feet contained a muddy puddle, and Trey realized the towel wasn't going to be enough either. "In fact, stay right here. If we hurry, your mom won't need to know about this."

He darted into the laundry room and got out a big towel. He wrapped it around TJ's body and dried him off, saying, "Okay, step on it. Yep, like that." Once the boy wasn't dripping anymore, he added, "Go get in the shower. I'll mop up out here."

TJ would be eight years old this year, and he did what Trey asked without an issue. He loved the boy as if he were his own, and since the adoption had gone through, he legally and technically was Trey's son.

He returned to the laundry room and got out the bucket. After filling it with TJ's muddy, cold clothes and putting them in the washing machine, he rinsed the bucket and put hot water and cleaner in it.

He'd finished cleaning up the area in front of the door when Beth, his wife, said, "What happened?"

Trey turned to find her dressed and ready for the day, a sleepy-looking Fern on her hip. She surveyed the house, her eyes landing on the kitchen sink last.

"TJ had some trouble with some mud," Trey said. "No big deal. I'm working on it, and I'll have it cleaned up in a minute."

"Okay," she said. "Trish and Taylor are almost here."

Trey looked at the clock, realizing they had to leave almost the moment TJ went with his biological father's parents. "It's just mud," he said. "It'll clean later, right?"

"I'm sure it will."

"Are you getting her dressed this morning?"

Beth looked down at Fern, who'd snuggled into her chest. "She keeps crying. I think she's hungry."

"The surgery is soon enough," Trey said, dunking the mop and leaving it in the bucket. "Let me go check on TJ.

I'll get him ready, and you make sure we have everything for the hospital."

Beth already had everything ready for the hospital, and Trey dismissed the fact that he hadn't had time to make her coffee yet. They could get some once they got Fern off to her surgery. He went down the hall to the bathroom and knocked on the door. "Teej," he said. "Trish and Taylor are almost here."

He didn't mind sharing TJ with the Dixons. They'd been his grandparents for years, and just because their son had died didn't mean they should be cut out of their grandson's life. Right now, it was especially helpful to have more people around, as Spur and Olli couldn't watch TJ due to Olli's pregnancy.

Ginny's mother had just moved in with her a week or two ago, so Trey didn't want to ask them. There weren't any other children in the Chappell family the same age as TJ, and while they could've asked one of Beth's siblings to help, the Dixons had come to the forefront of Trey's mind and it had felt right.

The shower turned off, and TJ called, "Okay, just a second."

The boy could get distracted by the wind, so Trey didn't go far. His son came out of the bathroom with a towel around him, nothing but skin and bones. "Get dressed quick," he said. "We all have to go."

TJ ran into his room and started rummaging through his drawers. Trey went to help him find jeans and a T-shirt, and the boy had just pulled them on when the doorbell rang. "I didn't get breakfast."

"Ferny can't eat," Trey said. "Trish and Taylor will get you something." He handed his son his coat. "Grab your shoes. Kiss your momma. Be good today."

"Okay." TJ struggled to get his arms into the coat as he walked, and Trey followed behind him, the one who'd grabbed the boy's shoes.

He hugged Trish and Taylor, who didn't come into the back of the house, and TJ sat on the formal couch to put on his shoes. Once that was done, he hugged Beth and kissed his sister, and then the three of them left.

"Ready?" Trey asked as a sigh left his mouth.

"We better get going," Beth said. "Yes." She hefted a bag onto her shoulder, still carrying Fern in her other arm. "We've got to check-in in about a half-hour."

Outside, the snow had stopped, but it had covered the world in an inch of whiteness. Trey hadn't had time to come out and start the truck or clear it off, and he did the quickest job possible of it while Beth buckled Fern in her car seat and then got the heater running.

He got behind the wheel, cold and wetness seeping up his jeans. Panting, he buckled and looked at his wife. Time stopped for a moment, and Trey enjoyed the charge moving through him at the speed of lightning. When he and Beth had first started seeing each other, the charge between them had always been hot like this.

He loved his wife, and he loved being attracted to her. "Ready?" he said, breaking the freeze over time.

"Yeah," she said. "Let's go."

* * *

By lunchtime, Trey was pacing. "She should be done soon, right?"

Beth had put her phone away at least an hour ago. "She'll be done soon."

"What if something's gone wrong?" Trey glanced at his wife. They knew the risks of this surgery. Fern would have incisions behind her ears. The surgeon would put the implant into her cochlea. That way, Fern would be able to translate the sounds she heard into meaning. Right now, she couldn't.

The surgery was supposed to take a couple of hours, but could take longer. Up to four hours. Fern had been gone for three. Trey told himself that she wasn't necessarily in surgery that whole time. He and Beth had been able to stay with her all the way through putting her to sleep, and he'd kissed her as her eyes had drifted closed.

"They'll come out and tell us," Beth said. "Your mother is here."

Trey turned, almost frantic for some comfort. Mom did walk toward him, her hand looped through Daddy's. They didn't move fast, due to Daddy's hip, and Trey started in their direction. "She's not out yet," he said, hearing the gruffness in his voice.

Daddy opened his arms, and Trey sank into them. "I just keep thinking something's gone wrong."

If his mother told him to have faith, he might go nuts on

her. Instead, she wrapped her arms around him from behind and said, "I'm sure the doctors will be out soon."

Beth joined them, and Trey moved to his wife's side to find the comfort he needed. He gripped her hand, his fatherly feelings so strong inside him. "I just want her to be okay," he said. "We should've maybe just been okay with her hearing loss."

"This was the right thing," Beth said, and her strength shone through. She'd always been so strong, and Trey leaned on her will for a few moments. "Let's go sit back down. They said it could take up to four hours. She's little. They want to get the implant in the right place."

Trey nodded, and he went with his wife to the uncomfortable couch they'd been sitting on before. He looked at his phone, which had the after-care instructions for Fern's incisions, her stitches, and more.

She wouldn't actually get the microphone or speech processor for another month, at least. Possibly longer. She had to heal from the surgery first, and Trey hoped he could explain to her when she was older that he and her mother had wanted the very, very best for her.

Please don't let her be scared, he prayed. She was only a year old, and he couldn't soothe her the way he did TJ.

"Trish just sent a picture," Beth said, tilting her phone toward Trey. "They love him so much."

Trey took in the picture of Trish, Taylor, and TJ, who did have some similar facial features to the Dixons. They stood in front of a huge buffalo outside of a restaurant, grins from ear to ear on all three faces. "I'm glad we called them."

He leaned over and brushed his wife's hair back off her face and kissed her. "She's okay. She's going to be okay."

Beth's tension filled the space between them, and she looked over to the door they'd come through after kissing Fern before she'd fallen asleep. "Chappell?"

"Right here." Trey exploded to his feet, Beth not far behind. "How is she? How did it go?"

Their surgeon, Dr. Reynolds, smiled at them. "It went really well. No complications at all. They've moved her to a recovery room, and we'll have to keep her there for a little while." He gestured to them as he turned. "You can both come back."

Trey started that way, then quickly turned back to his parents. "She's okay. He said it went well. Let everyone know, will you?"

He didn't want them at the hospital, and they wouldn't come anyway. Fern was supposed to be able to go home that night, and he had no doubt he'd find trays of food in his oven and fridge. Olli and Ginny, Mariah and Lisa, Tam and Ryanne, would make sure of that. Not to mention his mother.

"I'll let them know," Mom said. "Text us anything else."

He promised he would, and then he hurried after Beth and Dr. Reynolds. They went past the room where Fern had first been sedated, the hallway yawning before them. Dr. Reynolds said, "She is a darling girl. There were no problems with any other nerves in her head. She's got a few stitches behind each ear. You'll come back in a week to get those out."

Beth nodded, but Trey just wanted to see his daughter. He needed to see her chest rising and falling.

"The nurse will go over more care with you," Dr. Reynolds said, pausing outside a room. "When to wash her hair, the swelling to expect that's normal and not normal."

"Okay," Beth said.

"I just wanted to stop right here for a minute," the doctor said. He wore a big smile, and Trey had always liked him. He'd spent a lot of time with them in the months leading up to this surgery, and he always felt like Dr. Reynolds had nothing but time for him.

"Her head is going to be wrapped in bandages. It shocks some parents. It's okay. It's normal. She did great, and everything went exactly right." He looked from Beth to Trey. "We want to keep the incisions clean and dry, and right there behind the ear it's hard to do that without wrapping the whole head. That's all."

"Okay," Trey said. "Can we see her? Is she awake?"

"She's coming out of the anesthesia," Dr. Reynolds said. "Let's go see how she's doing." He opened the door and waved for Beth to go first. Trey put his hand on his wife's back, everything inside him coiled tight and praying for his daughter and his wife.

Baby Fern lay in a tiny bed—almost like one of the plastic bassinets they'd put her in when she'd been born, and Beth sobbed as she moved over to her. "Hey, baby girl," she cooed at her, swiping her hand along the tuft of dark hair that poked up from the top of her head. The bandages went around both sides and the back, and even once under her chin, but right on the very top, a patch had been left open.

Trey's love swelled as he saw his daughter's chest rise in a breath, and he too took up a position on one side of the bed and put his hand on his child. He rested his palm against her belly, feeling her body heat and her breath. He looked up and met Beth's eyes.

"She's okay," he whispered.

"Hopefully, in a few weeks, she'll be able to hear," she whispered back, tears in her eyes. They both looked at Fern again, her big, brown eyes fluttering.

"Hey, Ferny," Trey said. "It's Daddy. You did so great." He leaned over and kissed her, the little girl not trying to wake up or move after that.

The nurse who'd been in the room with her excused herself, leaving Trey and Beth alone with Fern. He didn't care if he had to sit there from now until the end of time. For his daughter, he'd do anything.

He eventually did sit in one of the chairs, only an arm's length from Fern, and checked his phone. Everyone in the family had texted on the family string to tell him and Beth how much they loved them and how they couldn't wait to see Fern soon.

Trey closed his eyes and sighed, wrapped in the arms of his family though they couldn't be there with him right now.

CHAPTER 24

Ian pulled on his leather gloves and let Blaine step over to the conveyor belt first. Spur hadn't let him back into the loft, but hay still needed to be moved from one spot to another. Ian kept both feet on the ground as he took his turn pulling the bales from the belt and stacking them on the flatbed.

The work wasn't hard, and he liked Blaine and Conrad. They let him be quiet, and sometimes Ian needed that more than anything.

"That was the best book," Conrad finally said, breaking the silence. He reached up and took out his single earbud. "Just finished it." He grinned at Ian like he'd run a marathon, and Ian smiled back.

"It's the last one in that trilogy, right?" he asked, reaching for another bale. He'd worked with the conveyor since his injury, but he couldn't help thinking about his ride down on the contraption. The way everyone had stared at him. Nita's concerned eyes.

"Yeah," Conrad said. "I'm going to go into withdrawals."

"Just start something new," Blaine said, and Ian ducked his head.

"I can't do that," Conrad said. He always ended a series on a high, and he'd mope around for a couple of weeks while he tried to find something else that sounded half as good as the books he'd just finished.

Somehow, he always managed to do it, and Ian knew he would again.

"You don't have time to read anyway," Blaine said. "The wedding is in three weeks. It's crunch time."

"That's why he started audiobooks," Ian said, giving Conrad a look. "He's going to queue one up and help me move into the homestead this weekend."

"I can come too," Blaine said, giving Ian a look that said he had more to say. Blaine would bide his time, but Ian would rather he just spat it out.

"Sure," Ian said. "I'm not going to turn down help. I have a super nice bed, and I'm not sleeping in one of those things at the homestead."

"Other than that, he can fit it all in his own truck," Conrad said dryly. He'd apologized about a hundred times for making Ian move out of the corner house. Ian didn't blame him at all. He understood that a man and his new wife wanted a house all to themselves.

Ginny and Cayden had insisted he move in with them,

even before her mother had come to live at the homestead. Afterward, Ian had told them he could find an apartment in town, and Ginny had shown up on the doorstep with Boone in a stroller and a turkey sandwich from his favorite deli.

"You will not rent an apartment," she'd said as she'd handed over the sandwich. "There are four bedrooms upstairs, and you can have any of them you want."

Ian had agreed, and while she'd said he could pick a bedroom, Cayden had asked him to pick one over the back of the house. Ian hadn't had a problem doing that, and he'd selected the second floor master suite, which had a private bath attached to it.

He really was moving his own bed into the house, because everything in the homestead was a leftover or old, and Ian didn't want to sleep on a mattress from another century.

"I still need help with the heavier stuff," Ian said. "Don't be tellin' him he doesn't need to come." He grinned at Conrad and back at Blaine. "I'm planning to have muffins and orange juice there."

"I'm sure you'll get everyone then," Blaine said with a chuckle. "We act like we haven't eaten carbs before sometimes."

Ian laughed, the sound flying up into the sky. Sometimes it did seem like the Chappell men turned into animals when food made an appearance.

"How are things with Nita?" Blaine asked, and as Ian turned back to the belt after depositing his bales of hay, he caught the exchanged look between his two brothers.

That set his nerves on fire, and ire shot through him. "Things are fine with Nita." He gave Conrad a look too, and his brother raised his eyebrows as if to say, *What?*

"Maybe you two will get married soon," Blaine said. "Conrad says she has a place only a few minutes from the ranch."

"Is that what Conrad is saying?" Ian moved in front of him and took Conrad's bales out of turn.

"I'm not gossiping," Conrad said.

"You're talking about me behind my back." Ian didn't look at him as he moved the few feet to the flatbed. "What do you call that?"

"Concern," Conrad said. "She hasn't been over to the house in a couple of weeks. You never leave in the evening. You say you're not broken up, but you don't see her." Conrad stood still, and the three of them all looked at one another as the hay bales kept coming.

"Things with Nita are fine," Ian said, shaking his head and walking over to get another couple of bales.

"Fine," Blaine said. "That's not good. Or even great."

"It's almost bad," Conrad said. "Given how enamored they've been with one another. Eating lunch together every day, sneaking off all the time, that kind of stuff." He went to get the piling bales.

"It wasn't that much," Ian said, though he recognized the lie as it came out of his mouth. "I still see her. Just because it doesn't happen at night doesn't mean it's not happening."

"Yeah?" Conrad asked. "I never see you leave the training facilities."

"Maybe she's sneaking in the back," Ian said. He did see Nita every single day, whether his brother knew it or not. He'd told her he wasn't going anywhere, and he hadn't. He did see her at lunchtime, and he always went by her stables. He went and watched her train, and they talked a lot.

He'd also told her the truth—he wasn't sure she could put him into the first spot in her life. He didn't have to be there all the time. He knew the life of a trainer, and sometimes horses came first. He certainly didn't want to be behind Sampson, and right now, he still felt like he was.

Despite everything she'd said, and despite holding her while she cried, Ian still had work to do to believe her. He'd get there, he knew.

"Listen," he said. "I'm just trying to go really slow this time, okay? It's really none of your business." He gave both of his brothers a scathing glare as he turned and hefted another couple of bales off the conveyor belt.

"What do you need to know?" Conrad asked. "Maybe we can help you with it."

Ian said nothing as he stacked, and he climbed up onto the flatbed, as they'd layered the hay high enough now to require a man up there to move the bales around.

"Hey, I'll get up there," Blaine said, but Ian ignored him.

"I'm fine." He glared down at the two of them. "Do you really want to know?'

"Of course," Conrad said. "Remember when Ry was

going through all of that stuff with her sister and her therapist and everything?"

"Yeah."

"You kept me sane by saying everyone needed time to move past the hard things in their life. I gave her the time she needed, because you encouraged me to do that."

"Really?" Ian asked.

"Yes, really." Conrad tossed up one bale and then another. Ian bent to move them toward the front of the flatbed. "Just tell us."

Ian considered it, the words lining up perfectly in his head. "It's really stupid." He gathered another bale and turned his back on his brothers.

"Tell us," Blaine said, leaning against the flatbed and panting. "We're not going to judge you."

Ian took an extra moment to make sure the bale corners matched up. "She got a new horse, right?" He walked across the lumpy surface of the bales already on the bed and bent to get another one. "Her first stable purchase. It's a gorgeous gray Thoroughbred. I actually wanted her."

He blew out his breath, glad it didn't hang in the air in front of him anymore. The cold snap that had moved through Kentucky had given way to warmer temperatures, and Ian was glad about that. "She named her Sampson's Girl."

He couldn't watch Conrad's or Blaine's reactions, so he moved to the front of the bed again. Their silence told him everything he needed to know. He said, "I'm not sure she's quite ready for a new husband, despite everything she says," anyway. "So I'm going slow. No one can blame me for that."

"No," Blaine murmured. "No one will blame you for that."

Ian went back toward them, trying to read their expressions. Conrad had covered his over, his jaw jumping as his mind worked. "Did you talk to her about it?"

"Yes," Ian said. "She insists I make her happy. That I'm special to her. That of course she's over Sampson and that I am everything she wants."

Blaine's eyebrows went right up. "Wow. She said all that?"

"Yeah," Ian said miserably.

"Bro," Conrad said, and he cocked his hip and folded his arms. "Why haven't you proposed yet?"

"What?" Ian picked up two more bales and stood there, waiting. "Why would I do that?"

"What's she going to have to do to convince you?" Blaine asked.

Ian looked at him—really looked. "I...I don't know."

"Women don't usually say things that aren't true. It's what they don't say you have to try to decipher."

"I know all about what women say and do," Ian said, some of his latent bitterness creeping into his soul and his voice. He pushed it away with Mom's words about how he'd punished himself for long enough. He wasn't stupid. He wasn't a child. He'd always had a good head on his shoulders, and his parents trusted him.

He was still learning how to trust himself, that was all.

He got the bales of hay where they belonged, the conveyor still running. Duke and Spur kept tossing bales down, and Ian really wished they'd stop. His one saving grace was that the machinery made it impossible for up-top conversations to be heard down below, and vice versa.

Spur already knew all of this anyway, as Ian had dropped by for their brotherly pizza night only a couple of days ago. Conrad had so lied; Ian did leave the house in the evenings, and he hadn't told him he'd gone to Spur's. For all Conrad knew, Ian had spent his time at Nita's.

"I say it might be time for a leap of faith," Conrad said.

Blaine gave him a troubled look and said, "I think Ian knows what he needs, and he can take as much time as he wants to make sure he's going to be happy."

"Thank you, Blaine," Ian said. "I can't leap, Conrad. Doctor's orders."

Conrad rolled his eyes. "Ha ha."

Ian gave him a grin and turned again, his muscles straining with the hay bales.

"Hey!" Spur yelled from the loft window. "Why is Ian on the flatbed?"

"I'm fine," Ian started to yell back, twisting to look at Spur. His brother wore a livid look, and even Ian cowered.

"I told him," Blaine called up. "He said he's okay."

"Nope," Spur said, his dark eyebrows drawn all the way down. "Not okay. Someone switch him. He could stumble and fall and re-break his leg. Come on, guys."

Ian stood there and faced his older brother, and Spur's powerful personality had him jumping down while Blaine climbed up onto the flatbed. "I'm really fine," he called up to Spur.

"I'll decide when you can do stuff like that," Spur yelled down. "I'm not watching them cart you out of here on another stretcher, Ian." With that, he pulled his head back inside, and the brief break they'd gotten in hay bales soon started up again.

Ian kept his head down and picked up bales and moved them, one after the other after the other. His mind had seized onto one specific sentence that had been said before they'd all been chastised. *What's she going to have to do to convince you?*

"Con," he said, almost under his breath. "What are you doin' tonight?"

"Ry's working late," he said. "She's trying to get her summer catalog off to the printer. I'm going to take her dinner and drop it in the sewing room. Why?"

"Can I tag along?" Ian asked. "I'll just sit in the truck while you go inside."

"Sure." He watched Ian for a moment, turned, and gave his bales to Blaine. As he came back he asked, "You need something?"

"Yeah," Ian said, glancing at Blaine as he turned around. "Help with Nita. Maybe I'm ready to move past this, but I don't know what to do."

Conrad's face split into a grin, and Ian wanted to swat it away. He glanced at Blaine again. "Stop it," he hissed.

"You know what to do," Conrad said, not bothering to

remove his smile. "You can still ride along tonight, but you know what to do with Nita."

"What's he gonna do with Nita?" Blaine asked.

"Great," Ian muttered.

"He's gonna go tell her she's number one in his life, and he'll be patient while she gets him to the top spot." Conrad smiled and smiled at Ian, who just shook his head.

He'd already said a version of that. Things between him and Nita were still a little stilted. There was still something between them. He needed to figure out what it was and pluck it out. Only then would he be ready to accept whatever place on her list that she'd give him.

"I changed my mind," he said. "I don't want to ride along tonight."

"No?" Conrad's smile slipped. "What are you going to do instead?"

"Take dinner to Nita," he said, taking a leaf out of Conrad's book. "Seemed to work for you." He shrugged. "Maybe it'll be the magic sauce for me too."

Conrad burst out laughing, and Ian joined in. Even Blaine said, "Tam loves it when I bring dinner home. Smart move, Ian."

A smart move. Ian needed to figure out what that was exactly, and then make it.

CHAPTER 25

Nita's fingers flew across her screen. Ian had just offered to bring dinner to her house, but he couldn't do that.

She'd already ordered his favorites from Blue's.

I already got dinner, she typed out. Wait. That wasn't true. She quickly tapped the screen to call him.

"Hey," he said. "You're eating already? It's barely three."

"No," she said. "I've ordered dinner...for me and you. I was seriously just going to call you." She looked out the windshield at the white barn where she'd just dropped of the gray horse.

Her stomach vibrated, and she cleared her throat. "I had a couple of errands in town, and I ordered barbecue to pick up at five. I can bring it to you."

"I can come to your house."

"We can meet at the stable," she said, smiling despite her throbbing pulse. "Whatever is okay with me." She'd seen Ian fairly often since she'd broken down in front of him in her kitchen. Their exchanges weren't very long, and she felt like she'd been demoted to lunchtime with him, which was where couples started their relationships.

Lunch wasn't as serious as dinner. Lunch was casual. Lunch was what friends did to catch up after a long time apart.

Nita knew the root of the problem between them, and it wasn't Sampson. It was her continued attachment to including him in the realization of her dreams. The truth was, Sam hadn't been here for the past six years. The memory of him might have driven her to continue on her crazy quest to own and operate a training stable of her own, but she'd put in all the work.

She would continue to do that, and she could remember Sampson in subtle ways—like using the name he'd suggested. What she really wanted right now, though, was a future with Ian Chappell in it.

She wanted to kiss him good morning and lay in his arms in their bed at night. She wanted his face to light up when she happened upon him in his training ring, and she wanted to have a best friend and lover who she was completely comfortable with again.

Sampson couldn't give her any of those things, and he hadn't been able to for a long time.

"I'll come to you," Ian said, making Nita blink back to the present. "What time? You're picking up at five?"

"Whenever is fine," Nita said, glancing over to the passenger seat. She'd brought her laptop with her, and she could go to the library to use their Internet. She'd already narrowed her choices down to three anyway, and she wouldn't pick a new horse until she spoke to Ian.

Her foot bounced against the floorboard of the old pickup as Ian said, "I can be there about six, six-thirty. Spur is seriously whipping us to get the hay out of the loft, as if we need it all cleared before dark."

Nita grinned and giggled at the darkness in his tone. "You guys have a lot of horses to keep fed."

"Yeah, and he won't let me up on the flatbed. He seriously made me get down so Blaine could take over."

Alarm pulled through Nita. "I actually agree with him on that, sorry."

"I knew you would." Ian sighed. "I know I'm not one-hundred-percent better, but I can walk."

"Hay bales shift," Nita said. "They're not flat."

"Okay, yes, thank you, Spur," he growled, which only made Nita laugh again.

"Come on," she said. "I get to have an opinion on this. I just don't want to see you with that crutch again. Then I get Grumpy-Gus-Ian."

"Grumpy Gus?"

"That's right," she shot back. "It's a miracle you even have people still talking to you."

Ian inhaled on his end of the line and said, "You're right. I'm sorry. I will not be grumpy about Spur trying to make sure I can keep healing."

Nita grinned at her faint reflection in the driver's side window. "There you go, cowboy."

"Mm, you haven't called me cowboy for a while."

"We don't see each other enough," she said, all of her laughter drying up. "When you come tonight, will you stay longer than an hour?"

"Yeah," he whispered. "I will."

"Great," she said, though she didn't want to make light of the situation they were in. "I need your help with something too, okay?"

"What?"

"It's a surprise." Her stomach flipped, but Nita was going through with this. She was. She'd already sold Sampson's Girl, and the horse had already been delivered to her new owner. All Nita had to do was back away from the barn and get off the farm.

She'd taken the afternoon off to take care of this problem, and she was going to see this all the way to the end, whatever that was.

"A hint?" Ian asked, a teasing quality to his voice.

"Sure, I'll give you a hint," she said. "It has four legs."

"A horse," he guessed, no question mark in sight.

"See you tonight," Nita said among the giggles, and she ended the call.

She managed to back away from the barn and get off the farm. She stopped by the bakery and got a box of brownies before she drove out to her house and unhitched the horse trailer. Then she went back to town and picked up the barbecue she'd ordered.

By six, Nita had everything ready. Dinner sat on the table. Candles had been lit. Her computer sat open, with three windows waiting for Ian to look at the horses Nita had been studying.

The check she'd been given that afternoon sat at Ian's place. She'd rehearsed her speech. All she needed was the sexy cowboy she was in love with to show up.

The minutes ticked by until finally, Goliath jumped up, already barking for all he was worth. "It's just Ian," she told the little dog, and they went to get the door.

Ian was just getting out of his truck, and Nita took a quick moment to admire him before he saw her. Then his eyes lifted to hers, and Nita knew she was going to cry. She sucked back on the emotion now, telling herself to get through the next twenty minutes before letting the tears out.

She could do it. She'd sat with Sampson as he'd taken his last breaths, and she'd told herself to cry later. She'd done exactly that, and she could do it again.

"Howdy, Nita," Ian said as he clomped up her steps.

"Howdy, cowboy." Her voice stayed steady, and Nita threw herself into his arms. "I've missed you."

The way he held her told her that he'd missed her too. He kissed her neck, steadily working his way toward her mouth, and when he finally claimed it, Nita kissed him back enthusiastically.

"I'm sorry," he breathed.

"About what?"

"I don't know. This distance I've put between us." He steadied her with his hands on her waist and kissed her again. "I've missed you too. A lot."

"Come in," she said. Her neighbors lived far enough

away that no one had seen anything, especially as the sun had gone down twenty minutes ago.

"I brought dessert," he said, lifting a brown paper bag. "I couldn't help myself. See, I was going to bring this big dinner and make everything right between us."

"I got Blue's," she said. "Ribs, and I'm going to eat them in front of you this time, so I hope you're prepared." She closed the door and stepped to his side.

"You lit candles," he said, staring at the small dining room table across the room.

"I guess we had the same idea about getting a big meal and making things right." She looped her arm through his, the way she had many, many times in the past. She'd done it before to steady him as he moved on his crutches. Now, she did it to be near him and to steady herself emotionally.

"Go sit in your spot," she said, taking the bag of desserts. "I'll get the food out."

He did what she said, but she'd only put one foot in the kitchen when he said, "Nita, why is there a check for one hundred and fifty thousand dollars on my plate?" He held it up, his dark eyes blazing with more intensity than she'd ever seen.

"That's how much I have to buy another horse," she said.

Ian's confusion almost made her laugh, but she didn't want to play tricks on him. She forgot about the food for a moment and detoured toward him. She grabbed the open laptop as she went and faced it toward him.

"I'm going to buy a new horse, and I need you to help me pick. I've narrowed it down to three."

Ian looked at her, the computer, and then the check. "I thought you didn't have enough to fill the fourth stable."

"I don't," she said simply. "I sold Sampson's Girl."

The check drifted down as Ian dropped it. "You did not." His voice came out of his mouth in a haunted way.

Nita smiled and held up the computer a little higher. "I did," she said. "She's what broke us, Ian, and I couldn't keep her. Not if I want to keep you, and I do."

Ian inhaled and ran his hands up his face. He removed his cowboy hat and then scrubbed his fingers through his hair. Nita had seen him do all of this before when he was trying to find the right thing to say.

She knew exactly what to say, and she opened her mouth to get the words out. Maybe then her stomach would stop fighting with her.

"I love you, Ian Chappell," she said, and his eyes flew back to her. "I want you. I won't let a silly horse come between us. I won't let *anything* come between us. So I sold Sampson's Girl. I'll do anything to fix things with you and to be with you."

Ian moved the two steps to her and took the computer. He set it on the table and cradled her face in his hands. "You didn't have to do that."

"Yes," she said. "I did. If I want you, Ian—and I do. Can't you see that I do?—then I had to get rid of her. It wasn't just the horse I dropped off today. I got rid of Sampson's Girl to make room for Ian's Wife."

She hoped. Oh, how she hoped she could become this man's wife. She'd never wanted anything more, because she could finally, *finally* see a future that didn't include lonely nights and bleak days.

Ian searched her face, his dark eyes intense and hopeful and filled with desire. "You're not lying to me." He wasn't asking, and he said the statement with awe.

"I am not," she whispered.

"I love you, too," he murmured as he lowered his mouth to hers for a kiss that felt full of fire, electricity, and adoration. He controlled it, because Ian could control anything, including all of the chemistry between them in this moment.

He broke the kiss, a laugh bursting from his mouth. "I can't believe you did this." He fell back and looked at her, pure disbelief in his gaze now.

"I love being with you," she said. "I get to be my best self and my worst self, and if you're not ready to be your best self and your worst self with me, that's fine. I'll just stick around until you're convinced."

He ran his hands through his hair again. "I'm convinced, Nita. You just sold a horse you were really excited about training." He shook his head. "I'm not worth that."

Nita shook her head too, her smile not going anywhere. "You are, Ian. To me, you are everything." She stepped over to the table and flipped open her computer. "Now, are you going to help me pick one of these? There's only three to look at."

"No," he said, the word almost a bark.

"No?" Nita straightened as he came toward her.

"No," he said, taking her into his arms again. "First, I'm going to tell you again that I love you. I love you, Anita Powell. Then I'm going to say that I believe that you love me. Like, legit love me."

She grinned up at him, because she did love him, and she sure did like hearing him say he loved her too.

"Then I'm going to kiss you again," he whispered, and he did just that.

"Then we can look at horses, right?" she teased, breaking their kiss long enough to get the words out.

Ian only growled and kept kissing her.

CHAPTER 26

Ian tore his eyes from Nita as she put dinner on plates for the two of them, his disbelief raging through him. He picked up the check Nita had placed at his spot, the numbers so huge to him. The top of the check read *Bastian Brothers Horses*, and Ian's mind percolated.

"Don't even think about it," Nita said, putting the plate with barbecue ribs, cole slaw, and mashed potatoes with country gravy on it where the check had just been. She plucked the check from his fingers.

"Think about what?"

"I know what you're thinking." She moved around the table and put down her plate too. She took her seat and looked at him with a cocked-eyebrow glare. "You're not buying back this horse with some of your billions of dollars."

Ian narrowed his eyes at her. "I wasn't even close to

thinking that." He pulled out his chair and sat down. "Okay, fine, I was."

Nita grinned at him. "I could see it in your eyes." She nodded to his plate. "Let's eat, and then I really do want your help with choosing my next horse."

Ian picked up his fork, the scent of the food making his mouth water and his stomach grumble. Now that he'd told her he loved her, everything felt new and fun and comfortable with her.

Across the table, she'd already picked up a rib and taken a bite. He grinned at her and reached to get some mashed potatoes. "Do you have ideas for your second wedding?"

Nita coughed and choked, abandoning her rib. The bone clattered on the plate, and she stared at him while she scrambled for her napkin. "Second wedding?"

"Yeah," he said, enjoying her reaction. "I love you. You love me. I'm seriously moving in with my brother, his wife, and his wife's mother next weekend... I'd rather marry you and move in here."

Her surprise lessened with every word he spoke. She put her napkin down but maintained eye contact with him. "You could move in here instead of the homestead."

"Only if I want my mother to freak out," he said, shaking his head. "Which I don't. Trust me, we do *not* want that." He smiled at her. "It doesn't have to be a big deal, like some of my brothers have done. We could even just go down to City Hall or something. Whatever you want."

"What was your first marriage like?"

"I was the second son to originally get married," he said. "It was a huge deal. Like, *huge*. Minnie was this socialite, and you've met my mom a few times, but back then, she was all about appearances. We rented this massive garden reception area, and I swear every single person in Kentucky came."

"I don't think we'd moved from Louisville yet," she said with a smile. "I'm guessing you don't want a big wedding. That doesn't sound like you at all."

"No," he said. "I'd prefer something small, but again, I'm fine with whatever you want."

"Do you think I'm the type to have a huge wedding?"

"No," he said honestly. "Most of my brothers have gotten married at Bluegrass. Conrad and Ry will in only a few weeks." His father's words about doing a double wedding ran through his mind. He didn't speak them, though, because he didn't want to get married on the same day as Conrad.

He didn't think his brother would like it either. He wouldn't tell Ian no, though, and that meant Ian couldn't ask.

"My dad has a small farm," she said. "We could get married there. Or rent somewhere. Or honestly, we could do it in my backyard."

"Once the weather gets a little warmer," he said. "I'm fine at the homestead. I was just wondering what you were thinking."

"I'm thinking of sunsets," Nita said, scooping up a bite of baked beans. "Me and you on horses, my dress trailing off the back of mine. We ride in together, and we can get married, and then we ride off into the sunset. There's a truck waiting, and we jet off to some amazing destination."

Ian laughed, though he didn't think Nita was kidding. "That sounds great," he said. "What's an amazing destination for you? Are we talkin' beach, mountains, big city, what?" He hadn't done a lot of traveling outside of work, and part of him wanted to.

"I don't know," she said. "I've been to a few places, but all of them are down here in the South. Might be fun to go north. Or west."

"Northwest," he mused. "I'm sure we can find somewhere." He took a bite of his potatoes and swiped on his phone. He pulled up his map app and zoomed out from his position at her house. "Northwest of here is Mount Rushmore. Montana. We could go visit some ranches there. Ride horses. See some National Parks. Yellowstone is up there." He looked up at Nita, his eyebrows raised.

"I don't really care," she said. "It all sounds great." She gave him a smile. "Something small, Ian. I have a few friends and my family."

"My family makes the wedding bigger than small," he said dryly. "Mom is also still involved in all of her charity stuff, and she'll want to invite everyone."

"Then let's have a really small, intimate ceremony, with a reception back here after we go to Yellowstone."

"You don't have to convince me to do small," he said.

"Hmm," Nita said, her bright blue eyes twinkling with mischief.

"Hmm?" he repeated. "What does that mean?"

"Seems like I had to do quite a bit of convincing to get you to believe I wanted to be with you."

Ian picked up a rib and took a messy bite. With barbecue sauce on his face, he grinned at her. After wiping his mouth, he sobered. "Nita, I just needed my heart to heal, that's all."

"I know."

"You helped with that, and I just had to learn to trust myself."

"Do you?"

"Yes," he said. "I do. Now, I do."

She nodded, and they got on with dinner. After he'd cleaned up their plates, Nita brought her computer to the couch and handed it to him. She curled into his side and pointed. "I like that brown and white one. She has really long legs."

"Let's see," Ian said, reading the specs on the horse. After several seconds, he said, "Yeah, she'd be great."

"Flip over to the other tab," Nita said, and he did. He read about all three horses, and went back to the brown and white one.

"I'd get her," he said, sliding the computer onto Nita's lap. "She'll be ready later this year too, and you can break her before January."

"True." Nita studied the screen for a while longer, and then closed the computer. "I think I'll get her."

"What are you going to name her?"

"I don't know," she said, reaching to set the computer on the coffee table. She snuggled into him again, and Ian put his arm around her and held her against his side. "Do you have any ideas?"

"No clue," he said. "My daddy names our horses. I just go with it."

"Maybe like Heart of Gold or something." She looked up at him, and Ian couldn't help smiling at her.

"Sure, baby," he said. "That sounds nice." He leaned down to kiss her, still a bit in disbelief that this evening had turned out the way it had. "How long are we talkin' until we get married?" His lips caught against hers, and he kissed her again before she could answer. "Because I'd really like to stay right here with you."

"I should probably give my mom a couple of months," she said, her voice as heated as his. "May or June?"

"Let's go with June," he said. "Before the Summer Smash in July."

"Are you asking me to marry you, then?"

"Not right now," Ian murmured, matching his mouth to hers again. "I'll do it properly." As he kissed Nita, he couldn't think of a good way to propose. He'd need a ring first, he knew that. Other than that, all he could think about was kissing the woman he loved.

"Yes, I want that," Ian said, squaring off with Conrad. "You never even use it."

"The house will have an empty spot without it," Conrad argued back.

Ian couldn't believe his brother wasn't going to let him take the recliner he sat in every single evening. "Ry will probably have ten things to fill this corner with," he said. "We're taking it." He gestured to Blaine and Spur. "This chair."

Conrad stepped back, his arms folded. He didn't say anything, and Blaine and Spur hefted the chair and started out the front door.

Trey came inside, TJ right behind him. "What else, Ian?"

"There's a box or two in the kitchen," he said. He wouldn't need his dishes and whatnot at the homestead, but he did like his cast iron skillet for making cornbread. It would all keep in a corner of the closet for now.

He'd told only Spur and Conrad about his amazing evening with Nita, and they'd both agreed that a shorter engagement would suit him better. Conrad had said he could move in with Ry if Ian was going to get married so soon.

Ian had refused the idea. He'd always thought he'd end up in the corner house, and he still might. Right now, though, Conrad needed it, and Ian could move in with Nita. The situation might change in the future, but Ian felt at peace with things how they were and how they'd play out in the next couple of months.

"We got the stuff in your bedroom," Duke said, coming down the steps from the second floor. "It's cleared out. Just needs to be cleaned."

"I'll come back and do it," Ian said, going outside with him. "I think that's it." The back of his truck seemed really full compared to what he'd thought he had. He supposed his fan and his guitar took up a lot of room. His bed sat in the back of Spur's truck, and everyone loaded into a vehicle somehow, and Ian made the drive back toward the epicenter of the ranch.

He couldn't quite see the corner house in his rearview mirror, and he wanted to.

"You'll be back there," Cayden said. "Your cars are in that shed, and Ry's not going to survive out here."

"You don't think so?" Ian asked, glancing at him.

"I give her six months," Lawrence said from the back seat. "Tops."

Ian chuckled, as did the other brothers in the truck. "You might be right," he said. "She works a lot in town, and it's not a short drive."

"They'll buy some land halfway between," Trey said. "Build there. You and Nita can have the corner house."

"Me and Nita?" Ian asked. "Who says we're gettin' married?"

"Oh, please," Cayden said. "I saw your face when she texted you this morning. It was all sunshine and rainbows and hearts."

Ian shook his head, chuckling some more. "Fine," he said. "I'm probably going to marry Nita."

That brought a stunned silence to the truck Ian should've anticipated. "Don't clam up on me now," he said. "I need ideas for what kind of ring to buy."

"Really?" Lawrence asked at the same time Trey did.

"Yes, really," Ian said, a slip of darkness moving through

him. "So everyone start talkin'. Conrad was no help; he and Ry went to Louisville to buy her ring."

CHAPTER 27

D uke Chappell burst through the back door of the house he shared with his wife. "Lise?" He didn't see her in the expansive kitchen, dining room, or living room. "Lisa? Where are you?"

"Coming," she called, and as he hurried through the kitchen, she appeared at the end of the hall.

He took the diaper bag from her. "I could've gotten this." He scanned her from head to toe. "You're sure we need to go?"

"My water broke," she said, one hand on top of her belly and the other beneath it. "I changed my clothes right after I called you. We need to go."

"Are you having contractions?"

"Yes," she said. "Every six minutes or so." Her face held a whiteness to it Duke had never seen before.

He put his arm under hers and turned to step at her side. "Okay," he said. "Let's go."

Harvey's Stud Farm sat out in the rolling hills of Kentucky, and they had quite the drive to the hospital. "How fast will the contractions progress?" he asked.

"I have no idea." She sucked in a breath and stilled, and Duke watched in utter helplessness as pain filled her face, causing her to hunch over and groan.

"What should I do?" he asked. He'd taken the birthing classes with her. He knew how to support her once they were at the hospital. Getting there? Someone needed to design and teach a whole class for dads on that. "Should I pick you up?"

She shook her head, her eyes pressed closed. The contraction didn't seem to last long, but Duke had no idea how much time had actually passed.

Six minutes, he told himself. *You can get her to the truck in six minutes.*

"They're already coming faster," she said, panting. "Let's go." She took another tentative step, and Duke helped her as much as he could. He did manage to get her in the truck before the next contraction came, and then he jumped behind the wheel and got them moving toward civilization.

Lisa did not want to have the baby on the farm or the side of the road. She'd been very adamant about that.

"Did you text your brothers?" he asked.

"No," she ground out between her clenched teeth. She edged up on the seat, her fingers around the handle above the door cinching tight. "I don't want anyone there."

Duke nodded, though he'd have invited his whole family. He wanted to keep her calm and help her, but he had no idea what to say. Lisa endured several more contractions before they reached the hospital, but some measure of relief filled Duke when they did.

No matter what, now that they were here, everything would be fine. He carried the bag while a nurse wheeled Lisa up to the maternity ward. Everything moved at lightning speed, and the next thing Duke knew, he stood in the corner of the room while Lisa lay in bed, already hooked up to beeping machines.

At least four other people were in the room, with a baby warmer and blankets, and Duke told himself to focus on his wife. "How are you?" he asked. "Okay? The epidural is working?"

"It's working," she said as a monitor beside her started to increase its beeping. "There's still quite a bit of pressure, though."

A nurse came to check her, and when she turned, she said, "Page Doctor Veracruz. She's progressed really fast. She's at a nine."

Duke actually looked at the ceiling as a female voice paged Doctor Veracruz, and within four minutes—two more contractions—the Peruvian doctor walked into the room. She looked a bit harried, but she grinned at Lisa and Duke. Her dark hair had already been tied back and contained beneath a surgical hat, and she said, "Third baby of the day."

"You're kidding," Duke said.

"I am not." She sat down in front of Lisa and not three

seconds later, she looked up again. "Okay, Mama. You're ready to push on this next contraction."

"Already?" Lisa asked. "Really?" She looked up at Duke as if he had any medical knowledge at all. Yes, he ran all the breeding for Bluegrass and had even done quite a bit around Harvey's since marrying Lisa. Horse births he understood.

Humans? He did not.

"Yes, already," Dr. Veracruz said with plenty of intensity in her voice. "Now, Lisa."

Duke held his wife's hand through each and every contraction, saying, "All right, love. You can do this," until the high-pitched wail of his son entered the room.

"It's a boy," the doctor said, and tears pricked Duke's eyes. Dr. Veracruz wrapped the tiny baby and gave him to a nurse, who immediately stepped to the head of the bed and gave him to Lisa.

Duke couldn't look away from the blotchy baby. He was pure perfection.

"All ten toes and fingers," the nurse said. "We'll take him in a minute."

In the bed, Lisa cried as she gazed down at their beautiful boy, and Duke let his tears snake down his face too. He leaned down and pressed a kiss to Lisa's forehead. "I love you," he whispered. "He's wonderful, and you brought him into the world."

She looked up at him. "We're still naming him after Daddy, right?"

"Yes, ma'am," Duke said, looking up as the nurse approached.

"I hate to take him," she said, reaching for the baby. "We'll get him all cleaned up and back to you, Lisa." She looked at Duke. "You can come along, Daddy."

Duke hesitated, but Lisa said, "Go with him, Duke. I'm okay."

"You sure?"

"Yes, I don't want him to be alone."

Duke nodded and went with the nurse. Once they left the room, she said, "You can bathe him. I'll show you how."

Duke couldn't seem to form words, so he simply nodded again. In the nursery, he watched and listened as the nurse showed him how to cup the water in his hands and drip it over the baby. She held the slippery infant, and he washed him, stroking his fingers along his son's belly and arms.

"He's so perfect," he murmured. He could not be more in love, and he couldn't wait to introduce Wayne to the rest of his family.

"Do you have a name for the birth certificate?" another nurse asked, and Duke straightened from the sink to answer her.

"Yes," he said. "Wayne Jefferson Chappell."

Spur tipped his head back and laughed at the joke Cayden had just told. Around him, the people he loved most chattered and ate. He kept glancing over to Olli on the couch, and she hadn't moved yet. He'd told her they could have this party after church for Duke and Lisa and their new baby Wayne if, and only if, she let him handle everything.

She'd not been sleeping very well for the past week, as their second baby was due any day now. Technically, on Tuesday, so she still had a couple of days.

Spur had not gone out on the ranch for the past four days, because Olli needed him at home with Gus. He also wanted to make sure he didn't have to find her on the bathroom floor next time she went into labor. She'd told him he was being a bit overprotective again, but he didn't care.

He didn't want to raise two boys by himself, and if he stayed home and helped with his son and made sure she was doing well, so be it.

She caught him looking, and she smiled at him. He grinned back at her and nodded toward the kitchen, clearly asking her if there was anything she wanted. She nodded, and Spur stepped away from Cayden and Lawrence. They were already talking about the Summer Smash, which he supposed they should be.

Sometimes all of it just made Spur tired.

"What do you need, sweetheart?" he asked. "There's plenty of those German chocolate brownies left."

"One of those," she said, lifting her empty cola can toward him. "More to drink too."

"You got it." He looked over to Ginny, who sat next to Olli on the couch. "Ginny? What can I get for you?"

"Potato salad," she said, giving him a red plastic cup that had clearly contained the stuff previously. "Thanks, Spur."

"Yes, ma'am." Spur went into the kitchen to take care of

what his wife and her best friend needed, and once he'd delivered the soda and dessert, as well as the salad, to the ladies, he turned to find Duke standing there with his son.

"How's fatherhood?" he asked, reaching to take the infant from his brother. "He's adorable. Lighter than all of us." He grinned at Duke, who couldn't seem to look away from his son. "He has the Chappell chin, though."

"He does, doesn't he?" Duke asked. He sighed next and looked around the room. "Things are good. Busy. I'm tired." He chuckled, and Spur recognized the sense of being completely overwhelmed. Duke and Lisa ran a very busy stud farm, and Duke had plenty to do at Bluegrass still.

"Take another week or two off," Spur said. "The horses are fine here. You got Conrad up to speed. We're fine."

"Conrad's getting married this weekend," Duke said.

"Ian can handle it."

"What can Ian handle?" Ian asked as he walked by. He joined Spur and Duke in a three-way huddle.

"The covering," Spur said.

"It's almost done, honestly," Duke said. "We've only got three mares left to give birth too."

"I can handle it," Ian said, smiling at both Spur and Duke. He'd changed so much in the past few months, and Spur's heart was so glad Ian had found a way to heal. He'd wanted that for him for so long.

"See?" Spur asked. "You'll take another week." The infant in his arms started to squirm and fuss, and Duke hurried to take him back.

"Lisa said he needs to eat," he said. "Sorry." He hustled

away, and Spur watched him go for a few seconds before focusing on Ian.

"When's the big day?" he asked quietly.

"Friday," Ian said just as softly. "I'm not going to steal Conrad's thunder, right?" He looked genuinely worried about it too, the nerves right there in his dark eyes.

"He's getting married on Sunday," Spur said. "You're not asking her to marry you *at* his wedding. It'll be fine."

"We're thinking June."

"Mom will be thrilled," Spur said sarcastically, lifting his soda can to his lips to conceal his smile.

Ian didn't even try to hide his. "She hates short engagements."

"She should know by now that that's what you'll do," Spur said after swallowing. "She'll be fine." He found his mom talking to Mariah and Ry, and they all seemed to get along fine with her.

"She will," Ian said. "You're right."

A commotion behind him drew his attention, and he turned as someone said, "Spur."

Ginny half-stood from the couch, both arms reaching toward Olli. "Spur!" she yelled again. "She's bleeding."

Spur didn't even know what happened to his soda can. One moment he was holding it, the next he wasn't. He ran the few steps to his wife, trying to take in everything at once. The coffee table had been moved and bumped—probably the noise he'd heard, as it held dishes and candles. Olli had candles *everywhere* in the house.

"Bleeding?" he repeated, arriving at the scene. Had Olli passed out? Why hadn't she said anything?

She looked up at him, her face white as a sheet of paper. "Spur," she said, the word almost slurring.

"I don't know how long she's been bleeding," Ginny said, plenty of panic in her voice. "I noticed it coming out the side of her leg. I asked her if her water broke, and she sort of seemed to pass out."

Her head lolled now too, and Spur didn't waste another second. "Clear the way to the door," he commanded. "Ian, help."

Ian stepped to his side as Spur scooped Olli into his arms. "Out of the way," Ian yelled. "Everyone move away from the door."

That got people to move, and Spur hurried with Olli in his arms for the exit.

"I've got a blanket," Ian said behind him. "I'll help you get her in."

Spur had so many flashbacks to when Gus had been born. He and Blaine had done this exact thing, and he did not want to do it again. "Call the hospital, will you?" he yelled over his shoulder. "Tell them we're coming, and she's bleeding, in labor, and on heparin."

"I'm coming," Ian said, laying out the blanket on the front seat before Spur put Olli there. He pulled her seatbelt into place and turned toward his brother. "Give me your phone," Ian said, holding out his hand. "I'll call the hospital and the doctors on the way."

Spur did what Ian said, and then they both got in the truck. The last thing Spur saw as he tore away from his house with his unconscious wife in the passenger seat was every member of his family out on the front porch, steps, and sidewalk.

"Pray," he muttered under his breath. "Ian, text them all and tell them to pray."

CHAPTER 28

Olli came back to consciousness with a gasp, the way she might have done had she broken the surface of the ocean after a long time beneath it. Her first thought was: *Where am I?*

Machines beeped around her, and Olli instinctively knew she was in the hospital.

Ginny's words rushed at her. *Olli, you're bleeding.*

"Spur?" she asked, finally getting her eyes to flutter open.

"Right here, Olli," he said. "Wake up, sweetheart." The pressure of his fingers in hers came to life, and she blinked and blinked until he came into focus. "She's awake," he called, and that got more people to come into her field of vision.

"Olivia," her doctor said, his face one of seriousness and grim reality. "Do you think you can deliver this baby?"

Olli wanted to say yes, but everything still seemed so swimmy around her.

"I'd really like to not have to do surgery, in your condition," he said. "We've given you something to counteract the blood thinning, but that has its own problems."

She looked at Spur, who wore an expression of guarded love, worry, and determination.

"What'll be easiest for her?" he asked. "We need to make sure she's okay, and the baby is okay."

"The baby is fine for a minute," the doctor said. Why couldn't Olli remember his name? So many things seemed out of her reach. Another man came into view, and she knew him.

"Doctor Blake."

"I think she should try to deliver if she can," Dr. Blake said, giving her a small, cursory smile. "She's still bleeding quite badly."

"Let's do it," Spur said. "Olli, you can do this. You've done it before, and you're ready."

She nodded and started to push herself up. Spur helped her, and Dr. Blake and Dr. Rosenthal—Dr. Rosenthal!— moved to the foot of her bed.

"Did I get an epidural?" she asked her husband. "How long was I out?"

"Almost an hour," he said, positioning himself behind her. She could lean into him, and he was rock-solid. So strong and so steady and so wonderful. She could do this, and she would.

She'd obviously gotten an epidural, as Olli felt no pain as she went through the delivery of her second baby. It went

much faster than the first, or maybe Olli was simply somewhere outside her head.

No matter what, it only seemed to take a few contractions and a few rounds of pushing to deliver her second baby
boy. She wept as the nurse wiped him and wrapped him, and
she gave him to Spur, not her.

He gazed down at their son and then her, his joy full and
evident. "You want Liam for a name, right, baby?"

"Yes," she said as he tilted the infant toward her. She
reached for him, but Spur wouldn't give him to her.

"They said I can't," he said. "You need a blood transfu-
sion, and they said you might pass out again at any
moment." He stepped closer and leaned in. "He's right here.
Here's your mama, Liam."

She leaned over to kiss the baby's head, not sure what
Spur had said. She felt okay. She wasn't going to pass out.
"Hey, baby," she murmured. "Mama's right here." She
looked up at Spur. "Where's Gus? Did Ginny take him?"

"I'm sure someone did," Spur said. "Everyone was at the
party. He's fine."

"Party?" Olli asked, noting the alarm in Spur's eyes when
she did. She hated the cloudy feeling in her head, but she
didn't know how to get rid of it. She looked up as the doctor
said something, and then she laid back, utterly exhausted.

As long as the baby was okay, she'd be fine.

"Don't go to sleep, Olls," Spur said. "Doctor."

"Olivia," someone said, and her eyes snapped open. "I
need you to stay awake."

She did what the doctor said, and she let the people

around her work on her. Spur had to step back with baby Liam, and then he left the room altogether. *They'll be back,* Olli told herself. *Don't go to sleep. Hold on. Gus needs you. Liam needs you. Spur needs you.*

Olli managed to stay conscious and minute by minute, she came back to herself. She blinked, looked at the IV in her arm, and asked, "Where's Spur?"

He entered the room, their baby now clean and dressed in the clothes she'd packed for him in their baby bag. "Hey, sweetheart." This time when he approached the bed, he lowered the baby into her arms.

Olli gazed at him, realizing everything that had happened. She cried, her tears thick and furious down her face. "I didn't realize my water had broken," she said. "I'd been sitting on that couch for so long. I just thought the cushion was warm. I didn't know it was wet." She looked up at Spur. "I swear."

"It's fine, Olls." He pressed a kiss to her forehead. "You're fine. He's fine. We made it."

She had no idea what he'd had to go through though, and she let herself cry for a few more minutes. Then she stitched everything back together and looked up at him again. "I love you," she said.

"I love you too." He smiled softly down at her, the way Spur only did for her. "My parents came. They'd love to see him. Can I take him out to them? I'll bring him right back."

"Of course." She passed Liam to Spur. "What did you put for his middle name?"

"Hudson," Spur said. "You were out of it when I asked, so I just made a family decision."

"Liam Hudson," she said, smiling. "It's perfect, Spur. Thank you."

He kissed her again, and Olli watched her handsome cowboy husband and new son—who had her maiden name as his middle name—leave the room.

"Feeling better, Olivia?" a nurse asked.

"Yes," she said. "Tons."

"It's amazing what a little blood can do." The nurse smiled, checked something, and left the room too. Thankfully, Spur wasn't gone long, and when he returned, he had Gus with him too.

He lifted the boy onto the bed with Olli, and then gave her Liam too. "Let me take a picture," he said.

"I can take one of all of you," a nurse said, and Spur got in the picture too. For Olli, nothing would ever be better than the four of them, her and her three boys.

Conrad Chappell finished buckling his belt when someone knocked and then opened the door. "Just me," Daddy said, entering with his stunted steps. "My, you look fit to be married."

Conrad chuckled and turned from the mirror that had been brought into the living room at the corner house. He covered the distance between them and hugged his father, saying, "Thanks, Daddy." He held him tightly for several long seconds, only stepping back when he felt fully in control. "How's Mom handling the non-formality of the wedding?"

"It's a good thing you gave her a few months to get used to the idea." Daddy smiled and reached up to reset his cowboy hat on his head properly. "She's fine. You know how your mother gets."

That he did, and Conrad turned back to the mirror. "Everyone should be here in a few minutes."

"I saw Spur stopping to get Cayden," Daddy said, limping over to the couch. "The back of his truck was full of flowers."

"Perfect," Conrad said. Despite Olli's scary delivery only a week ago, she'd made a full recovery, and when Conrad had talked to her about getting someone else to do the flowers, she'd given him a fiery look and denied that he needed to do that.

Ry had tried talking to Olli then, and it had gone about the same. He'd get married without flowers pinned to his lapel, but his bride-to-be loved flowers. He'd never seen her wear any article of clothing without some sort of print on it, and ninety percent of the time, that print boasted flowers.

The door opened again, and this time Blaine and Ian walked through it. They too wore dark slacks and black jackets over white shirts. Every Chappell male had been given a tie made from the same fabric, courtesy of Ry's sewing machine and genius mind.

"Lookin' good," Ian said, grinning from ear to ear. He reached Conrad and flipped his tie. "I can't believe you're doing this." They laughed together as they embraced, and Conrad closed his eyes and prayed for Ian's well-being in the few seconds he had before his brother stepped back.

"It'll be you soon," Conrad said. "Right?"

"I think so," Ian said. His engagement plan had been derailed when he couldn't get the ring he'd wanted by Friday. So he'd put it off until he could get the correct diamond. Last Conrad had heard, it should be here on Tuesday or Wednesday this week.

Conrad and Ry wouldn't be here on Tuesday or Wednesday, and even if Ian waited until the weekend, he wouldn't be here for the engagement. Conrad told himself it didn't matter. He'd be present for the wedding, and that was what really mattered.

He'd be in Europe with his new wife, and he couldn't wait to start his married life.

Spur opened the door next, but a white bucket preceded him. "A little help here," he said, and Blaine went to help him. All told, he, Blaine, and Cayden brought in three buckets of flowers, and Spur started passing them out while consulting a piece of paper.

"Why are there so many?" Ian asked, peering down into a bucket Spur hadn't touched yet.

Before anyone could answer, Lawrence and Mariah arrived, along with Trey and Beth. More flowers got passed out, and Mariah picked up the extra bucket of flowers and lugged it with her down the hall to the room Ian had been living out of since he hurt his leg.

Ry was back there with her mother, getting ready for the

wedding. She'd asked Beth to come do her hair, and Mariah to help her finish getting ready. Olli, Ginny, Lisa, and Tam were on baby duty that day, and they likely had Fern and TJ with them.

Conrad expected Duke to arrive any moment, and when the doorbell rang, he turned toward it. "That's weird," he said.

Ian practically sprinted toward the door, and suddenly it wasn't so weird. Nita stood on the doorstep, and Conrad couldn't help watching and smiling with every fiber of his being as his prickly, never-going-to-get-married-again brother stepped out and spoke to the pretty blonde in a soft tone. He leaned down and kissed her, and Conrad wished them every happiness in the world.

They entered the house together, the door almost closing before Duke called for someone to hold it. Ian opened it up again, and all the brothers were finally there.

Yes, they got together often, and Conrad had the opportunity to get all of his brothers in the same room all the time.

"I'll see you soon," Ian said, kissing Nita again. Then she hustled down the hall and out of sight, leaving only men in the main room and kitchen of the corner house. They seemed to group themselves naturally in a circle, and Spur lifted his arms and put them around the brothers closest to him—Ian and Cayden.

Those three always did seem to trio up. Ian could always be found at Conrad's side too, and he hoped not too much would change after the I-do's were said. Duke lived so far away now, and Conrad missed having him so close.

He put his arm around Duke on his right and Trey on his left. Blaine meant a great deal to him too, and he looked across the circle to Lawrence, who was so steady and so even. Conrad had a lot to learn from him too, and he returned his smile.

"You boys have been the highlight of my life," Daddy said, his voice hushed and awed. He'd been quite the taskmaster on the ranch, but soft as marshmallow at home. "I hope you know how much I love you all, how much I respect each of you, and how proud I am of the men you've grown into."

"Love you, Daddy," Conrad murmured, and everyone else said some form of endearment for their father.

"I'm thrilled the two rebellious sons are finally settling down," he said, which caused Ian to protest. "Then maybe I can finally get your mother to let us retire."

"Oh-ho," Spur said as he laughed. "Daddy, you're the one still out on the ranch every day."

Daddy grinned around at all of them, and Conrad let time slow down so he could too. They'd all shown up here dressed well, cologned, and wearing their best dress hats for him and Ry. To celebrate their love.

He appreciated them so very much, and he cleared his throat. He hadn't planned a speech or anything, but he found himself saying, "I'm glad I have so many brothers to look to when I need a good example of a man," he said. "Or a cowboy, a brother, a father, a husband, or a grandfather. I love you guys."

"Ditto," Duke said, beaming at Conrad.

"We're all learning, every day," Spur said, and Conrad could agree with that.

"Okay," he said, taking a big breath. "Who doesn't have a flower? Everyone has to have one. You lot best get over to the tents too. I'll wait here for Ry."

"She's ready," Nita said behind him, and Conrad wondered how long she'd been standing there. The circle broke up, and Ian went to collect his girlfriend and go with her over to the tents that had been set up.

Mom had complained about the wind and weather this early in April, but so far, Mother Nature was proving her wrong one beam of sunshine at a time. Conrad smiled to himself over it—and then thanked the Lord for answering his prayers.

The corner house emptied of people until only he remained in the living room, waiting for Ry to come out of the bedroom. They'd agreed that they'd walk down the aisle together, hand-in-hand. No one needed to give her to him. She *wanted* to be at his side, and he wanted to be at hers.

Footsteps came closer, and he told his stomach to play nice. Ry was here, and she wasn't going to back out. Anything else, like running out of sweet tea, wouldn't be the end of the world.

She came into his view, and all he could do was look at her. Head to toe, she was perfection in human form, wearing a white dress that looked like it had been made with rose petals or feathers or both.

"Wow," he managed to get out of his throat. The dress hugged every female curve and went all the way to her knees, where it flared slightly. The straps over her shoulders were thinner than spaghetti noodles, and she looked like she'd been painted into the dress.

She wore bright blue heels that clearly had a rose pattern on them, and that kicked a grin onto his face. "Get over here," he said, gesturing for her to come closer to him so he could kiss her.

She smiled in her graceful, sophisticated way and advanced toward him. "I see why we're all wearin' blue flowers now," he murmured, running his hands up her bare arms.

Ry shivered and leaned into his chest. The scent of powder and perfume came with her, and her neck looked elegant and long as her hair had been pinned up into some sort of curled up-do.

"You look spectacular," she whispered, adjusting his tie slightly. "The vest is very vogue."

"You would know." He wanted to kiss her right now, but she'd told him if they walked down the aisle together, she wouldn't be kissing him until they leaned over the altar as husband and wife.

He'd agreed, and he was going to keep his promise.

"Should we go?" he asked.

"We better," she said. "I'm pretty sure we're late by the Julie clock." She grinned up at him while he laughed about his mother's timeline. He offered her his arm, and she slid her hand through it.

"I sure do love you," he said.

"I love you too," she responded. They drove over to the

same site where Lawrence had married Mariah last year, and some of the tent flaps did blow in the breeze.

He didn't care. A single spot had been saved for them, and he parked in it. The crowd inside the tent rose to their feet, and while Conrad wanted to wait a few more minutes, he knew he better not.

He got out of the truck and went around to the passenger side to let Ry down. She emerged from the vehicle like a monarch butterfly coming out of its cocoon for the first time. A gasp moved through the crowd, and Conrad couldn't help smiling at her.

"What's this made of?" he asked, tracing one fingertip down the tiny strap going over her shoulder.

"Lace, leather, fabric, and feathers," she said.

"It's gorgeous." He leaned down so his mouth sat right at her ear. "You're gorgeous."

Her hand in his tightened, and Conrad counted himself among the luckiest men on earth in that moment.

They arrived at the end of the aisle, and they faced their parents, who stood in front of the altar to receive them. Step by slow step, Conrad moved into the future with the love of his life right beside him, just as he'd dreamed and hoped and prayed for.

They'd come a long way together, and he couldn't wait to finish the race.

CHAPTER 29

Nita might try to put on a hard exterior, but she loved a good wedding. Conrad and Ryanne seemed so perfect for each other, and as they read their vows to each other, tears gathered in her eyes.

"I do," Ry said first, and then the pastor asked Conrad if he'd take Ryanne unto himself to be his legally wedded wife.

He said, "I do," as well, and as the pastor pronounced them husband and wife, the cowboy cheers blew the top off the solemnity of the occasion. Only a row in front of her, Conrad kissed Ry, the two of them grinning for all they were worth.

Nita stood and clapped, her voice trapped somewhere behind the emotion in her throat. When Ian finally quieted —Conrad was his best friend. They'd lived together for years —and turned toward her, he too wore a grin the size of Texas.

"Hey, are you okay?" he asked, coming right back to her side.

"Yeah." She nodded, glad some of her feelings were breaking up. "That was just so beautiful."

Ian slung his arm around her and faced the happy couple, now embracing their parents and other loved ones. "It was, wasn't it?"

At least two hundred people had gathered for this wedding, and Nita didn't even want half that. Ian had assured her before the ceremony had started that they wouldn't have to have a huge guest list. She could name ten people on her side of the family, and that included her living grandparents, her parents, her father's new wife, her brother and his wife, and her favorite aunt.

The Chappells had sixteen adults and a handful of children. Ian didn't have any living grandparents, but he had pointed out a few aunts and uncles who'd made the trip for today's festivities. He said they could come to the reception.

For Nita, that made thirty people, with a few babies added on, and that was plenty for her.

Ian hadn't even asked her to marry him yet, though, so she wasn't sure why she was already planning their wedding. Perhaps because they'd talked about it several times, and she'd already started shopping for a wedding dress and circling dates on the calendar.

Ian's arm slipped from around her, and he took her hand. He led her over to Conrad and Ry, where he released her to embrace his brother and his new wife at the same time. "Congrats, you two. I'm so happy for you."

They both hugged him back, and Nita could feel the joy and happiness radiating off of Ian and into the surrounding air. He turned back to her, and she instantly stepped into his sunshine, right where she always wanted to be.

* * *

Thursday found Nita frustrated with the progress she'd made with Powerplay. Which was to say, she hadn't made hardly any. The horse was more of a diva than she'd given him credit for, and he'd been extremely slow to break.

Just when she thought she'd have him figured out, he'd toss his head, throw his bit, and bolt. She'd come off him twice that day, and her aching back had had enough.

"Come on," she said crossly to the horse. "Back to the stall with you." She'd still brush him down and make sure he was conditioned and as comfortable as possible. Then she had feeding chores to do, and then she and Ian were going to pick up the new brown and white horse she'd bought.

She'd named her Two Hearts in her mind, though she hadn't told anyone that yet. She wanted Ian to know that it took two hearts to love completely, and that he was the other half of her that was required to feel whole.

The air held very still this afternoon, and Nita wished a wind would breathe some life into the day. Everything seemed so quiet too, and Nita kept her head down as she got on from the training ring to her stables.

She loved seeing the GMP banners with the running horse logo she'd designed. She loved coming to work every single day, even if the training was hard. She reminded herself of this with every step, and before she knew it, she'd arrived back at Powerplay's stall.

He nickered, and she turned and looked at him. "What's that about?" The horse loved getting bathed and pampered about as much as he loved sweets. Nita wasn't going to give him either.

She reached for the handle on his stall door, sure she'd left the top half open when she'd come to collect him a couple of hours ago. Apparently not, as it now sat closed.

The door swung open, and Powerplay nickered again, this time adding a hefty amount of air to his lips at the end so they flapped.

Someone chuckled, the sound coming from inside the stall. Nita's heartbeat flew into a frenzy, and she instinctively stepped behind Powerplay slightly, using the tall horse as a shield.

She knew that laugh, though...

Ian appeared in the sunshine, dressed in his usual jeans, cowboy boots, black and white plaid shirt, and that beautiful cowboy hat. "Afternoon, Powerplay." He reached for the horse and ran his hand down the side of the horse's neck.

Nita narrowed her eyes at him. "What are you doing in there?" She looked past his shoulder to the stall behind him. "You didn't even clean it out."

Ian's eyes flickered to hers, plenty of nerves there. She'd once yelled at him for encroaching on her horse's space, but she didn't believe he'd do anything nefarious inside Powerplay's stall.

"I'll help you put him away," he said, completely ignoring her questions. They unhitched the saddle and he wiped it all down while she worked on the horse. When he joined her in the stall again, he stood far too close for his visit to be casual.

Their relationship definitely wasn't casual, and Nita looked up at him. He'd looked over his shoulder at something outside, but when she followed his gaze, she couldn't see anything.

"Nita," he said. "Will you come out of the stall for a minute?"

"I'm almost done."

"Now would be great." Ian backed the couple of steps out of the stall, and annoyance sang through Nita. She'd had a lousy day, and she just wanted to finish the job and go home, preferably with Ian at her side. He'd make or get dinner, and all she'd have to do was lament how the wildly expensive horse was going to be a bust.

She went outside too, immediately stalling when she saw every single cowboy from her stable there. "Hey, guys," she said, trying to figure out where Ian had gone and when her men had shown up.

Around the corner came Spur Chappell, and then Cayden. Every Chappell brother marched as if they had an internal beat they were born with, until they all stood in front of her—except for Conrad, who was on his honeymoon.

"Nita," Ian called, and it took her a moment to find him standing on the roof of the rowhouse across from hers.

"I'm in love with you, and I want to shout it from the rooftops."

"My goodness," she said with a giggle.

"I want a merger between the two of us. Me and you. Forever. Will you marry me?"

Spur stepped forward and held out a diamond ring that made Nita's eyes double in size. When she dragged her eyes from the gem, Ian wasn't on the roof anymore. He came jogging around the rowhouse and toward her, and Nita moved through the sea of cowboys to meet him.

They laughed together as they met, and he swept her right off her feet. He held her in his arms as he circled, and when he lowered her to the ground, he pressed his forehead to hers. "I love you."

"I love you too," she whispered.

"Was that a yes or a no?" Blaine asked. "I couldn't hear."

Nita turned to face the crowd that Ian had gathered. "It's a yes!"

They swarmed then, and Nita let his brothers get to Ian while she hugged anyone willing to give her an embrace.

The cowboys disappeared as fast as they'd come, leaving her alone with Ian and a half-brushed-down Powerplay. She couldn't make herself get back to the horse, though. She stayed in Ian's arms, kissing him and kissing him so he'd know she couldn't wait to become his wife.

CHAPTER 30

Ian looked up from the newspaper Cayden had dropped on the table a few minutes ago, his blood starting to simmer. Someone had just come in from the garage, and little footsteps accompanied bigger ones.

"Slow down, Gus," Olli said from the dark dregs of the hallway before her son appeared.

He did not slow down, and in fact went barreling past the refrigerator and the end of the peninsula—and right toward Ian.

The little boy brought a smile to Ian's face, and he scooped the eighteen-month-up up off his feet, both of them laughing.

"Heya, bud," he said. "What are you doin' here?" He glanced over to Olli, who had her two-month-old strapped to her chest. She'd made a miraculous recovery once Spur had gotten her to the hospital and Liam had been born.

She was slated to get a heart procedure done in a few

weeks, just to prevent any clots from going into her heart. As far as he knew, from what Spur and Olli had told the family, she was fine, but it was a precautionary measure they'd decided to take so she didn't have a massive heart attack one day.

She was on blood thinners still, and she looked healthy to Ian.

"We brought you some cookies," Olli said, smiling at him. She'd put a plate of them on the counter and came toward him. "Come on, Gus. Go find Aunt Ginny." She took the little boy and pointed him in the direction of the hall that led toward the back of the house. "She's in the sunroom with Booney."

"Boone," the little boy said, running on his chubby legs in that direction.

Olli drew in a deep breath and watched her son leave the room. Ian suddenly felt like he'd just entered an intervention, and his nerves doubled.

"What's up?" he asked. He'd been over to Olli's and Spur's only a couple of nights ago, his last pizza party with his brother before Ian and Nita got married.

Olli's eyes traveled back to Ian's. "I just wanted to come give you a hug." She took him into an embrace, and Ian's eyes closed as he hugged his sister-in-law. "I know you're in a bit of turmoil, and that stupid article your mom put out has upset you."

He didn't deny it; he just held Olli tightly for another few seconds. He cleared his throat as he stepped away. "I'm okay. Cayden just showed it to me."

"Yes, Ginny called and said you were here."

"So y'all are watchin' out for me." He gave her a smile, not really asking her a question.

"Of course we are," Olli said, leaning a little closer to him. "The in-laws have to do that for you Chappells. You've lived with your mom for decades, but we haven't, and wow. You guys need some support with her sometimes."

"She means well," Ian said with a sigh. "She's been an important person in the community for years." He looked down at the Society page, where a picture of him and Nita stared back at him. Truth be told, he'd like to burn this paper, then the office that had printed it, and then storm over to his mother's and demand to know what had been in her head when she'd okayed the article.

"No one cares about Southern society anymore," Olli said.

"They do," Ian said. "I am a renowned trainer. Nita made news several months ago. I just wish she hadn't made it about how everything is a secret and more about how happy we are together." He flipped the paper over. "She almost made it a scandal."

"That's why I brought you the cookies," Olli said with a smile. "I think Mariah is bringing dinner—but don't worry. It's not for you. It's for Ginny and Wendy."

"I'm sure there'll be enough to feed an army," Ian said dryly. "I should call Nita and have her come over. She should probably see this mess anyway."

"You'll be married tomorrow night, and it'll be done. She won't care."

Married tomorrow night.

Panic struck Ian right in the throat, but it dissipated quickly. "I can't believe I'm getting married tomorrow night."

Olli grinned at him, and the back door opened. "...have to wash, Teej. You look like you've been dipped in straw." Trey came inside, then stalled to hold the door for his son, who did look like he'd been mudded and strawed.

Ian thought the boy should be hosed off outside, but he came into the homestead instead, and Trey told him to go use the sink in the garage. He sighed as the boy did, dropping pieces of straw along the way.

"I swear," he said, and nothing else. He looked from Olli to Ian. "Did you see it?"

"I saw it," Ian said.

Trey shook his head. "Sorry, brother."

"It's fine. It's not going to change anything. No one but us knows where the wedding is. We'll be back from Montana in a week or so, have the reception, and no one will even care." As he spoke, he heard the truth of his words. "Let Mom have her fifteen minutes."

Trey picked up the paper and looked at the offending article. "You're amazing, Ian." He folded it in half and then in half again. He stepped into Ian and gave him a hug, then took the paper over to the recycling bin.

The garage door opened, and Spur entered, calling hello to anyone within earshot. Lawrence and Mariah followed him, bringing with them the scent of something roasted and something delicious.

From there, everyone began arriving, and Ian was glad Trey had gotten rid of the paper when he had. Conrad stood close to him, as did Blaine, while a few people worked in the kitchen, and just when Ian was starting to wonder where his fiancée was, the door opened one more time, and Nita walked in.

A love so powerful Ian couldn't name it moved through him, and he greeted her with a smile and a kiss.

"All right," Cayden yelled above everyone else. They were a loud bunch when they got together, and after one more attempt, Lawrence whistled through his teeth.

"Thanks," Cayden said, a hint of color coming into his cheeks. He hadn't always been the loudest brother, and Ian knew that was hard for him.

Nearby, Fern began to cry, and Lawrence sucked in a breath. "I'm so sorry. I forgot about her microphones."

"It's okay," Beth said, pressing Fern's face into her chest. "Trey already adjusted them, but we'll turn them down again." She gave Lawrence a smile, but he still looked upset with himself.

Fern had done really well with her cochlear implants, and she'd been fitted with the external pieces that allowed sound to enter her ear the way it should. In the past four months, she'd been vocalizing more and learning the language, and everyone—doctors, Trey, Beth—had been pleased with her progress and ability to adapt with the implants.

"I won't whistle again," Lawrence said. "If y'all would just settle down when Cayden asks."

"It's okay," Beth said again. "Really. She's just sensitive to louder noises, and she's okay." The girl had already stopped sniffling, and Conrad moved over a few feet to take the girl from her mother. All of the kids adored Conrad, and Fern perked right up.

"Ian and Nita are getting married tomorrow," Lawrence said, his face fixed with a smile. "We wanted to have this dinner, since they're not doing anything but the ceremony. I didn't make it, so it should be delicious." He grinned at his wife, and Mariah grinned on back at him.

"Let's pray," Daddy said, reaching up to remove his cowboy hat. Ian had already hung his near the garage entrance, so he just squeezed Nita's hand and bowed his head. His father began to pray, and Ian opened his eyes and looked up and around at his family.

Duke held his baby, swaying slightly and patting the boy's back with his eyes closed. His wife next to him was angelic, and the perfect complement to Duke.

Blaine and Tam each had charge over a twin, and Blaine put another cracker in front of Caroline to keep her quiet. Ian grinned at them, such love filling his chest.

Lawrence stood with his arm around Mariah, the two of them leaning on each other for support. He loved them too, and the steady way they simply lived their lives. They didn't have to be loud or in the spotlight. They were just good.

Trey and Beth had been through a lot in the past couple of years, and they'd weathered every storm with grace and optimism. Ian admired them for that, and he grinned at TJ when their eyes caught.

Cayden held Boone in his arms while Ginny stood next to her mother, holding her steady with her arm looped through her mom's. Their example of dedication to family and an open-door policy astounded Ian, and he wanted to be as freely giving as they were.

Conrad held Fern in one arm and kept Ry tucked into his side in the other. He'd already texted Ian that he and Ry were looking to move closer to town, and that Ian and Nita should plan on having the corner house on the ranch.

Daddy and Mom stood hand in hand while Daddy continued to pray for good health and blessings, while also thanking the Lord for His bounteous favors he'd poured out on their family.

Spur stood with Gus in his arms and Olli in a chair next to him, baby Liam still strapped to her chest. Spur's eyes were also open, and he met Ian's. With such silence around them, as well as the rays of heaven, Ian could only feel love and gratitude for his oldest brother. For the way Spur had incorporated Ian into his life, for listening to him, for not judging him, and for letting him be who he needed to be at any given time over the past decade.

A smile touched Spur's lips, and Ian returned it. They didn't need to speak. They had a strong brotherly bond that marriage wouldn't change, and Ian appreciated that.

"Amen," rang through the house, without Ian's voice in it. He hadn't heard much of the prayer, but he'd felt the familial bonds he'd needed to experience.

"Let's eat," someone said, and for the first time in years, Ian stepped out of the crowd and moved toward the front of the line. He couldn't quite beat TJ or Duke to the food, but being third wasn't all that bad.

The following evening, Ian let Spur adjust his hat. He let Duke straighten his tie. He let Conrad hold the reins of the horse he'd be riding to get married. Everyone had gathered to the barn, just like they had to the corner house for Conrad's wedding.

Blaine gave him a hug, because Blaine was always the best at expressing emotion and not being ashamed of it. Lawrence helped him pin on his boutonniere. Trey said, "Your truck is waiting along the back fence. It's packed and full of gas."

"Thank you, brother." Ian's own emotions swelled up at the kindness his brothers had shown him in the past few weeks. Always, really, but especially as he prepared to do something really hard for him. Good, but hard nonetheless.

Cayden handed him an envelope, and said, "Our gift to you and Nita. From all of us." He glanced around at all the men in the barn. "Don't open it right now. Just know it's from all of us, and we love you."

He hugged Ian, both of them vibrating just a little bit in the chest. The rest of them joined in, making the embrace a group affair, with Ian right at the center of it.

He closed his eyes and breathed in the sense of brotherhood and family, love and camaraderie.

"All right," Spur said. "It's time."

The group broke up, and Ian swung himself into the saddle on the black horse he'd chosen, and Conrad handed him the reins. The two of them locked eyes, and they'd been through so much in the past year. Last June, Lawrence had gotten married, and Conrad and Ian had tried to sit at the back table, away from the family.

Things felt so different now. Things *were* different now. He was different; he'd changed.

"Love you, Con," he said. "Thank you."

"You're ready for this," Conrad said, stepping back and pressing his palm to the top of his hat, smashing it down. Ian recognized the sign of nerves, though he wasn't sure what Conrad was anxious about.

"I am ready for this," he said, and he hoped that would calm his brother. All of them.

"Yes, you are," Daddy said, patting Ian's thigh. "Let's go boys."

"All right," Spur said, obviously the designated timekeeper for the wedding. "Give us a few seconds to get out there, and then we're a go."

Ian simply smiled at him, because he knew what came next. Everyone left the barn, and he stayed. Nita would come in the other side, having been helped by her mom, sister-in-law, and a few of the Chappell wives.

He'd kiss her there, and they'd open the doors together to ride down the aisle.

He waited in the shade in the barn, wishing it were a bit cooler. He told himself it would be outside, because Mom had insisted on misters and fans, even though the guest list hadn't topped thirty.

After a couple of minutes, the back barn doors opened, and sure enough, Nita entered, her bright white wedding dress getting illuminated by the remaining sunlight in the day. A grin exploded onto his face, and it took all of his willpower to keep his horse right where it stood.

She came toward him, and Ian reached for her reins as she got closer. He took them, guiding the horse right up beside his so he could lean over and kiss her. "Wow," he whispered just before touching his lips to hers. *Wow, wow, wow,* moved through his mind.

They parted, and she scanned him while he drank in her dress. "You're majestic on a horse," she said. "I don't get to see you ride very often."

"We should change that," he said. "Your dress is gorgeous."

She looked down at the form-fitting dress that flared around her legs and hips, the fabric spilling over both sides of the horse and around the back. "It's not custom, like Ryanne's, but I do love it."

"I love you," he said.

"I love you too."

They'd wait inside the barn for Spur and Cayden to open the doors, and Ian thought that should be happening any moment. Any moment now...

When it still didn't, his heart began to throb. "What do you think they're doing?"

"I don't know," Nita murmured. He reached over and

took her hand in his simply to comfort himself but also to comfort her.

Just as he was about to swing down out of his saddle and go find out what was holding things up, a crack of light appeared between the two doors separating them from the rows of seats that had been set up for the wedding.

Ian saw instantly what had been the holdup. Only one row of chairs remained, and Nita's grandparents sat in that. The pastor in front of them sat atop a horse, as did everyone else.

Spur and Olli, Blaine and Tam, Trey and Beth, Cayden and Ginny, Lawrence and Mariah, Duke and Lisa, Conrad and Ry, Daddy and Mom—they'd all saddled up. There were enough adults to handle the children, and they rode with their parents or an aunt or uncle.

Tears pressed behind Ian's eyes, and he glanced at Nita. "This is incredible."

Her brother and his wife rode, her father and his new wife, her mom, her cowboys from her stables, and a few of Ian's choices friends—every single one of them had found a horse and sat in the saddle, ready for the ceremony.

Nita nudged her horse forward as the classical music continued to play, and Ian's horse went with hers. She'd chosen to ride a bay with a golden coat and a black mane and tail, and he hoped his family was taking pictures of the two horses side-by-side, their riders about to get married.

They went to the fence that Spur had erected to act as an altar, and someone had twined vines of flowers around each rung to decorate it. Ian's mind buzzed, and he forced himself to pay attention to the advice of the pastor.

When it was time for vows, his were very simple. He looked at Nita, keeping their horses facing the pastor, as she said, "Ian, I've known *about* you for a long time, and I've always admired what you can do professionally. Getting to know the man behind the trainer has been a joy, and something I hope to continue to be able to do for the rest of my life. I love you, and I can't wait to share my life with you."

He'd known her vows wouldn't be long, so he didn't feel bad that his were short too. "Anita," he said. "You opened my eyes to a future I thought had long passed me by. Thank you for convincing me to take a step out of my comfort zone, and for loving me for who I am. I love you with everything I have, and I'm excited to be at your side moving forward."

They faced the pastor, and pulses of joy moved through Ian as he and Nita were pronounced husband and wife. He leaned toward her; she leaned toward him; they met in the middle and kissed, the final part of Ian's life and heart that had shattered so many years ago finally becoming whole again.

Around him, whistles and cheers filled the sunset-colored air, and they swung their horses around to face their family and a few friends.

He lifted both arms and waved to them as if in silent applause. He found Nita doing the same thing, and after a few seconds, he asked, "Ready?"

"Ready," she said, and they moved around the fence and

past the fans, misters, chairs, horses, and people and faced west. He urged his horse to pick up his feet, and soon, he and Nita were trotting into the sunset, happily married as husband and wife.

Once all the noise was behind them, and only the rolling, green ranch extended in front of them, he slowed and reached for her hand. He brought it to his lips, kissed her wrist, and said, "I love you."

She leaned toward him, and he held her steady so she wouldn't fall on the moving horse. She cradled his face in one palm, the way she'd done before to make him feel adored and cherished.

"I love you, cowboy."

* * *

Keep reading for a glimpse of the first book in my next series, *LOVING HER COWBOY BEST FRIEND* - **now available in paperback.**

Sneak Peek - Loving Her Cowboy Best Friend - Chapter 1

Regina Barlow pushed her shopping cart out of the grocery store, the familiar sight of the huge trees only paces away reminding her of where she lived now.

Back in her parents' house.

"Only for now," she told herself for the tenth time that day. She'd given herself the same caveat at least a hundred times since returning to Chestnut Springs five days ago.

As she pushed the groceries past the trees and toward her car, she muttered, "You have to find a job. Today."

A job would mean she could afford an apartment. A job would mean she wouldn't lose her car and her dignity. Yes, she had a little bit of money from the severance package from the high-end restaurant in Dallas, but not enough to support herself independently for longer than a couple of months.

She pushed her hair back, semi-disgusted she'd let Ella

talk her into all the highlights. Her sister loved getting her hair done, and she'd been shocked at the state of Gina's upon her return to their small, Texas Hill Country town.

Truth be told, Gina had been somewhat shocked she'd let her hair get as frayed and as dim as it had, and she did feel better now that the blonde shone, and the sun caught on different hues of color. It was just a little too much, and it had cost her a small fortune.

With the groceries all loaded in her truck, she pushed the cart over to the return. A couple of men stood there, both cowboys of course, with a woman. In Chestnut Springs, Gina could throw a stick and hit a cowboy.

"Excuse me," she said, her voice taking on some Texas twang she'd left behind a long time ago. Confusion ran through her at the same time the three people turned toward her, one of them edging out of the way so she could return her cart.

She pushed her cart into the chute, but her body froze immediately after that. Her arms fell to her sides like lumps of ice.

"Regina Barlow?" one of the men said. Calvin Rowbury. Of course she'd run into the most popular boy from high school, the one who'd known everyone, who'd come to Gina's eighteenth birthday party fresh from his win in the state rodeo.

Before she could even offer a forced chuckle and a whispered hello, Cal engulfed her in a big hug. Of course. His spirit had always been as big as the Montana sky, and he would know, as he'd traveled all over competing in the rodeo.

He laughed and twirled around, all while Gina stayed still, her arms pinned to her sides by his. He set her down and backed up, his face aglow with life and love and laughter. Gina wondered what it would be like to feel those things again, actually, and her heart pinged out a twist that hurt.

"Hello, Gina," the woman said. Tawny Grossburg. The way she linked her arm through Cal's, it was obvious she was Tawny Rowbury now.

"Hi," Gina said, looking to the other man. Todd Stewart. Her heartbeat knifed through her body, and she couldn't look away from those dark hazel eyes. He didn't look exactly like his older brother, but close enough.

Too close.

"Gina," Todd said formally, with a nod of his cowboy hat. "Well, I best be goin'." He looked back to Cal and Tawny. "My daddy has a whole bunch of interviews today, and he hasn't been feelin' the best. Needs this ginger ale."

"Yeah, go," Cal said. "We'll pray for him." He still grinned like he'd been deemed Santa Claus, and Todd started to walk away.

Gina couldn't help her interest in him. Not because he was handsome, though he was. Not because she'd known him real well growing up, though she had. She had spent countless days and hours out at his family's dude ranch, because she'd dated his older brother for quite a long time.

Yeah, she told herself. *Back in high school.*

Which was almost twenty years ago now.

No, the reason she was interested in Todd was because

he'd said his daddy was interviewing, and well, Gina needed a job.

Not at the Texas Longhorn Ranch, she thought. Immediately a war started within her. *Why not there? You don't even know if Blake is still there.*

There certainly wasn't anywhere else in this small town, and Gina was done with big-city living.

She looked at Cal, who grinned on back at her. "You should come to dinner," he said. He glanced at Tawny, who clearly didn't share his same sentiments. "Shouldn't she come to dinner, baby?"

"Sure," Tawny deadpanned.

Gina wasn't sure what she'd done to Tawny, but she shook her head. "No, I can't," she said. "Thank you, though." No reason to make Cal's light dimmer. "What are the Stewarts hiring for?"

"A chef...something or other," Cal said, turning away from the cart return too. "I guess they've been in a real hurt."

"I can't imagine they have that many people applying," Tawny said, going with her husband.

Gina couldn't either, and she watched as Todd swung himself into a huge pickup truck the way men did to get in saddles. Without thinking too hard, she started jogging toward him. With any luck at all, she might be able to flag him down.

Turned out, luck and the Lord were on her side, because he backed out and pointed his truck right at her. Needlessly, she waved both hands above her head, hating herself and what her life had come to in that moment strongly.

He took care of that truck, because she could clearly see his eyebrows lift through the impeccably clean windshield.

Can't back out now, she thought, and she continued over to his window. "Hey," she said breathlessly. She hadn't been in a kitchen in a month now, and she didn't subscribe to exercising all that much. "What job out at the ranch?"

This time, Todd's eyebrows shot toward the sky. "You want a job at the ranch?"

"I need a job," she said, not appreciating his attitude. "Cal said it was for a cook."

"Pastry chef," Todd said, reaching to rub the bridge of his nose. "Does Blake know you're back?"

"No," Gina said. "Listen, Todd, you know *I'm* a pastry chef, right?"

"I've heard," he said wearily.

"Would your daddy interview me?"

Todd appraised her, and wow, the Stewarts had always had eyes that could dive right into a person's inner-most secrets. Blake had done that to her countless times, but his whole family could achieve the same thing. "I'm not going to keep this a secret from my brother."

"But you don't need to tell him right this second either," Gina said. Desperation clogged her throat. "Listen, what about this?" She put one foot on the runner of his truck and boosted herself up so she was more eye-level with him.

"I come interview. If your daddy likes me and my résumé and I get the job, then you can tell Blake. Or I'll tell him."

She swallowed, her fear and all of the past she shared with Blake and his family lodging in the back of her throat. "But if I don't, then...no big deal. He'll find out I'm back in Chestnut Springs when he comes to church or...something."

Both Todd and Gina knew Blake didn't make the trip to town for church. Or much of anything. He had brothers and sisters who brought him his groceries and took care of his errands. He ran the family dude ranch, at least if his daddy had started thinking about retiring.

Maybe she was wrong, because Max Stewart was obviously conducting the interviews.

Todd cocked his left eyebrow, but he was considering her proposal.

"Please, Todd," she said, stopping herself from adding a plea that she needed a job. She'd take one almost anywhere, but if she could get something that actually utilized her education skills? That was the job she wanted.

"Fine," he said with a sigh. He scanned her down to her toes, though he couldn't possibly see below her chest. "Can you come out this afternoon? I know Daddy wants to get this done today."

"What time?"

"Come on out any time," Todd said, and discontent wove through Gina. She didn't want "any time." She didn't want to show up and wait for an hour while others got interviews.

"I have my mama's groceries," Gina said, stepping down off the runner. "I'll come after that?"

"Should be fine," Todd said, looking out the windshield.

Another car came their way, and Gina fell back to the parked cars so it could pass.

"Thanks, Todd," Gina said, and Todd nodded his hat at her and eased down the row.

Gina took a deep breath and looked around. The wind blew across her face, and Gina shivered in the late winter weather here in the Hill Country. She didn't even know what she was doing, standing here in this parking lot.

"Car," she muttered, finally spotting her father's semi-old truck and striding toward it. "Groceries. Job interview."

* * *

An hour later, Gina turned and went under the massive arch that announced her arrival at the Texas Longhorn Ranch. "That's new," she said to herself and all the perfume that had come with her in the car.

There'd always been a sign here at the Longhorn Ranch, but not one that nice, and never with hand-carving. She wondered if one of the Stewarts had done it, or if they'd hired it out.

The roads, which had always been dirt, seemed nicer. They were still dirt, but it was packed and dark, and almost as smooth as the asphalt she'd driven on from town. Twenty minutes it had taken her to get from the house where she'd grown up to this ranch, and that hadn't changed.

The lampposts along the quarter-mile stretch between the entrance and the lodge had, as had the hanging flower pots which actually boasted colorful blooms. The parking lot was still dirt, but at least three more buildings had been added to the epicenter of the ranch, which was the lodge itself.

An ice cream shack sat to the left, and two big barns took up quite a bit of land on her right. *The south*, she heard in Blake's voice. His hearty, deep chuckle accompanied the words, because he did everything in proper directions, and she used her left and right. For him, things were universal. For her, it was her perspective.

Her stomach swooped as she pulled into an available parking space, one of only a few. Things seemed very busy at the ranch today, and she hoped with everything inside her that all of these cars didn't belong to prospective pastry chefs.

She wasn't sure how that was possible, as Chestnut Springs wasn't exactly a hotspot for the culinary arts. She'd left this small town for precisely that reason in the first place.

Still, her legs shook as she went up the steps—again lined with flowers attached to lariats—and to the big, heavy double-doors of the lodge. Those hadn't changed either, though someone had stained them a different color since the last time she'd been here.

She didn't need to knock, and she didn't. She went right inside, the scent of coffee and chocolate meeting her nose. Blake had joked that his daddy never went anywhere without a coffee mug in his hand, and it was obviously someone's birthday today, because a small card table had been set up several paces inside the building. It bore two half-eaten pans of brownies, and three melting cartons of vanilla ice cream.

Definite life and activity buzzed here, but no one sat at the desk just inside the door. It wasn't quite check-in time, and it wasn't even close to mealtime, which she knew were two of the busiest times here at Longhorn Ranch.

She didn't see a row of chairs with people waiting in them, their legs bouncing nervously while they held a manila folder with their life's credentials. Gina swallowed as she gripped her folder tighter, wishing she had more directions than just "come on out anytime."

Out where? The interviews could be happening somewhere else, and Gina wouldn't know. She hadn't gotten Todd's number, and she glanced around nervously, the war inside her raging.

She wanted to see Blake.

She didn't want to see him.

She wanted to hear his voice.

She'd rather bury herself alive than hear his voice.

"Ma'am?" someone asked, and Gina blinked her way out of her inner struggles. "Can I help you?" A cowboy stood there—where he'd come from, Gina would never know—his smile genuine and soft at the same time. He wasn't a Stewart, and that only added a gold star to his stature.

"Yes." She cleared her throat. "I'm here for the pastry chef interviews?"

"Oh, sure," the cowboy drawled. "They're in the back, by the kitchen. I'll take you." He started weaving past the huge dining hall on the right, where the lodge fed their guests two square meals each day. On her left sat a variety of desks, some with cowboys at them, but most without.

They were probably all outside at this time of day, tending to cattle or fields, because while the Texas Longhorn Ranch was first and foremost a dude ranch, it was also a functional cattle ranch. Just on a very small scale compared to others surrounding Chestnut Springs.

No one seemed concerned about the dripping ice cream, and Gina wanted to rescue it. She told herself to ignore it as she followed the man in the red plaid shirt.

Blake would never wear red and black. He was more of a blue and yellow type of cowboy, and Gina schooled her thoughts. She really had no idea what kind of cowboy Blake Stewart was anymore.

"Thank you," a man said, his voice diving deep into Gina's chest. "We'll call you." She knew that voice. She'd heard that voice whisper her name right before the man it belonged to kissed her, and she'd heard that voice beg her to come back to him here in Chestnut Springs.

Around her, or maybe beside her, a woman moved.

"That's the last one," Blake said from somewhere beyond Gina's sight. He stood in front of the red-plaid-shirted cowboy, a sigh slipping from his lips. "No one good. Daddy's not gonna be happy."

"I've got one more," the man who'd greeted her at the door said.

Before Gina could yell that she'd made a mistake and run for the exit, he stepped out of her way.

"You do?" Blake asked, his words warping in her ears.

Their eyes met, and the whole world froze. Gina took in the glorious cowboy in front of her.

Blake Stewart. He still had deliciously dark hair, with long sideburns that connected to a full beard. He stood tall and tan and trim, and wow, he'd bulked out a lot in the shoulder department over the years.

His thick eyebrows drew down, breaking the spell over time. "Regina Barlow," he said, not forming her name into a question.

Her heart thundered through her chest, sounding like the hooves of a hundred horses sprinting over dry ground.

"What are you doin' here?"

"She came to interview," the other cowboy said.

Blake settled his weight onto one cowboy booted foot. He wore jeans too—Gina had never seen him wear anything but jeans—but he'd paired his with an equally denim shirt in a light blue that made his dark features even more handsome.

Her mouth watered, and it wasn't for the brownies and ice cream out front.

He folded his arms, and she cleared her throat to speak.

"Is that right?" he asked. "Well, I think the job's filled." He held her gaze for one more moment, turned toward the other cowboy, and said, "Thanks, Baby John." Then Blake turned and headed down a hallway Gina hadn't seen yet.

Baby John turned toward her, surprise and confusion on his face simultaneously. "Oh-kay. I guess the job's filled?"

Gina watched Blake until he disappeared, and then her muscles thawed enough for her to move. "No," she said, her vocal cords tight but functional. "He just said there was no one good for this job." She smiled up at Baby John, though by the look on his face, it wasn't a happy gesture. More like terrifying.

"*I'm* good for this job," she said. "I'm just gonna head back and see what he thinks of my résumé, okay?" She started after Blake, her step as sure as his now. She'd driven all this way. He couldn't just dismiss her like that. Not after everything they'd been through.

He'd been her best friend for years. Her boyfriend. Her everything. So she hadn't come back. All that sentence needed was a *yet*, and she wasn't going to let the stubborn cowboy close the door on this opportunity she needed so badly.

In the hallway, several open doors greeted her, and Gina took a deep breath. She'd poke her nose into all of them until she found the one with Blake inside. Then...well, then she'd deal with whatever she had to in order to leave the Texas Longhorn Ranch as its newest employee.

Sneak Peek - Loving Her Cowboy Best Friend - Chapter 2

Blake Stewart's pulse leapt through his body like some sort of jackrabbit. The big kind. The kind that had just seen a coyote and run for its life.

"You can't hire her," he said to his reflection in the mirror on the inside door of the coat closet in his office. He turned away from it, the other side of the room his goal now. He paced in front of the open doorway, his breath coming in spurts.

Regina Barlow. Gorgeous, flirty, fun, kissable Regina Barlow.

He'd been in love with her once, even if he was only eighteen years old. He'd told his mother a bunch of times that love didn't have age boundaries. Of course, Gina had fled Chestnut Springs by then, and she'd written him for the duration of her culinary education.

He really thought she'd come back.

He'd been a fool.

"A darn fool," he whispered to himself when he reached the lamp in the corner. A recliner sat there too, and Blake didn't think he'd ever actually reclined in it. Todd would sit there while Blake would rant about something from the safety of his desk. Sometimes Kyle would text from the recliner while Blake went over the finer points of their meeting.

His sisters sat there and told him about the problems out on the ranch or in the lodge, and it was up to Blake to solve them all. All of his brothers and sisters came in and out of his office at-will now, especially since Daddy had announced his partial retirement at the New Year. He'd be out of his office and living duty-free by June first.

The weight of the world sagged onto Blake's shoulders, the fire Gina had relit inside him burning up against it. He turned and rolled his eyes as he started striding toward the other side of the office again.

On one step, he was alone, and on the next, he'd collided with a very solid, warm body. A grunt and a grumble escaped his mouth, and his hand slid down cloth and over bones as he tried to steady himself and the curvy woman in front of him.

He and Gina came to a standstill, his hands on her waist and hers braced against the outside of his biceps. Dang it if his pulse didn't turn into a jackhammer then.

"Blake," she said, the word mostly breath. "There you are."

He could only blink at her. It was definitely her, with all that shiny blonde hair, and those deep, gorgeous, ocean-blue eyes. She even had the freckles dashed across her nose she used to cover up with makeup.

She wore makeup today, especially on her eyes, but she hadn't used anything to blot out those freckles. Blake wanted to kiss them the way he once had, but just as quickly, his desire to get away from this woman shot through him.

She seemed to get the same idea, because they backed up simultaneously, his hands falling back to his sides. They knew the shape of Gina's body though, and his nose understood the scent of her perfume.

She'd changed over the past couple of decades, but she was still herself too. Stunningly beautiful, full of fire, and completely confident. Who else would've followed him down this hallway and started poking her head into every room until she found him?

Along with the makeup and perfume, she wore a pair of jeans, sneakers, and a sweatshirt in a shade of purple that made her eyes almost seem violet too. It was a tie-dye actually, that started out purple, and faded into blue near the hem.

He sure did like it, and Blake curled his fingers into fists to keep himself from grabbing onto her again.

Friends, whispered through his mind. Gina had been his best friend since the fifth grade, when they'd been paired in a science experiment. She had the brains, and he had the fearlessness, and they'd taken first in the district fair.

They'd been inseparable since, even when she started dating Tony McCollins in ninth grade, and he'd had a fairly terrible stint with dating Veronica Turnby. After that, Blake had only had eyes and feelings for Gina, and it had taken him all of his sophomore year to tell her about them.

They'd gone from friends to more, and he'd sure enjoyed their last couple of years of high school. He'd known about her wings from the age of ten, and he wasn't sure why he'd thought he'd be able to clip them.

He cleared his throat and headed for his desk. "When did you get back into town?"

"Four or five days ago."

He sat and shuffled some papers around his desk. He couldn't switch them around too much, because they had to be signed and given back to Lindsey before the end of the day. He picked up his pen to get his signature on the lines where it belonged. "And? Just visiting?"

If she was here about a job, she wasn't just visiting, and he knew it.

"No," she said, coming closer.

Blake steadfastly refused to look at her. He could resist Gina for several seconds, but if she stayed in this office for much longer than that, he'd look at her and fall for her all over again. He practically scribbled his name as she sat down.

"Do you run the ranch now?"

"Not entirely," he said, sliding the now-signed paper behind another one. "Daddy's semi-retired." She didn't need to know more than that.

"Todd said you need a pastry chef," Gina said, her voice like warm, pleasant music in his ears.

Blake lifted his head then, his pen point coming to a halt. "Todd did?"

"I ran into him in the grocery store parking lot," Gina said with a small, single-shoulder shrug. "Blake, I have a bachelor's degree in pastry arts."

"I'm aware," Blake said, his shock still waving through him in pulses. Todd had run into Gina? When? Why hadn't he said anything to Blake? Out of all the siblings, Todd alone knew how broken Blake had been when Gina had taken her first job in New Orleans instead of coming home.

"When did you talk to Todd?"

"About an hour ago," she said.

The fire licking through Blake quieted. "What happened to your job in Dallas?"

A flicker of a smile touched her mouth, which she'd painted a light pink. Blake tore his eyes from those lips he'd kissed before and went back to signing papers. He didn't care about her previous job. He didn't care about her.

Lies, he thought, but his pen scratched out another signature.

He looked up when she remained quiet. That was new for her, and he caught the hint of apprehension in her gaze.

"The restaurant went out of business," she said. "Sort of." She licked her lips, her tell that she was about to say something hard. Blake paused, because he found he wanted to hear it. "The previous owner was doing something illegal. Embezzlement or something? He sold the restaurant, and that's when it was discovered. Of course, Paulo is gone, off to some South American country or something, and the rest of us—"

She cut off, her eyes widening. She gave herself a little

shake and ground her voice through her whole chest. "I got a small severance package. We all did, but the new owners wanted to start fresh."

"Makes sense," Blake said. He didn't believe for one second that Gina would do anything like embezzlement. She didn't even know what that was. Heck, Blake barely knew. "So...you want to make desserts at a dude ranch?"

A smile brightened her whole face, extending way down into her very soul. He loved that look on her, as he'd seen it several times in years gone by. *Not for a while,* he told himself, but that didn't make her any less shiny to him.

"I would literally sacrifice a goat to make desserts on a dude ranch," she said.

Blake blinked, then burst out laughing, all of the tension gone between them. *See?* his mind whispered. *Friends.*

"All right," he said, reaching for her folder. "Let me see your résumé."

She dutifully handed it over, then sat back, her hands clasped in her lap. Blake just needed her to think she might not get this job. Gina wasn't stupid, though, and she'd heard him tell Baby John there wasn't anyone good.

She'd be perfect here, and his heart started making plans to ask her to dinner too. He shut those down real fast when he saw the four premier restaurants she'd worked at over the years.

"Hmm," he said, keeping his voice real neutral. "This last place was only for two years." He flicked a look in her direction and went back to her credentials. "Why'd you leave...The Tall Texas Grande?" He looked up then, surprised he'd been able to keep his tone so even.

The Tall Texas Grande was a five-star resort-hotel in Corpus Christi, and somewhere he'd never even *dream* of visiting. Families who never got dirty went there. Billionaires and politicians. Gina had probably met celebrities while they dined spa-side and presented them with upscale caramel cheesecakes, all fancied up with chocolate curls and strawberry sauce she'd labored over for hours.

"Are you kidding?" she asked.

"No, ma'am," Blake said, clearing his throat and snapping the folder shut. He set it on his desk, making no move to give it back to her. Their eyes met, and Blake determined he'd win this time. She'd speak first, and she'd tell him what he wanted to know.

"They weren't paying you enough?"

Gina's eyes narrowed. "The head pastry chef quit. He was my mentor, and I followed him to The Parisian in Dallas."

"Was he the embezzler?"

"No," Gina bit out.

"He must've lost his job too."

"Yes."

"Where did he go?"

"Miami."

"You didn't go with him?"

"Obviously." With every answer, her shoulders had lifted a little higher. Finally, she exhaled out. "I know where you're going with this."

"Do you?"

"I dated him once," she said. "Five years ago. But after it fell apart, we were just colleagues."

"And he didn't take you to Miami." Blake leaned forward, steepling his fingers. "So you left your job at a resort-hotel on the beach for him...but he didn't have a place for you when you needed it."

Gina's eyes blazed with blue fire, and oh, Blake had missed that so very much in his life. He held up one hand. "Never mind." He took a big breath and looked down at the paperwork on his desk. Daddy would be thrilled with the addition of Gina to their staff. Heck, everyone would. He couldn't even imagine the culinary delights she could put on the table here at the Texas Longhorn Ranch.

"Do you want the job?"

"Is that a real question?"

Blake bent to get the hiring paperwork out of the bottom desk drawer. "I asked it, didn't I?" So she'd made a long-lost joke about sacrificing a goat for something she wanted. They'd been doing that since they were twelve.

"Yes," she ground out through clenched teeth, though he couldn't see her. "I want the job."

"Great." He plunked the paper down on top of her folder and slid everything toward her. "I need this filled out, and I think you should come out in the morning and meet with the head chef. She does her weekly meetings on Tuesdays as we gear up for the weekend, and you'll get a feel for how the two of you will work together."

Gina took the folder and simple tax paperwork. "Is she hard to work for?"

"Depends on how you define that," Blake said, standing with a smile. "I'm used to her, but our last dessert master *did* quit because of Starla..." He clucked his tongue like that was just too darn bad, and he chuckled at the horrified look on Gina's face.

"Starla Masters is the head chef here?"

Blake could've been imagining it, but he thought he saw her swallow. More like a gulp, in all honesty.

"Yes," Blake said, drawing the word out. "Is that a problem for you?"

Gina looked like she might throw up, but she shook her head. "No," she said, her voice somewhat tight. "No, sir."

Blake took a step around the desk and then kept going. "Gina," he said quietly. "You don't have to call me sir." He stood in front of her now, and he might as well have been naked for the way she looked at him with such a sharp edge in her eyes.

"We were friends once. We can be friends again." He took a breath, because he'd nearly choked on the word *friends*. Twice. He wasn't thinking of her in a strictly friendly way, that was for certain. The longer he looked at her, the further she pulled him in with those ocean-y eyes and the more he thought about kissing her. "Right?"

She simply gazed up at him, and Blake thought for sure he'd just made the biggest mistake of his life, but whether that was saying he and Gina could be friends or hiring her to be the ranch's pastry chef, he wasn't sure.

Why wouldn't she answer him?

"Listen," he said, sighing. "If we can't be friends, I'm not sure you should take the job." He couldn't stand to watch her walk out of his life again, not when she'd only been back for ten minutes. Working with her when they couldn't have a conversation would be torture, though.

"Well?" he asked, unsettled by Gina's long silence.

Another second chance romance set back in Chestnut Springs - I hope you're excited to read it. You can read *LOVING HER COWBOY BEST FRIEND* now. It's available in paperback and starts a new cowboy romance series with the Stewart family at Texas Longhorn Lodge.

Texas Longhorn Ranch Romance

Book 1: Loving Her Cowboy Best Friend: She's a city girl returning to her hometown. He's a country boy through and through. When these two former best friends (and ex-lovers) start working together, romantic sparks fly that could ignite a wildfire... Will Regina and Blake get burned or can they tame the flames into true love?

Book 2: Kissing Her Cowboy Boss: She's a veterinarian with a secret past. He's her new boss. When Todd hires Laura, it's because she's willing to live on-site and work full-time for the ranch. But when their feelings turn personal, will Laura put up walls between them to keep them apart?

BLUEGRASS RANCH ROMANCE

Book 1: Winning the Cowboy Billionaire: She'll do anything to secure the funding she needs to take her perfumery to the next level...even date the boy next door.

Book 2: Roping the Cowboy Billionaire: She'll do anything to show her ex she's not still hung up on him...even date her best friend.

Book 3: Training the Cowboy Billionaire: She'll do anything to save her ranch...even marry a cowboy just so they can enter a race together.

Book 4: Parading the Cowboy Billionaire: She'll do anything to spite her mother and find her own happiness...even keep her cowboy billionaire boyfriend a secret.

Book 5: Promoting the Cowboy Billionaire: She'll do anything to keep her job...even date a client to stay on her boss's good side.

Book 6: Acquiring the Cowboy Billionaire: She'll do anything to keep her father's stud farm in the family...even marry the maddening cowboy billionaire she's never gotten along with.

Book 7: Saving the Cowboy Billionaire: She'll do anything to prove to her friends that she's over her ex...even date the cowboy she once went with in high school.

Book 8: Convincing the Cowboy Billionaire: She'll do anything to keep her dignity...even convincing the saltiest cowboy billionaire at the ranch to be her boyfriend.

CHESTNUT RANCH ROMANCE

Book 1: A Cowboy and his Neighbor: Best friends and neighbors shouldn't share a kiss...

Book 2: A Cowboy and his Mistletoe Kiss: He wasn't supposed to kiss her. Can Travis and Millie find a way to turn their mistletoe kiss into true love?

Book 3: A Cowboy and his Christmas Crush: Can a Christmas crush and their mutual love of rescuing dogs bring them back together?

Book 4: A Cowboy and his Daughter: They were married for a few months. She lost their baby...or so he thought.

Book 5: A Cowboy and his Boss: She's his boss. He's had a crush on her for a couple of summers now. Can Toni and Griffin mix business and pleasure while making sure the teens they're in charge of stay in line?

Book 6: A Cowboy and his Fake Marriage: She needs a husband to keep her ranch...can she convince the cowboy next-door to marry her?

Book 7: A Cowboy and his Secret Kiss: He likes the pretty adventure guide next door, but she wants to keep their relationship off the grid. Can he kiss her in secret and keep his heart intact?

Book 8: A Cowboy and his Skipped Christmas: He's been in love with her forever. She's told him no more times than either of them can count. Can Theo and Sorrell find their way through past pain to a happy future together?

ABOUT EMMY

Emmy is a Midwest mom who loves dogs, cowboys, and Texas. She's been writing for years and loves weaving stories of love, hope, and second chances. Learn more about her and her books at www.emmyeugene.com.

Printed in Great Britain
by Amazon

20327868R00202